THE
HISTORIES THAT
HAUNT

BOOK FOUR

a  *Regency Mystery*

SANDRA & TAYLOR
PREISLER

ISBN (ebook): 979-8-9929861-1-2
ISBN (Paperback): 979-8-9929861-3-6
ISBN (Hardcover): 979-8-9929861-4-3

Library of Congress Control Number: 2025927185

Cover design by Sandy Robson.

Dedicated to our readers, without whom this journey would have been impossible

England 1812

Chapter One

The clear view of the night sky caught Zoe Huxley's attention before the large manor house did. Looking up as she stepped out of the carriage, she couldn't help gasping softly in astonishment. The sky was swathed in a vast silken veil. The thousands of lights twinkling from the white expanse contrasted against the deep and endless black, taking her by surprise.

Mesmerized by the view, Zoe wasn't paying attention to her feet and she stumbled, too impatient to wait for the carriage driver to assist her. Fortunately for Zoe, her husband Quinton was right behind, and he reached out to steady her, his large hands gripping her waist. He glanced up as well, and Zoe could see in the way his jaw slackened and his breath caught that he was just as taken with the night sky as she was.

Though the London smog didn't allow for much stargazing, Zoe had seen a clear night sky before—in her childhood in France, and on the boat to London when she and her mother had fled the country, and then on the boat to and from America this past year. She was sure other instances didn't come to mind, simply a byproduct of the opportunities her upbringing allowed. But Quinton's upbringing had been very different than her own, with few trips to the country or boat rides to distant shores. A life spent entirely in the haze of London did not allow the full vision of beauty to shine through from above. Especially in summer, the sooty, heavy air kept one's eyes ahead, not up.

That had all changed for Quinton now. During their extended honeymoon across the continent, they had experienced many wonders. But still, they had spent their weeks in cities and had travelled during the day in between. The starry heaven itself had never quite revealed its wonders, not like this. Zoe wondered if Quinton had ever seen a clear sky like the one on display tonight.

"It really does look like spilled milk," Zoe said quietly. "If spilled milk was beautiful, that is."

Quinton nodded, clearing his throat and looking down at her. "It's beautiful."

His gaze then turned to the massive building before them. In the bright starlight, the pillars and stone towered above them, an impressive monument to the wealth and status of the family Quinton had recently claimed as his own. Such a strange twist of fate which had made this house theirs to share.

Zoe took Quinton's forearm in her hand, enjoying the feeling of his warmth even on a muggy summer night. He placed his opposite hand over hers, turned them towards the steps, and began to climb toward the imposing front door. Before they reached their destination, the door swung open.

A tall, ramrod straight man stepped before them, his beakish nose silhouetted by the light streaming through the doorway from inside the house. Zoe wondered briefly if it was a requirement for butlers to be tall with painfully straight posture.

"Lord Coleville, Lady Coleville, welcome to Cedarbrook." The butler stood back, arm extended, inviting them to enter Quinton's new home.

Only this last year had Quinton discovered his heritage and claimed his rights as an heir. Before that, he had been an agent for hire, the orphaned son of an actress. Together with Zoe, he had recently solved his mother's murder, which had led to the discovery that his previously unknown and long-dead father was a nobleman, and a firstborn at that. Even more shocking, they had discovered indisputable proof that his mother and father had legally wed. He was born in wedlock, the firstborn son of a first-born son. A legal heir.

Quinton's grip on Zoe's hand tightened as they stood inside the entrance of the great house while servants scurried outside to retrieve their trunks from the second carriage and the staff who accompanied them from the third. Zoe's lady's maid was shown upstairs to ready their room while the two of them were led to a parlour, painted a dark blue with oversized chairs clustered in groups.

Soon a light repast was before them, and Zoe found herself quite famished. They had travelled far that day and made little provision for stops, knowing they would arrive late as it was. As the two of them piled the small plates with cuts of cheese and bread and delicate cakes, another tall young man came in bearing a bottle of claret and stayed to fill their glasses as they emptied them. Zoe would have preferred whiskey, and she knew Quinton felt the same, but she could see the stiffness begin to leave his shoulders after the second glass. It was good to be able to relax. Whatever this new future brought, at least they were finally here.

Suddenly the door to the room was thrown open and an older man stomped in, already shouting before the door even closed behind him. "Don't grab at my arm like a nagging wife, Evans. I've earned the right to say my piece before I leave." His glare zeroed in on Quinton. "I didn't think you had the gall to actually come out here, but I just had to see the usurper while I had the chance. I'll be gone before the week is out."

Following the outburst, the butler followed hurriedly, announcing the man belatedly. "Mr. Ellis Langford, land steward. I did tell him to come back in the morning, but I'm afraid one of the footmen had already let him inside by then, my lord."

"It wasn't no footman, it was you who let me in," snapped the interloper with a sneer. "Quit lying to save your own hide, you weasel."

The butler's face went a particular shade of red. Zoe raised an eyebrow but said nothing about his attempt to place the blame for the breach elsewhere.

"It's fine, thank you . . ." Quinton trailed off, and Zoe realized they didn't know the butler's name.

Fortunately the butler seemed to interpret the pause correctly. "Evans, sir."

"Right, thank you, Evans."

Evans hesitated, then retreated, closing the door quietly behind him. Quinton stood slowly, watchfully chewing a piece of crusty bread.

The older man stared angrily at Quinton, having apparently run out of words. If he was intimidated by the fact Quinton stood a full head taller and was decades younger, he did not let it show.

"Would you care for some brandy, Mr. Langford?" said Quinton, gesturing toward the sideboard. "I believe the bottle might be quite a good vintage."

The young serving man filling their glasses immediately made his way to the bottle and brought three glasses back with him, offering one to Langford. At least Evans had trained the staff to be responsive.

Langford stared at Quinton, as if he had carefully rehearsed this conversation in his head but now it wasn't going at all the way he had thought. After a long moment he accepted the glass.

Zoe took a deep sip from hers, again wishing it was whiskey, and spoke quietly. "How long have you lived here, Mr. Langford?"

What she wanted to do was tell the old man he was impertinent and to get out, but Quinton had obviously chosen to entertain this behaviour, and Zoe was willing to back him up if that's what he wanted.

Zoe had chosen that question for its simplicity, and it worked. Langford answered without thinking. "Grew up a village over, and me and Lord Philip used to be friendly when we were boys. When the old land steward retired, Lord Philip thought of me."

Langford took a long swallow of the brandy, and Zoe followed suit. Despite the fact it was not whiskey, it was, as Quinton had surmised, an excellent vintage.

Quinton took advantage of the silence and spoke quietly as well. "Mr. Langford, I understand you may be unhappy with the new arrangement, for whatever reason. However, it was my grandfather himself who suggested that my new wife and I come here and familiarize ourselves with the estate. He wrote to say some oversight was needed here and suggested we make it a priority when we returned to British soil."

"I see." Some of the bluster had been diffused from Langford's demeanour, replaced by an expression Zoe could only describe as calculating. "Lord Philip and I always had a good working relationship—at least I thought we did. But I'm too old to learn the ways of a new master, and since he seems to think the estate needs so much oversight and couldn't be bothered to tell me himself, I'll leave it in your hands."

Zoe couldn't really blame the man for his surprise—it had come as a shock to her and Quinton as well when they received the letter from Philip Coleville inviting them to come when they returned from their honeymoon. Considering his previous lack of acceptance of Quinton, the invitation was an unexpected turn, but Zoe hoped it meant he was coming to terms with the reality of the situation—an olive branch of sorts.

"If that's the way you feel about it, I'll respect your choice." Quinton might be trying not to burn bridges, but Zoe knew her husband wouldn't grovel. "I would appreciate your input before you leave," continued Quinton. "Or at least a tour of the grounds."

Langford started as if he had been shot. He hesitated briefly, and Zoe wondered if this whole thing had been a ruse, perhaps hoping for a pay rise, and Langford wasn't sure what to do now that Quinton had called his bluff. Too bad for him—one shouldn't bet it all if one weren't able to pay the price.

"Very well," said Langford. Apparently he was willing to pay the price rather than swallow his pride and apologize. "I will tour you the house and garden, as well as the tenant farmers, on the morrow if you please. After breakfast."

"My wife and I need some time to get settled, and my in-laws will be arriving in two days," Quinton responded. "Would you be willing to give me the tour in three days' time?"

The old man hesitated, then nodded stiffly and stomped back the way he had come.

Once he was gone, Zoe leaned her head back and pinched the bridge of her nose. "You were much kinder than he had any right to expect." She didn't add what she would have told the old man given the chance.

"I want to build bridges, Zoe, not tear them down." He sighed. "I don't suppose they have whiskey around here?"

Zoe laughed. "You're the master of the house for now. I'm sure all you have to do is ask."

Quinton laughed too, but it didn't hide the exhaustion from the lengthy travels etched into his features or the dark circles under his eyes. What they both really needed tonight was sleep.

Chapter Two

LONDON

Eyeing a passing hackney, Mary Fletcher briefly regretting her decision to walk from her mother and father's house back to where she lived with the Dovefields. The weather was hot and sultry, and she felt another bead of sweat make its way down her back. She rarely left her mother's presence in a good mood, but the London summer heat certainly did not help.

Mary had always been fond of London, and though she knew it was irrational, she felt that her affection for the city deserved some kind of reward—that London should be kinder to her as a result. After all, she had been born and raised on its streets, spending her whole life there, except for that godforsaken trip across the demonic ocean to America last year with her former employer and friend Zoe Demas. Mary had been seasick that entire voyage and had vowed to never leave the shores of Britain again.

Zoe had not felt the same way, relishing the experience of travel and life beyond her home. She was currently on her newlywed trip across the Channel. Zoe and Mr. Quinton Huxley —or Coleville now, Mary wasn't sure how that worked—had danced around their attraction to one another for over a year, but being an overly honourable man who always thought he knew best, Quinton had refused to admit to his feelings due to their social inequality. But then this past winter when Quinton's circumstances had changed, he suddenly felt he had something to offer a lady like Zoe.

Mary was of course very happy for both of them, but now that Zoe no longer needed a companion, Mary was left a bit adrift in life. So here she was in the thick summer heat, walking instead of taking a hackney.

Mary's thick black curls were always held back by numerous pins and a wide band when she was out in public, but the humidity seemed to give them a life of their own. By the time she made it to the Dovefield house and around to the back entrance, several strands had escaped their prison and were pasted onto her brown skin, and her less-than-cheerful mood had soured even more.

When the cool walls of the home enveloped her, some of her heated mood dissipated. She found herself walking past Zoe's room on the second floor and paused. The truth was, she missed Zoe. Mary had almost more sisters than she could count, but they were all younger than her, and Mary had fallen into more the role of a third parent than a sibling or friend. The bond she held with Zoe was different. Though they were as different as night from day, from the colour of their skin to their experiences in life, Zoe was her closest friend. Mary was lonely without her around.

"Mary, wait." Lady Simone Dovefield's voice broke into Mary's musings, and she turned to the stairs as the woman hurried up. Seeing a woman like Simone hurrying was odd. She was too dignified to rush anywhere.

"I'm glad I caught you, dear." Simone smiled at her, more animated than Mary had ever seen her. "Wonderful news! They are back! Zoe and Quinton are at the Coleville country estate and soon we shall be as well!"

Simone's eyes shone with anticipation of seeing her daughter again, and Mary could not help but smile back. "It will be nice to get out of this hellish heat. But are you sure you wish me to accompany you? This seems like more of a family occasion."

"Of course you should come," responded Simone without even a pause. "You are family." She continued past Mary toward her own rooms with a parting timeline. "We must settle the girls at The Haven and arrange our affairs, so we'll leave in two days' time, which gives us plenty of time to pack."

With that Simone disappeared before Mary could respond. Mary shook her head, laughing internally at how certain Simone was in everything. She was a woman who always knew—and got —what she wanted. Mary wondered what it would be like to live in her shoes, but dismissed the thought quickly. That wasn't the kind of woman Mary was, and she had accepted that.

Glancing back at the door of Zoe's bedroom, Mary's thoughts returned to her loneliness. Hesitating for a moment, she finally turned the knob and went in. The room was as Zoe had left it—or rather, how the maids had left it after her wedding day—bed made and books stacked neatly on shelves. Memories popped into Mary's mind of when she and Zoe would end up in this room to whisper of their secrets and discuss the stupidity of men and puzzle through a mystery. As her chest faintly ached at the remembrance, her thoughts drifted back even farther down the path of her memories, to the very day she met Zoe Demas.

Zoe had been in need of a lady's maid when Mary's cousin John introduced them. Her previous maid, Lucy, had been murdered, and through the ensuing events Mary and her employer had bonded, and Zoe had become acquainted with the characters who populated Mary and John and Quinton's lives— Rory the resurrectionist and Charlie the underworld hustler, as well as Charlie's mother Katy and sister Savita. Eventually Mary had become Zoe's companion, rather than maid, and the cast of their lives had moved from acquaintances to friends.

Now that Zoe was married, she had no more need of a companion, of course. In her absence, Mary had been helping at The Haven, Simone's home for unwed mothers—another indirect result of Lucy's death. The situation was only temporary until Mary figured out what was next in her life, but it did make her feel less like a leech in the Dovefield home.

Much had changed since those early days. Now Mary's cousin John, a Bow Street Runner, had wed Charlie's little sister, Savi. They had been married a few months longer than Quinton and Zoe, and had recently announced they were expecting their first child. Savi was truly glowing: if possible even more beautiful with the bloom of motherhood upon her.

Even the other two, though confirmed bachelors, had a new business venture consuming their thoughts and time. Though she found their project of dubious value, she had been the one to ask Charlie to check in on Rory last winter, as he was going through a rough patch. Now the two were thick as thieves and business partners, blending something that was near and dear to their heart with a chance to make some actual legal money. In a fit of possible madness, they had bought a distillery. Despite her doubts, both seemed happy as could be, discussing blends and sampling the results.

They all seemed quite . . . happy. Which made her oddly sad.

Everyone had found a partner or a passion. Everyone but her.

Chapter Three

Holding the sight of Zoe in his mind's eye, Quinton closed the door to his bedroom quietly. She was lying there asleep, her face peaceful and her dark curly hair surrounding her head like a halo, but it would be a mistake to think of his wife as angelic. Some men might have found that a drawback or a flaw to be put up with, but as for Quinton, he would change nothing about her.

At the estate they had each been given their own bedroom, as was the custom for couples of their status, but being so newly married they still preferred to sleep together. On their newlywed trip, their rented facilities had also always provided each with a bedroom, which had come in handy, mostly when Zoe needed to cool off from an argument. Her eyes would darken with storm clouds and her chin would come up, and Quinton knew the hurricane was arriving. That's when he had learned it was best to give her some space to let the wind blow itself out.

In the early months of their acquaintance, the storm clouds in Zoe's blue eyes had put the fear of God into Quinton. As a man who craved control over his life and his fate, she had made him feel quite unstable. Now he understood that, like all storms, this one would pass. He had accepted he would never control her, nor did he want to. Quinton knew the tempest did not mean she loved him any less. As he made his way downstairs, he reflected that her temper came with her, and he had learned not just to accept it but to love it.

Breakfast was served on the sideboard, and though the hour was early, the food was hot and ready within minutes of Quinton's arrival. He helped himself while a servant poured his coffee. The bread was the same he'd eaten the night before, which he happened to remember was crusty and divine, now served with a tasty marmalade spread. He also added eggs and sausages and cooked mushrooms, then looked around to find a spot to enjoy the feast.

The breakfast room had comfortable seating as well as sideboards and a table, and the large windows overlooked the beautifully kept grounds. Quinton took his plate to a large armchair next to the window and made himself comfortable, tucking into the food with appreciation. The footman brought his coffee to the small table next to the chair and Quinton took a deep breath, enjoying the aroma of good coffee and the view of the estate grounds—his new home.

As he brought the cup up to take a sip, movement caught his eye at the end of the grassy estate.

His interest piqued, Quinton leaned forward to get a better look, waiting and watching for another flash of movement. His patience was soon rewarded. A figure slipped from the grass to the bordering woods and, after a quick glance back toward the mansion, disappeared among the trees.

Quinton was up and out of the room in a flash, letting his plate clatter on the table. In a mere minute or two, his large frame carried him to the spot in the woods where the figure had disappeared. Most of his thirty years had been spent in the working class of London, and he had considerable speed, not to mention legs longer than most.

He crept into the brush quietly, looking for any sign of the person he had seen. He quickly came upon a path continuing deeper into the woods and followed it, keeping his steps light and quiet. After about ten minutes of walking, Quinton came upon the ruins.

The house must have been significant at one time, many years past. But now the roof had collapsed and ivy covered the crumbling walls, the native woods having called the structure back to nature and the wildness that resided there. As if to stake its claim, an actual tree grew in what had undoubtedly once been the foyer, sprouting tall and wide in a space made for people where no tree should grow. But despite the claim the forest had staked, the bones of the building were still there, proudly enduring after years of neglect and wear. Quinton could still see the sitting rooms from where he stood, as well as the grand staircase, still partially intact and leading up to a second floor which Quinton wouldn't trust as being structurally sound.

Sitting in a chair he must have set up himself, in the cover of the partial roof of the dining room, sat Mr. Langford, with a steaming cup of coffee.

There was something so surprising about the comfortable way he sat—a small table drawn close, and a footstool to boot. The older man, so surly the night before, looked completely at ease. Like he owned the place.

Quinton started towards him, not bothering any more with light steps. At the sound of his footfalls crunching on the gravel, Mr. Langford glanced up. Even from that distance, Quinton felt the heat of his glare. The two weren't destined to be friends, Quinton decided. Fortunately he didn't need any new friends, only answers.

"I said I would meet you in three days' time. Is listening always this difficult for you?" spat the old man as Quinton approached.

"This is my family's land, sir, and you work for my family," retorted Quinton, growing tired of the man's disrespect. "You may address me with respect or take your leave now. For good."

A long pause ensued as Langford's eyes narrowed, clearly

considering his next words carefully. He finally seemed to come to a decision, relaxing back into his chair and cocking his head. "Understood, my lord," he said.

Quinton did not miss the heavy sarcasm on the last word, but it was progress and he would take it. Taking a deep breath to calm himself, Quinton raised his eyes to the skies. His temper was different from Zoe's. Hers sparked often, flaring brightly but then abating just as quickly. Quinton's on the other hand took longer to build, but once it did it burned hotter and longer. He didn't wish to say something he later regretted.

The still-standing edge of the roof caught his eye, as if he had just missed movement somehow. A bird no doubt, but it brought the original reason for Quinton's quest into the forest back to him. He looked down, locking eyes with Langford. "I saw someone running into these woods from the house. I know it wasn't you, as he moved as a young man. I am concerned about the safety of my wife."

Langford's eyes widened in surprise, and having had quite a bit of experience reading the emotions of others, Quinton suspected the reaction was genuine. He could generally tell when someone was lying, and he didn't get that impression from Langford.

"First I've heard of it. Might have been a lad from the village," said the old man. "It was known you were coming. Maybe he wanted a glimpse of the new lord."

Quinton nodded. "Is your house near here?"

As a land steward, Quinton assumed Langford was given the use of a small home on the property. It would have to be close to for the coffee to still be hot.

"It's a short walk away." Langford gestured vaguely towards the back of the ruins, confirming Quinton's suspicions. "But I sometimes take my coffee here." Glancing up at the structure, Langford continued, "It's still got a life to it."

The sentiment wasn't something Quinton shared. All he felt was decay and disuse and neglect, and it made Quinton's skin crawl. But he knew better than to speak those thoughts aloud. "It must have been an impressive home at one time." A true statement at least. "Perhaps I will take the time to explore it this summer when we have settled."

This was apparently the wrong thing to say. Langford's mood immediately darkened. "This manor belongs to the past, my lord." Langford's words were clipped and sharp. "It's got no place in this future you have somehow gained."

The hair on the back of Quinton's neck suddenly stood up. For a moment he thought it was his temper reigniting at Langford's attitude. But then he instinctively glanced around, recognizing the pinprick feeling.

He was being watched.

There was another small flash of movement at the point where the tangled branches wrapped around the crumbling roof of the sitting room, and just as suddenly the feeling of being watched was gone. Whoever it was had fled, and Quinton was not prepared to scale the top of the tree and give chase.

Shaking off the strange feeling, Quinton returned his focus to the person he could engage with—though Langford had turned back to his coffee and was studiously ignoring Quinton. He didn't believe the old man was lying when he said he didn't know of a trespasser, but that didn't mean he didn't have secrets he was protecting. The real question was what those secrets might be.

Squaring his shoulders, Quinton turned to face him. "This is my home now, not by some travesty of justice but by my own blood. I am the heir, and your dislike of this fact does not change it. I will go where I choose and discover what I must to own this place in more ways than on paper. You can help, you can hinder, but I will do as I please here. Meet me at the manor in three days, or do not and I will take myself on a tour. It matters not to me."

He turned on his heel before Langford could respond. He didn't need to look back to feel the old land steward's eyes following him, boring a hole of burning anger into the back of Quinton's head.

Chapter Four

Practically vibrating with anticipation as she stared out the window, Zoe wrung her hands, trying to distract herself. She had chosen a deep blue walking dress, hitched high at the waist and flowing to the floor, along with a jaunty hat. She liked its comfort as well as how the blue complimented her eyes. For some reason she was anxious to look good for her family. She knew they would not care, but she cared.

"They should be here by now," she said to no one in particular.

"Perhaps their carriage lost a wheel," replied her husband from across the room where he was pretending to be engrossed in the newspaper.

"Don't even jest about that," said Zoe seriously before turning to face him. She took a deep breath and let her eyes peruse the room.

It really was a lovely sitting room, if a little stuffy for Zoe's taste. The windows faced the west, so they let in great deal of light in the afternoons. During the summer the housekeeper, a Mrs. Fox, had explained that the maids often closed the curtains to keep it cool during this time of day, but Zoe preferred to keep them open, even if it did get a little warm.

The decorations were old fashioned, done in dark tones with mahogany accents, but not tasteless by any means. Still, Zoe would change a few things when she became mistress of the estate.

It was a strange thing to think of—Zoe Coleville, future Countess of Cedarbrook. She ignored the stirrings of uncertainty about her own new role. Though noble blood ran in her veins, the thought of being the mistress of such a grand estate gave her pause. And worse, deep in her heart, she wondered not if she was capable, but if she was even interested.

It wasn't the life Zoe had pictured for herself, but the same couldn't be said of her mother. Simone—formerly Demas, now Dovefield—had always planned for her daughter to rise high in society. It hadn't happened quite the way she might have imagined it, but in the end, both mother and daughter were happy with the result.

"I just can't wait to see Mary and Brutus—and my parents and William and Phoebe and Gwen of course." Zoe turned her attention back to staring out the window.

"Of course." Quinton closed the newspaper, finally giving up the pretence of indifference. He had resisted any extensive upgrades to his wardrobe while on the continent, but Zoe still felt he looked dashing in his trousers and waistcoat. He had taken to wearing an ascot, as it was simple for him to manage himself. "I'm only teasing, dear. I am also looking forward to seeing them."

"Yes, I know."

Their honeymoon had been a wondrous time, full of new experiences and sights and people. Zoe had been having such a grand time that she'd really only thought of her family sporadically. But now it felt like it had been ages since she'd seen them, even though in reality it had only been a few months.

Distant motion drew Zoe's eye. She leaned forward, squinting, trying to make it out. "Oh, there they are!" she exclaimed.

Zoe raced down the stairs, Quinton not far behind. She knew it wasn't very dignified, but she didn't care at the moment.

Despite her breakneck speed, the butler managed to meet them at the door just in time to open it for them. Zoe was impressed at his agility, especially for his age, but something about it unnerved her as well. Butlers were supposed to be stiff and disapproving, not agile.

The two carriages were still a ways down the driveway when Zoe and Quinton emerged into the sunlight, but it didn't take it long for them to arrive at the doorstep. Two of the Cedarbrook footmen—Oliver and Lawrence, Zoe thought their names might be—rushed over, with as much dignity as was possible under the circumstances, to open the doors.

Her stepfather was the first to emerge from the lead carriage. Hugh Dovefield's face was marked by smile lines, and this occasion proved why this was so. His honest face broke into a wide grin at the sight of his beloved stepdaughter, his green eyes warm.

"Zoe!" Hugh pulled her into his warm embrace, and she breathed in the scent of lemon soap which was so familiar to her. "It's so good to see you."

"It's good to see you too, father." Zoe pulled away, returning his smile. "How was the journey?"

"Uneventful," he replied with a shrug before turning to Quinton. "Quinton, my good man! You are looking well—very healthy. Tell me, how was Italy?"

As the two men began to talk, Zoe turned her attention to the second passenger to emerge. Simone had already stepped down, standing like the pillar of dignity Zoe knew her to be. Although in her mid-forties, with her long blonde hair just beginning to grey, her mother was still more beautiful than any woman Zoe had ever laid eyes on, with her piercing blue eyes—not to mention her overall air. Or maybe she only was to her daughter and husband. Regardless, everyone who crossed Simone's path knew her as a force to be reckoned with.

"Hello, *Maman.*"

"Hello, *ma fille.*" Simone was more reserved than Hugh, but

Zoe could see the happiness shining in her eyes. "It is very good to see you."

Zoe took her mother's hand in her own and leaned forward to kiss her on the cheek. "And you. Walter and Phoebe are in the other carriage?"

Simone's brow furrowed. "Indeed, along with your great beast. Eight hours in a carriage is taxing enough without sharing space with a creature of his size. I feel quite sorry for the poor governess—I shall likely have to increase her salary to make up for the ordeal."

Behind Simone, Zoe caught sight of the third passenger disembarking—her dear friend, Mary. She was dressed in a plum-coloured day dress which flattered her generous curves and favoured her dark complexion. The familiar twinkle of mischief made her dark brown eyes sparkle.

"Mary!" exclaimed Zoe as she rushed over wrap her arms around her.

As she returned the embrace, Mary laughed. "Be careful, Z! You'll crush me."

"Oh, sorry." Zoe loosened her grip and stepped back.

"I'm only teasing." Mary grinned. "You look marvellous. Life by the sea must have agreed with you."

"I did enjoy it, except for the humidity. It wreaked havoc on my curls, despite Louisa's best efforts." The new maid had started only shortly before Zoe's wedding and didn't have Mary's experience dealing with said curls. And Mary hadn't had time to train her as she had trained Camille, the previous maid.

"You're also a shade darker than when you left."

A true statement. Zoe pulled up the sleeves of her dress, holding her arms out in front of her, showing off the tanned skin. "Also despite Louisa's best efforts. She wants me to stay inside as much as possible until it fades."

"It suits you." Mary looked up at the home. "I knew you were moving up in the world, Zoe, but this is something else. How are you settling in? Can you even settle into a place this big?"

Zoe laughed. "Honestly, it's a challenge. But we're getting used to it."

"Zoe!" The loud cry came from the left, where the children had all disembarked. The source was Zoe's younger half-sister, a miniature version of their mother with long golden blonde hair tucked into a bonnet, big blue eyes and a petite frame. Phoebe ran over and wrapped her arms around Zoe's waist without hesitation. Close to turning twelve years of age, she was still very much a child in body and mind, although she seemed an inch or two taller than Zoe had remembered.

"Hello, my darling girl." Zoe squeezed her tight, then turned her attention to the boy behind Phoebe.

Zoe's half-brother Walter was three years Phoebe's senior, having just turned fifteen. He was still young, but closer to adulthood than his younger sister, and possessed of a more serious disposition. His handsome young face resembled his father's, with the same straw blond hair, although his eyes were a mix of Hugh's green and his aunt Theo's grey. But his personality took after Simone.

"Hello, sister." Walter inclined his head stiffly in greeting. "You look well."

Zoe reached out a hand to affectionately brush a loose strand of hair from his forehead. "Hello, Walter. I swear you get taller every time I see you."

"What about me?" demanded Phoebe with a pout.

"You too, Phoebe."

Beyond her siblings stood their disapproving governess, as well as Zoe's dog Brutus, held on a lead by the dog's caretaker, young Gwen. Aged somewhere between Walter and Phoebe, she was technically employed to care for Brutus's needs, but in reality she existed in a sort of in-between space, acting as something of a playmate for Phoebe as well. Not quite a servant and not quite a member of the family.

A year and a half ago, Gwen and her deaf brother Ezra had been living as urchins on the street. That changed when their paths crossed with Quinton. Through quite a few series of events, Gwen had come into the household of the Dovefields, and her brother was currently residing at the Royal School for Deaf Children.

Zoe knelt down to greet her great beast, Brutus: once a bull-baiting dog, now turned massive house pet. He wagged his tail and leaned into her hand, clearly as happy to be back with Zoe as she was with him.

"Good boy." Zoe looked up at Gwen with a smile. "Hello, Gwen. How has Brutus been for you?"

"Oh, very good, m'lady." Gwen returned her smile—she was such a pretty girl when she smiled, which was often. Zoe noted her diction was much improved. "He's always a good boy."

"Somehow I doubt that," Zoe replied with a chuckle as she stood. She turned to include the whole group. "Well, who would like a tour?"

"I'm hungry, Zoe," said Phoebe, her pout back. "And my back hurts from sitting in the carriage."

"Of course." In her excitement, Zoe had forgotten the toll of the journey on her guests. She waved Oliver over. "Could you please take the children in and show them and the governess to their rooms? Tell Evans to have the cook prepare and send up their tea a bit early."

"Of course, my lady." Oliver took his new task seriously, shepherding his entrusted flock dutifully inside the house.

"What about the rest of you?" Zoe glanced over at Quinton, who then took her hand in response. "I'm sure it's been a long day. Would you like a chance to rest and freshen up first?"

Mary shook her head. "Absolutely not. I'm dying to see your new home."

The party spent the rest of the afternoon exploring the gardens of the estate, which were large enough to wander in for an entire day if one wished. But as tea time approached, Zoe could see the wear of travel was taking a toll on her parents. Though they were still in good health, the pair were undeniably aging, and a day's ride in a carriage would take a toll even on a young person.

"Why don't you go up to your rooms now and take a tray for tea?" suggested Zoe.

"Oh, no," countered Simone through a small yawn. "We don't want to go to bed when we've just got here."

"Nonsense." Her new son-in-law took Simone's hand into the crook of his arm and began to lead the way back to the house. "Take some time to recover from the journey, and then we'll reconvene for dinner."

"Well, if you insist." Simone patted Quinton's hand.

Though she hadn't always been in favour of Quinton and Zoe's interest, Simone had come around and was now his most fervent supporter. Sometimes Zoe thought Simone might like him better than her.

As they walked along the path a figure came into view coming in the opposite direction. Zoe's stomach dropped as she recognized Mr. Langford, their rude land steward. She really didn't want her parents or Mary to witness his behaviour.

There was a branch in the path ahead and Zoe moved forward to take the other way. Unfortunately for her, her stubborn husband didn't see her movement—or perhaps he chose to pretend he did not. So much for building bridges . . .

Quinton forged ahead with a gleam in his eyes Zoe had seen before. He was the more even-tempered of the two of them, but he could only be pushed so far. Once he'd had enough, he'd had enough. It was one of the reasons she loved him—and also one of the reasons he drove her mad.

Zoe hadn't thought it possible for Mr. Langford's permanent scowl to deepen, but deepen it did as he caught sight of the group. His pace quickened until he was within speaking distance.

"What is the meaning of this?" he snarled. "Does Lord Philip know you're having guests at his estate without his permission?"

"My *grandfather* has given me permission to do as I see fit at my family's estate." Quinton gestures to the others. "And as it happens, not that I have to explain myself to you, but these are my wife's parents, in addition to a dear family friend. I did tell you they would be arriving today, if you'll recall."

"Hmm," grumbled Langford, admitting nothing. "And I suppose you've been trampling all about the grounds?"

"If by trampling you mean taking a pleasant tour, then yes," Quinton sniped back.

"Indeed," interjected Hugh, ever the peacemaker. "The garden is spectacular, Mr. . . .?"

When only silence followed, Zoe stepped in. "This is Mr. Langford, the land steward . . . for now."

"Ah, well, as I said the grounds are quite lovely. We went as far as the west woods today and I still think we didn't see everything." Hugh offered his customary smile.

That wasn't enough in this case.

"The West Wood?" Langford spat. "You didn't go within, did you?"

Quinton was on the verge of steam coming out of his ears. "No, but why shouldn't we?"

Langford said nothing for a moment, looking Quinton up and down. "It's not safe. One of the maids thought she saw a wolf in the woods the other day."

"A wolf? That seems unlikely," echoed Mary.

"Why wasn't I told about it?" asked Quinton.

The tension was rising to be higher than the temperature. Zoe glanced over at Mary, and just as it had been in London, their thoughts were as one.

"Why don't we head inside?" Zoe took her father's arm. "I am dying of thirst."

"As am I," said Mary, taking his other arm. "Let's get out of the sun."

As they began to move away from Langford, only Quinton hesitated, clearly still ready to do battle with the man.

"Quinton," said Zoe in a low but sharp tone. "Come along, now."

He finally relented. "I will see you on the morrow then, Mr. Langford. I look forward to your report on this . . . wolf."

Then the party was back on track toward the house. Zoe breathed a quiet sigh of relief as they left the disagreeable man behind.

"What a horrid little man," said Simone once they were out of earshot. "I can't believe the earl would employ such an impertinent creature."

"I can," grumbled Quinton. "If it's true that servants resemble their masters."

Zoe frowned at him. "That's a very rude thing to say. Most of the servants here have been perfectly pleasant, and besides which, your grandfather is making an effort at least. Perhaps you could do the same."

"I suppose you're right," muttered Quinton, though the set of his jaw made Zoe doubt his sincerity.

"Anyway, we won't have to put up with Mr. Langford's behaviour for much longer." Zoe glanced back at the man, who was still standing there, scowling at their retreating backs. "He resigned as soon as we arrived. He's only staying long enough to catch Quinton up."

"Good." Simone shook her head. "In the meantime, I hope we shan't encounter him again."

Zoe hoped much the same, for his sake as well as theirs. As much of a temper as Quinton had, Zoe's was twice as wrathful. Langford was lucky he had not yet come face to face with it.

Chapter Five

"Where is that blasted land steward?" The words were spoken in a low grumble as Quinton kept glancing toward the door.

"Perhaps he overslept." Zoe took another sip of her bitter espresso, savouring the complex flavour. "As did my parents and Mary."

Quinton shook his head. "You've met the man. Does he seem the type to oversleep?"

Zoe chose not to answer, as the question seemed rhetorical. Her husband wasn't wrong though—missing an appointment did seem out of character for a grumpy old man who had already complained about Quinton not keeping to their set schedule. But on the other hand, perhaps it was simply another display of disrespect towards the man he had deemed so unworthy of inheriting the title of master.

Langford's behaviour was unacceptable. It grated against Zoe's grain to see her proud husband treated poorly, much less by a creature of Langford's character. If he hadn't already promised to resign, Zoe would have insisted on sacking him.

"Evans!" snapped Quinton suddenly, startling Zoe from her musings.

The butler moved fluidly to Quinton's side. Most butlers were masters at their craft—one didn't rise to such a high status of servant by being lazy or unskilled—but something about this one unnerved her to a small degree, though she knew her feeling was ridiculous. Zoe just expected butlers to be more like the one she had grown up with—stiff and disapproving, in a friendly kind of way.

"Yes, my lord?"

"Please send one of the footmen out to the land steward's cottage to retrieve Mr. Langford." Quinton crossed his arms. "I don't have all day to wait on the man."

"Yes, my lord."

As Evans disappeared from the room to carry out this task, Quinton sighed and looked out the window at the dreary morning sky. "The problem is I do have all day."

The discouraging statement caught Zoe by surprise. It wasn't that she was blind to the reality. Quinton hadn't grown up satisfied and comfortable like most gentlemen. He was used to being a man with a purpose—a man with a struggle. Now his biggest struggle was being kept waiting by a spiteful land steward. She hadn't expected the adjustment from a working man to a nobleman to be problem free, but so far Quinton seemed to have been taking the transition in stride.

Zoe reached across the table, taking his large, callused hand in her own. "Perhaps it's time to take a look at those letters my stepfather was keeping for you. Apparently quite a few gentlemen and ladies reached out to him when we were on our honeymoon, inquiring after your services."

"Yes, perhaps." Quinton turned his gaze back to her with a soft smile. "But not today."

Swallowing her frustration, Zoe returned his smile. She didn't understand this reluctance to even take a look at the letters, but she didn't want to start a fight over it—again—so she held her tongue.

"What of Rory?" she asked, changing the subject. "Has he settled on a date to visit?"

"Yes, he should be arriving within two days."

"Good, very good. And have you reached out to Charlie?"

"Charlie?" Quinton raised an eyebrow. "What of him?"

"I'm sure he is eager to hear of your travels abroad. Have you written to tell him we've returned to England?"

Quinton snorted. "I very much doubt he cares to hear of the Italian coast."

"You don't know that," scolded Zoe. "Besides which, he will be hurt if he hears you wrote to both John and Rory but not him. We should invite him to visit as well."

This time Quinton laughed out loud. "I can't imagine Charlie lurking these hallways, being waited on by the servants. He'd hate it here."

"His enjoyment of the experience is hardly relevant. This will be your home one day and your children's home." Zoe could almost picture that near future—little versions of themselves running around the sitting room, playing and laughing—but the thought of such a future filled her with equal parts joy and dread, so she quickly dismissed it. "Charlie is your family, not just your London mate. His presence in your life isn't optional, so I suggest you start acclimating him now."

"You make a fair point." His furrowed brow and clenched jaw conveyed he was still hesitant. "I'm not sure my grandfather would approve. Rory is a bit of a stretch as it is. When Philip asked me what his occupation was, I told him he 'works closely with the cemetery,' which we both know isn't the whole truth but sounded better than resurrectionist or grave robber or anatomist."

"Your grandfather isn't here," countered Zoe. "Besides which, he didn't just ask you to come and tour the estate—he asked you to provide oversight. In his own emotionally constipated way, that's a gesture of trust. It shows he's accepted you as his heir and wants you to start feeling comfortable in that role."

"I don't know if that's entirely true." Despite the dismissive words, Quinton nodded slowly. "But I take your meaning. I will write Charlie a note. If the messenger hurries, perhaps he could catch a ride with Rory."

Having won the verbal sparring, Zoe leaned back, satisfied. "Very good."

While they'd been having their discussion, Evans had discreetly returned to his post on the far side of the room, waiting to be called on for service. Quinton dictated the message to him, and he in turn sent the other footman for the messenger.

The door suddenly opened, revealing the first footman breathing hard. Evans had clearly conveyed that haste was of the essence.

The footman ignored Quinton and Zoe, striding over to Evans, whose disapproving expression made it clear the footman's breach of protocol hadn't gone unnoticed. But as the footman leaned in and whispered something in his ear, Evans's expression shifted. Zoe couldn't quite read it, but clearly something was amiss.

Quinton waited until Evans had dismissed the footman before speaking. "What is it?"

"Mr. Langford wasn't at the cottage," said Evans evenly, his posture straight and his expression giving nothing away.

"Well, then where is he?" snapped Quinton.

An uneasy feeling settled in the pit of Zoe's stomach.

"It seems Mrs. Langford told Oliver that her husband left shortly after dinner last night and has yet to return."

Zoe connected the dots first. "So Mr. Langford has been missing all night?"

"So it would appear."

A sudden flash of the old man tripping over a rock or stepping in a hole appeared in Zoe's mind. She could see him lying there in the darkness, calling out for help, but with no one near enough to hear him. When something went wrong with someone of Langford's age, it tended to go very wrong.

Clearly having pictured something similar, Quinton only paused for a moment before standing. "Evans, gather the staff. We need to search the property."

Chapter Six

Despite the reason for Quinton being out of doors, he still had to acknowledge that the grounds were beautiful. Over the past few days he'd taken a few strolls through the garden, and each time it had re-impressed him. Having lived his life in the dull greyness of London, the lush greens and purples and reds and blues of living plants sprawling as far as the eye could see was still awe-inspiring to Quinton. It was all just so . . . peaceful. The fact that this sheer amount of land also belonged to him, or would one day, made it even more surreal. In no world could his younger self ever have dreamed of this.

A scream suddenly tore through the still morning air, shattering Quinton's thoughts on the tranquillity of the place. He ran in the direction of the sound, heart pounding in his ears and chest heaving.

The time he'd spent searching had already left him with a shirt damp with sweat, but by the time he arrived at the source of the scream, Quinton's clothes were drenched. His first thought was that he would need a bath. A strange thought, considering the scene he came upon.

A kitchen maid stood, hand clasped over her mouth, face twisted into a horrified expression. The butler had arrived before Quinton and had a hand placed on her back to steady the maid. Both their gazes were transfixed on the ground—or rather what was on the ground.

Mr. Langford was laying on his back at the edge of the ruins of the old estate, his neck bent at an unnatural angle, his eyes open but unseeing. Eyes which would never see again.

Quinton cursed under his breath, unable to contain his shock.

Evans looked up at the sound. "My lord, I, eh—" He paused then, as if unable to form the completed sentence.

It was the first time Quinton had seen the man flustered. He couldn't blame him—finding a dead body was bound to unsettle anyone, even the most put-together butler.

Clearing his throat, Evans seemed to collect himself. "I heard Bridget's scream and happened upon the . . . scene . . . just a moment ago."

"Of course." It occurred to Quinton that he was the master of the house right now and the staff would look to him for direction. He nodded, clearing his throat. "Take her back to the house and have the cook make her a cup of tea. I'm sure there will be others headed this way who heard the scream, but try to head them off if you see them. I want to leave the body as it is for the constable, if it's practical with the weather."

"The constable, my lord?" asked Evans in a surprised tone.

"Indeed. Isn't that the standard procedure?"

"Well, there isn't a constable assigned to the village." Evans's tone had evened back out to his professional standard. "There isn't really a need."

"Ah, of course." Quinton had forgotten he wasn't in London. *What did people do out in the middle of nowhere like this?* "Well, what is the procedure in a situation like this then?"

The question seemed to take Evans aback. "There is a local magistrate, my lord," he said hesitantly. "But are you sure you want the scrutiny that comes with such an inquiry?"

"I would not seek it out, but a man is dead, Evans. There will have to be some sort of investigation."

"For an accident?" Evans looked up at the ruins. "Langford was known for spending time in the remnants of the old house. It seems his habit caught up with him and he likely slipped from one of the loose stones."

Quinton followed the butler's line of sight. He had to admit, the logic did make sense. The whole thing was likely just a tragic accident. But even so, it wasn't in Quinton's nature to accept things at face value.

"Perhaps," he responded. "But these things are not to be taken lightly. When you get back to the house, send a messenger for the magistrate."

After a moment's hesitation, Evans spoke again. "Very well. But the earl would not welcome the excuse for scandal. That is all I'll say on the matter."

With that he turned, guiding the maid back through the trees toward the main house. Quinton watched them walk away, pondering the conversation. Zoe would say the offhanded comment was impertinent, but that didn't mean Evans was wrong. Was Quinton jumping too quickly at the opportunity to involve the local authorities? He had to think of how these things would look to outside eyes now. Was he just looking for an excuse to try back on the skin of his old life, even for just a short while, at the expense of those around him? Quinton was a husband now, and his task was to protect Zoe.

But as he looked down at the lifeless body at his feet, Quinton knew he couldn't just turn a blind eye. He didn't have it in him. As disagreeable as the man had been, even Langford deserved the dignity of ensuring his death had indeed been an accident. If it had not . . . that would make Quinton's life more difficult, but Langford would also deserve justice.

Quinton let out a deep breath he hadn't realized he'd been holding, suddenly very aware of how his dampened clothes were clinging to his skin.

"You don't mind if I sit, do you, Mr. Langford?"

If the corpse could have answered, Quinton was sure he would mind, but since the poor soul was past caring, he didn't take it personally. Quinton quickly retrieved the chair he had first seen Langford sitting in from the dining room and took a seat of vigil. Suddenly the stress of the morning's events caught up with him and a wave of tiredness came over him, weighing his shoulders down and making Quinton want to close his eyes, just for a few minutes.

A burst of movement through the greenery cut his thoughts of rest short. Quinton bolted upright, a new burst of energy propelling him. Then he saw the source—his wife.

Zoe emerged from the shrubbery, her dark curls dishevelled and her light day dress torn in several places. "I heard the scream, but I was all the way on the other side of the grounds. Took me forever to get here."

She panted with exertion, clearly having run the whole way, and wiped away beads of sweat from her brow before they fell into her brilliant blue eyes. Quinton would have expected nothing less.

"Yes, I'm afraid poor Bridget was the first to find him." Quinton gestured to the body.

"Poor thing. She's barely more than a child." Zoe walked around the dead man, carefully examining the scene. "I never thought I'd say it, but poor Mr. Langford as well."

"Yes. It's probably just an accident, but I've sent Evans for the magistrate."

Zoe's nose wrinkled. "Yes, I encountered him on my way here. He informed me that I was to stay at the house and await your instructions. I didn't appreciate his tone."

"Well, in Evans's defence, I did tell him to head off any of the others." Quinton kept talking before Zoe could protest. "I obviously didn't mean you, but I didn't specify. He was quite put out I insisted on the magistrate."

She sniffed at his explanation but didn't press it further, for which he was grateful. "It's a good thing Rory will be arriving in the morning. I don't trust some country magistrate to deal with this."

"You haven't even met the man." Quinton shook his head, hiding a smile. "Perhaps he'll surprise you."

"I doubt it," replied Zoe with a raised eyebrow. "I'll wager you anything he's old, fat, and denser than rock, and that the most exciting things he's ever had to deal with is a property dispute."

Now Quinton laughed, despite the circumstances. How lucky he was to have married a woman who could make him laugh, even when standing over a corpse.

"You should go back to the house and let your parents and Mary know what's going on."

"And leave you alone in the forest with a possible killer on the loose?" Zoe scoffed. "I think not."

"My dear, he probably just fell. There likely is no killer at all."

"I said possible." Zoe took a seat in the chair Quinton had vacated. "Nevertheless, I'm staying."

Quinton leaned down and lightly kissed her forehead. "Thank you, darling. I feel much safer now."

The words were said lightly, but Quinton couldn't help but glance at the scar which ran along Zoe's left wrist and palm. It was never wise to underestimate his wife.

Chapter Seven

Z oe could not help but shoot a sideways glance at her husband as the magistrate walked his portly frame around the body of Mr. Langford. The man was exactly as she had predicted—old, fat, and dense—and she did love to be right.

Quinton returned the look with a slight quirking at the corner of his lips which told Zoe he was trying not to laugh, but then raised his eyebrow and shook his head. He needn't worry. She wasn't going to say anything she was thinking out loud. Despite what some might say, she did have some sense. For example, she hadn't even mentioned balding.

She deliberately avoided looking at the body on the ground. She might not have liked the man but seeing his broken neck twisted at such an unnatural angle unnerved Zoe.

Medley Dandridge paused after his circle of the body and raised his eyes upward. Zoe wondered how his eyesight was, considering he seemed to be aged somewhere in his sixties. She glanced up as well, taking in the partially collapsed roof jutting out unapologetically into the space above them, defiant of both the elements and humans, as if neither had a hold on it.

"If he were up there, wouldn't take much of a slip to find

himself down here." Dandridge straightened his hat carefully and waited for Quinton to speak.

"Is that your professional opinion of what happened then?" asked Zoe before her husband could form a response.

"It could be," said Dandridge in a neutral tone.

There was a lull as Quinton hesitated. It didn't take a mind reader to guess what he was thinking. A great deal of pressure rested on his shoulders, and any scandal was definitely unwanted right now—as if there was ever a good time to have one. Dense though he likely was, the magistrate would understand the system well enough to know that the word of a lord was law. If Quinton agreed, the matter would be dismissed.

After a moment, Dandridge seemed to take the silence as an invitation to speak further. "I have noted the area around this poor soul is quite clean, almost as if it has been swept." He pointed to some shadows in a corner of the ruins, where Zoe could make out a makeshift broom she hadn't seen before. "Did Mr. Langford spend time here in the old house? Or did you?"

"My family and I have just arrived at Cedarbrook, as I am quite certain you are aware." Quinton cocked his head as he looked at the magistrate. "My rise to nobility is assuredly the only conversation of late around bar stools and kitchen tables around these parts. Not that I hold any grudge on that. If the tables were turned, I would be curious as well."

Dandridge adjusted his hat again in what Zoe assumed was a nervous gesture and shrugged. "It's been a topic of interest, to be sure. What about Mr. Langford? Was he of a habit to enjoy these ruins?" He gestured to the chair Zoe remained in. "I assume you did bring that with you when you heard the screams. Someone was taking time to make the place more comfortable."

Perhaps the old magistrate was less dense than Zoe had thought. Still old and fat though. At least she was still right about that.

Quinton nodded, as if thinking the same thing. "Mr. Langford was known to spend time here, though I do not know why he felt such a connection to the place."

Settling his hat once again, Dandridge looked back up. "That roof is made of rock, to match the exterior wall of the foyer. No doubt beautiful in its time, but the edges are all crumbling with age, and I do find it peculiar that none of that rock managed to find its way down here if indeed the man was up there and fell."

Zoe started slightly in surprise, glancing up as one with Quinton. An astute observation. If Langford had fallen because he tripped or collapsed, surely some of the crumbled shale would now be around their feet, yet there was a shocking lack.

So perhaps he had not fallen at all.

When Quinton's eyes lowered, Zoe saw newfound respect for the man in front of him. "I would agree, sir. It appears Mr. Langford did not fall, which would indicate foul play of some kind."

"Perhaps, my lord, perhaps," said Dandridge in an even tone. "But there is no plain evidence either way. The official document is still at the pleasure of the people present now. In the end, you are the lord and this is your employee and your land. It is up to you as to how we proceed from here."

In other words, the magistrate knew his place. A coward's stance, but Zoe couldn't really fault him. The volunteer position of magistrate was considered one of honour and respectability, but that didn't mean it came with protections. In these rural areas of England, the lords of the manors held sway. A dispute with one could ruin a man like Dandridge.

"I assume you've had dealings with my grandfather before, Lord Philip Coleville?" asked Quinton.

"I have." Dandridge's tone remained even, but Zoe detected just a hint of edge.

Quinton nodded, crossing his arms. "I do not know what those interactions have been like, but my values and beliefs are different from his. I believe that that the need for justice is not divided somehow on class lines, nor should it be decided by the desire for discretion of those with more status than others. I did not know this man well, but his death will be investigated thoroughly, not swept under the rug."

Though the words were strong, Quinton's voice didn't raise above conversation level and his tone was friendly, not accusatory. It was just his way of letting Dandridge know what he expected.

Dandridge stilled for a moment, meeting Quinton's eyes squarely. Then with a tug on his hat, he nodded. "Then if I may, sir, offer a suggestion. You were correct before, your reputation proceeded you. I find it unlikely that anyone in this grand manor will cooperate willingly with a lowly old magistrate. I have no real power past the gates of the drive, and frankly most of my time is spent in property disputes."

If he noticed Zoe choke back a laugh, he said nothing.

Dandridge continued, "Since you have experience investigating these sorts of things, perhaps we should put off an actual ruling of cause of death and allow time for you to poke around a bit. I, in the meantime, will ask around the village itself to see what the talk is regarding Mr. Langford himself. He has been in these parts here all of his life, and that information will be there for me to dig through."

Zoe nodded appreciatively. "It's a good plan."

Of course she wished Langford had not been killed. The loss of any human life was a tragedy. But seeing the gleam in Quinton's eyes, Zoe couldn't help but be grateful. There was nothing like an investigation to bring her husband to life.

Chapter Eight

LONDON

"We cannot import peat from Islay." Pinching the bridge of his nose, Charlie Modi sighed. He didn't think he should have to have this conversation, yet here he was, arguing with the bloody Scot again.

The Scot in question waved his hand dismissively. "I realize there's an expense involved. But if you consider the return on high quality whiskey . . . we can start selling at a much higher price point—"

"Rory, there isn't a price point that would compensate for that kind of expense. The peat would have to be cut and dried there, then transported by ship here. We'd have to hire multiple people up in Islay, plus commission a ship captain. The sheer amount—" Charlie shook his head. "It's just not feasible."

"I understand what you're saying, but have you considered importing the malt already peated—"

"Rory," Charlie snapped. "Why don't we try making a quality product with what we have available to us here in England, and then once we are making a profit, we can discuss branching the operation out."

With clear reluctance, Rory Stewart finally nodded. "Very

well. But I do have considerable means at my disposal that I don't believe you're factoring into your calculations."

Now it was Charlie's turn to wave a dismissive hand. "You are correct, I am not factoring it in, because we agreed it would be a joint venture—50/50."

"True, true." Rory sighed. "I suppose we'll simply have to limp along for now with England's poor offerings."

Charlie rolled his eyes but didn't offer further comment. The pair were standing in their newly purchased distillery. The narrow building housed all the equipment they would need, and while it had once been a lucrative and thriving facility, the operation had fallen into disrepair in recent years—fallen far enough that together Rory and Charlie could afford to purchase it.

They'd already invested quite a bit of coin improving the equipment and repairing the building itself, besides the initial purchase. Neither Charlie nor Rory were men short of coin, but Charlie saw no reason to be wasteful. Rory on the other hand . . . Rory was a more fanciful man, driven by dreams and the nostalgia of a home he no longer lived in. Reining the Scot in was becoming a full-time job, and Charlie did have other considerations in his life.

That being said, he hadn't hated every moment spent on their new business venture together. The Scot kept things interesting, and the whole thing was exciting and—more importantly—legal. Charlie still had his hands in the criminal underworld where he had spent so much time building his little kingdom, but his life had changed recently. New factors needed to be taken into account.

His thoughts drifted to the boy who was likely still sleeping in the home Charlie kept for himself and his mother. He could clearly picture the innocent freckled face framed by red curls. This time of day, Charlie's mother, Katy, would just be getting up and brewing a pot of her famous chai. It wouldn't be long before the delectable scent awoke the boy, and he would go stumbling into the kitchen in search of sustenance.

The boy wasn't Charlie's by blood, but he had become an inseparable part of his life over the past few months. All Charlie wanted to do was go home and see him.

"Are we finished?" he asked. "I don't know why you insisted on meeting here so early in the morning. I haven't even had breakfast yet."

"I told you, I want to finalize as much as possible before leaving to visit Quinton and Zoe. They've arrived back from their honeymoon, as I'm sure you're aware. I'm bringing them a few bottles from the test batch, although in a perfect world we would have aged the barrels a few more years. But it will still give us an idea as far as flavour profiles go."

Rory had indeed told him that. But Charlie was still a bit sore he hadn't received any correspondence from his oldest friend since said friend's return to England, so he was pretending he wasn't aware.

"Ah, of course. Give them my best," said Charlie coolly.

Now it was Rory's turn to roll his eyes, but before he could offer a retort, a knock at the door interrupted their conversation.

Charlie walked over calmly, opening the door to reveal a scrawny young boy. "Yes?"

The thin, dirty arm extended, holding a note in its grasp. Charlie took it and deposited a generous amount of coin in its place. With that the boy scurried away, back into the shadows from which he had come.

"What is it?" asked Rory.

As Charlie quickly unfurled the crumpled paper, the name at the bottom caught his attention.

"It's from Quinton." Charlie scanned the message. "It looks as though I may be joining you on your journey to the estate." He reached the bottom of the note and sighed. "He wants me to bring his bloody cat."

Chapter Nine

"How are you doing, *ma fille*?"

Zoe glanced up from the fireplace, where she had been contemplating the dancing flames, to see her mother standing in the doorway. It was late at night, approaching the early morning hours, and Simone had let her hair down for the evening. The soft blond curls fell over her shoulder, framing the delicate features of her face. She wore her dressing gown, clearly ready for bed, but in her hands she held a bottle of claret and two glasses.

"I'm fine." Zoe gestured to the wine. "Not retiring just yet?"

Simone smiled. "No. I thought you might need a drink after the day you've had. And I wanted to visit with my daughter."

"Well, you're right about the drink." Zoe sighed, turning back to the fire, lit more for looks than for heat, wrapping her own dressing gown around her more tightly. "It's been quite a day."

Joining her on the chaise, Simone poured the wine into the two glasses. "Indeed. Has Quinton already gone to bed? And Mary as well?"

"Yes. Rory and Charlie ought to be arriving early in the morning, and he wants to be up to greet them. Mary did try to stay up, but she couldn't keep her eyes open, so I sent her to bed about an hour ago."

"Ah, yes." Simone took a sip of her wine. "Fortunate to have a resurrectionist en route, considering what's happened."

Zoe followed suit, enjoying the cool, bittersweet liquid as it filled her mouth. Zoe and Hugh had always preferred whiskey, but for Simone there was nothing better than a glass or two of claret, and Zoe had to admit that it could be quite refreshing.

Her mother wasn't wrong—it had been quite a day. As unlikable as Langford had been, Zoe was still having a hard time getting his eyes out of her mind. The way his head was turned, his neck bent, and his face pointed in the wrong direction . . . it was gruesome. Yet she had also felt a certain amount of exhilaration. That feeling was now gone, replaced by the weight of exhaustion as if someone were pressing down on her shoulders. And yet the thought of sleep seemed distant and far away.

"Yes. I feel sorry for Rory though. His time here won't be as relaxing as he expected." Zoe took another sip. "But there's nothing to be done about it."

"No, I suppose not." Simone glanced at her daughter. "What do you think? Surely it was just a terrible accident?"

Not too long ago, if someone would have told Zoe that her mother would sit next to her and ask her opinion on the cause of death of a land steward, Zoe would have laughed in their face. Much had changed over the past couple of years.

"It might have been." Zoe shook her head. "But I'm not convinced. Something's off about it. Quinton and the magistrate agree."

"Hmm. What a strange and unfortunate thing." Simone leaned back in the cushion, her expression contemplative. There were few places where she looked more beautiful than in the soft firelight. Even now, with her hair down and in a dressing gown, Simone still held a presence of dignity.

Zoe reached out and took her free hand in her own. "And

what about you, Maman? How have you and Hugh been these past few months?"

"I've been well. The Haven is progressing nicely—we purchased another home on the same block. And you know Hugh . . . he's been working on his cases. I swear, he spends more time in his study every day."

It was slight, but something in Simone's tone caught Zoe's attention. She looked more closely at her mother. Had those lines around her eyes been there long? Perhaps Simone was just tired and Zoe was reading too much into nothing. It had been a long day.

"And you, *ma cherie*? My Z, as Walter would say." Simone turned back to Zoe, the slight edge to her tone gone. "Are you happy, despite the day's grisly turn?"

Zoe smiled, both at the question and the childhood nickname, but she hesitated. "Yes. I am very happy, Maman."

Simone waited, and Zoe continued. "Most of the time."

Simone reached out to touch her. "Quinton treats you well, *oui?*"

"Quinton treats me very well, Maman," Zoe hurried to say. "And I love him with all that I am. It is not he that sometimes gives me pause."

"What, then?" Zoe saw the worry in her mother's eyes, and was quick to dispel it.

"It is . . . *absurdité.*" Zoe shook her head, trying to find the words to explain herself. "It was so exciting to get engaged to Quinton. And then we waited for months as Aunt Theo recovered, and the wedding was beautiful." Zoe reached out to take Simone's hand. "Thank you for that. I know you put much effort into making that day perfect. And the honeymoon was marvellous. But even through all of that, the thought would arise: what about the rest of my life? For some time I have been active helping to solve one puzzle or another, and now, I feel as if my time will be spent on the same *inutile* pursuits I often ridiculed other women for."

Zoe paused again, and her mother chose not to fill the silence that followed. Zoe felt the heat rise to her face as she finished. "I am not glad a man has been killed, but I can't deny that the idea of a new puzzle is . . . invigorating? Does that make me a terrible person, that I cannot be happy unless someone is injured or dies or is being swindled so I can amuse myself solving the puzzle?" The last words came out in a rush and Zoe lowered her eyes in embarrassment.

Simone drew her close in a familiar hug, and in the comfort of her mother's arms, Zoe relaxed, leaning in.

"Never put yourself in the same breath as those that cause that harm," said Simone softly. "You have an active mind and always have. You will find your way with this new life of yours, and for now, your quick mind will be useful in putting all of this behind us. Your mind is an asset, not a liability." Using her free hand, Simone drank of her wine and continued. "And an estate this size needs a woman's hand as well. Don't be too quick to dismiss it."

"Thank you, Maman." Zoe appreciated her mother's point of view, but the thought of spending her days tallying accounts and hiring scullery maids didn't fill her with joy for the future.

Simone changed the subject. "And Quinton? Is he happy as well?"

"Yes, he is happy too." Zoe hesitated. "Most of the time."

"Oh? What of the rest of the time?"

What of the rest of the time? It was a good question, one that Zoe had been pondering.

"His struggle is different, more with the transition to the peerage. When we were on the continent, there was always something to do to fill the days. But as it came closer to time to return home, something in him shifted. It's like he's trying to force himself to become something he's not."

"Hmm." Simone swirled her wine. "It's not an easy transition to make, entering society. It was not the same, but I remember when I was attempting it after I married Hugh. A Frenchwoman was tolerated, but not welcomed. Trying to find a way to balance who I was with who I had to be . . . it wasn't easy. I'm sure Quinton will find his own balance soon enough."

"Yes, I'm sure you're right." Downing the rest of her wine, Zoe sighed again. "I just hope he's happy when he does. As grisly as it is, perhaps this mystery will cheer both of us."

Chapter Ten

Quinton watched as his friend Rory entered the formal dining room looking freshly bathed and shaved. He was older than Quinton and Charlie by more than a decade, but his early forties had not stolen the youthful spring to his step. He caught Quinton's eye from across the room and walked over easily with a cheerful grin. Quinton usually associated Rory with either the scent of antiseptic of death, but a pleasing odour of bergamot and pine met Quinton first as Rory approached—or possibly rosemary.

Quinton stretched out a hand, but Rory ignored it, instead engulfing him in a hearty hug.

His Scottish accent was thick as Rory spoke. "Turns out cats dinnae make the best travellers, Q. I cannae be sure that carriage will ever be usable again." He paused and accepted a cup of tea from a footman. "And there is no certainty that Charlie will ever recover from the experience."

The glint of amusement in Rory's eye was good to see. The year before had taken a toll on his Scottish friend, with a stay at Newgate prison and an accusation of murder. Looking at him now, with his high-quality tailcoat, richly patterned waistcoat, and perfectly tailored trousers, Quinton couldn't help but smile. His friend was back. A Shakespearean quote was likely not far away.

Rory had a point about Charlie. The man had always had a soft spot for Quinton's cat Oscar, having been the one to save her as a wee mite. But this experience might test his loyalty. The odour from the carriage had actually preceded its arrival, and when the doors were opened, the human inhabitants had fled the interior as if chased by a wild boar. Interestingly, Oscar herself was sitting contentedly out of the carriage itself, next to the driver, and smelled better than any of the passengers.

"You bloody beggars better not be talking about me." Charlie stalked across the dining room. He also looked freshly bathed, with his comfortable linen shirt, grey waistcoat, and brown trousers highlighting his fit-though-compact physique. The light colours contrasted against his dark skin, highlighting his half-Indian heritage, as if that wasn't already obvious. He walked with ease and confidence, and if it weren't for the white scar which marred the left side of his face and blinded that eye, one would think he was born to a life of privilege. Quinton felt a pang of guilt that he hadn't thought to invite him at first.

"Of course not," replied Quinton soothingly.

"Mm-hmm." Charlie shook his head. "Your bloody cat can stay here for her lifespan as far as I am concerned, but I assure you, my friend, she will not ride back with me. And leaving at midnight was not the best choice either."

"Just out of curiosity, are there any choices you are pleased with, or is it your mission in life to grumble about everything?" teased Rory.

"Oh, like you enjoyed spending eight hours confined with that hellcat—"

"Your sacrifice is appreciated," Quinton interrupted. "I'm glad you're here, Charlie."

Charlie glared for a moment, but then his face softened into a smile. "It is good to see you as well, Q."

Returning the smile, Quinton reflected that Zoe had been

right. He could have his birthright, while keeping the people in his life that made up his family. He was a lucky man.

"Just be glad *Maan* stayed back with Finn. Either she or Oscar would not have survived the trip." Charlie turned to examine the various paintings that adorned the walls.

Rory rolled his eyes, but he too turned to look at the art. "Some of these pieces are very impressive, Quinton. One of your ancestors must have been quite the collector."

"I suppose so." Quinton glanced around. "I haven't really had much time to appreciate the artwork."

"I suppose not. We were very intent on getting into clean clothes, but did I hear you say something about a dead land steward as we entered the house?" asked Rory.

Quinton quickly laid out the details of Langford's unfortunate demise, the two men listening with rapt attention.

"Would you mind taking a look at the body?" asked Quinton. "I know it might not be the visit you were planning on, but—"

Rory laughed. "What would a trip to the country be without dissecting a body? No, of course I don't mind." He turned back to the wall. "But first, tell me about this?"

Quinton looked where Rory was pointing, at a large genealogy quilt that hung on the back wall of the massive room.

"What of it?" Quinton paused to grab a piece of his new favourite crust bread from the repast set out on the table before moving to stand closer to the quilt. "I don't know much about it."

"You ought to learn a little more about your own ancestry." Rory took a sip of tea and a bite of bread. "This looks to contain the names and dates of the Coleville clan going back two hundred years. This is really good bread, by the way."

Taking a closer look, Quinton saw Rory was right. The names, birth dates, and death dates had been embroidered beautifully with much skill over a traditional quilt with complementing squares. Sometimes symbols accompanied the names, and lines connected the names of those married, with their children and their children's children connected below by other lines. The symbols meant little to Quinton, and even the names seemed foreign. But after a moment, Rory laughed.

"I knew there was a reason I liked you, my boy. You have Scottish blood in you." Rory pointed to a name connected to his grandfather, not far from the names of Quinton's uncle Montgomery and his father Graham. "This lass is Scottish, sure as the moon in the sky."

Quinton squinted, trying to make out what Rory was talking about. Next to the name of his father's mother—his own grandmother—was a perfectly stitched picture of a unicorn holding a tiny blue cross.

Quinton turned to Rory. "A unicorn? That makes her Scottish?"

Rory opened his eyes wide in surprise, and if it was possible, somehow his accent became thicker. "Laddie," he explained slowly, as if talking to a child. "The unicorn is Scotland's national animal, for hundreds of years now. Every school boy kens that."

"A mythical animal is the national animal of Scotland?" scoffed Quinton. "You cannot be serious."

"Mythical? Maybe to the uneducated. We Scots are proud as can be of our unicorns." Rory said this without a bit of sarcasm, and Quinton opened his mouth to argue but Rory held up a hand. "But even for you naysayers, the wee beast is holding a saltire. That little blue cross is on the national flag of Scotland."

Realizing the Scot was right, Quinton let out a sound of astonishment. Looking over at his self-satisfied friend, Quinton felt a strange sense of connection, even though nothing had truly changed between them.

"I guess that makes us brothers, Rory," said Quinton with a smile.

"Don't be a bloody idiot." Charlie had made his way to their side and stood staring at the quilt as well. Quinton stood head and shoulders above Charlie, but what Charlie lacked in height he often made up for in pure will. "Brothers ain't about blood.

Brothers are about history, and you had that before." He paused as he studied the quilt as well. "More interesting, did you know about your aunt?"

Both Quinton and Rory looked past the proof of Scottish origins and saw the stitched entry Charlie was referring to. Below Philip and his Scottish wife were three names, not two. There was Montgomery, then Graham, and then a Catriona Coleville.

Quinton shook his head. "Montgomery spoke often of his brother, my father, but he never mentioned a sister to me."

"She was apparently quite a lot older," Rory answered easily, reaching a finger up to touch the relevant dates. "She was born first, and then four years later your father was born. Your uncle came along much later. There's no death date listed."

Suddenly a firm yowl caught the men's attention, and they turned to see Oscar sat in the middle of the biggest chair. She curled up and began an extensive grooming, including—but not limited to—her bum.

"By the way, you're not entirely wrong, Charlie, but you're forgetting that family is also about putting up with whatever comes, cat included." Rory paused, then added an additional thought. "And sharing Scottish blood? *A rose, by any other name would smell as sweet.*"

There was the Shakespeare Quinton had been waiting for. He was grateful to hear it.

Chapter Eleven

LONDON

"It still tastes like swill one would feed the swine." Despite the derogatory sentiment, the statement was offered with little emotion. Lady Theodosia Bexley, Dowager Duchess of Wentworth, was someone who believed a person should make their thoughts known whether emotion was attached or not.

She exaggerated her grimace as she drank the rest of the tonic. "Or perhaps what comes from the other end of the swine, though I don't know the taste of either from experience."

"That's how you know the tonic is going to work," responded Katy Modi with a tolerant smile. Taking the empty glass from Theo, the Indian woman stood to place it on the sideboard where the staff would pick it up. She then poured a cup of strong tea, which Theo knew would be sweetened with honey and milk, and brought it back her.

"Perhaps a good blend of tea will help alleviate any aftertaste," Katy said as she handed the cup over.

"I only have the best blends, my dear," retorted Theo.

Katy brought her own cup back, as well as a plate of cheese and bread, with a single small cake on the side, pointedly not acknowledging Theo's glare.

As Theo took a small sip of the excellent blend, she reflected on the many times this same conversation had taken place over the last number of months. Katy and she were an odd couple, Theo knew that to be true. Katy had come from India with two small children, Charlie and Savita, and their British father, only to be abandoned on the streets of London after their weak-willed father bowed to family pressure. Theo, on the other hand, was a childless aristocratic widow with excessive wealth. But true friends sometimes came in unexpected packages, and this tiny Indian woman had showed her friendship when it counted.

When Theo was first was affected by the apoplexy, her own doctor was nearby round the clock. But as the acute situation mellowed into the chronic weakness which now affected her left side, the doctors moved on and Katy all but moved in. She was a healer in her own right, having come from a family of healers, and her experience as a midwife had aided her in developing an array of tonics for any number of ailments.

She had come daily at first, her son's ward Finn in tow, and slowly Theo had healed. It was weeks before she could sit upright in a chair for any length of time, and it took longer still to regain use of her left leg. While the doctors advised bloodletting and purging, which only seemed to weaken Theo further, Katy drove her to push herself, both physically and mentally. She had also prescribed an assortment of tonics, tinctures, and teas of bitter-tasting herbs and roots. At times the fatigue was impossible to ignore, and Theo would sleep for an entire day. But when Katy came again, Theo would fight beside her, to find the independence she had taken for granted before.

At her beloved Zoe's wedding, Theo had been able to walk to her seat, escorted by her nephew Alexander. She had danced with Zoe's new husband at the reception which followed, though she knew Quinton had kept a supporting arm firmly around her waist. And now—though her staff still hovered obnoxiously—she could walk about her home and on outings very nearly the same as before the incident, with the addition of a cane.

Her array of canes, which she was at first reluctant to

embrace, became a part of her ensemble when she found out they could be custom made. She now sported one most of the time, especially when she left the house, her favourite made of ebony with mother of pearl adorning the handle. That one had a small compartment in which one could carry personal items. She even dabbled with the idea of having one made with a hidden weapon that would appear with the right movement of the handle. A bit impractical for her lifestyle, but the thought absolutely delighted her.

Realizing her musings had gone on longer than she thought, and surprised by Katy's quietness, Theo eyed her friend and commented, "You seem just a bit distracted, dear. Everything all right with the parents-to-be?"

Katy's daughter Savita and her husband John had recently announced they were expecting a baby in the spring, and Theo knew Katy was overjoyed.

"It is obvious to anyone how those two feel about each other. John and Savita are madly in love. But their life views often conflict," replied Katy with a sigh.

"Really? I am surprised. They seem so well suited." Theo took a small bite of the cake, enjoying the taste of the rosemary in the icing. She definitely would have another one once her overly strict friend left.

"They have much in common, but they also come from different backgrounds and cultures. Some friction is to be expected. However, the real source of conflict is their natures. John is naturally very protective of Savita, and I am glad for that. But now that she is expecting a child, he has become increasingly vigilant, fearful for her and the baby's health. As you can imagine, this has not gone over well with Savita, who does not appreciate being wrapped in silk."

Theo smiled at the thought. "No, I don't imagine it does."

Katy sighed. "Savita has been forging her own path in one way or another since her father left us to starve. It hasn't always been easy, and both my children are fiercely independent. They don't take well to being stifled. Now that Quinton and Zoe have returned, it has gotten worse. Savita wants to join Charlie and the others in the country, getting a reprieve from the heat. John wants to see his friends but does not want Savita to endure a bumpy carriage ride to get there, as he fears for the health of the child. Their clashes over the matter have been . . . memorable, to say the least."

Finishing her cake and small plate of cheese, Theo rose to fill her own plate, ignoring her ivory-handled cane. Katy said nothing as Theo chose another rosemary cake and two chocolate delicacies. Balancing the dish carefully, Theo slipped one of the chocolates onto Katy's plate, then sat down.

"Children cause us worry, my friend. The hours I spent anxious over both Zoe and Alexander have taken a few years off my life." Theo bit into the delectable treat, savouring the sweet herbal flavour. "But these kinds of issues often settle in the early years of marriage, if there is love to spare. Savita and John have no shortage of love, so I'm sure they will come to an understanding. In the meantime, I may have a solution for the carriage debacle. I happen to own one that is recently modified for an incapacitated elderly woman. It has every luxury—including an exceptionally smooth ride. Very few bumps. It may be a compromise the two young people can agree to make."

Katy took time to ponder her words. "That is a very generous offer—perhaps too generous. I don't wish to put you out."

Theo waved a dismissive hand. "It would not put me out in any way. I welcome the company. Take the offer to the young people and see what they have to say. For now, let's enjoy these sweets, though I know you say I should limit them, and move on to the torture you have prepared for me today. That should cheer you."

Laughing out loud, Katy relented and ate her cake.

Chapter Twelve

Mary hovered outside the shed, holding a lavender-scented handkerchief to her nose. It hadn't really been long enough for the body to start to smell, but the action made Mary feel better anyway.

Within the shed she could see Rory holding up a lantern to illuminate the dim interior. His expression was not cheerful.

"I need more bloody light," he snapped.

Quinton and Zoe obliged, each of them holding their own lanterns higher, but Rory's disposition did not improve.

"This would be much easier in my own shed—I had custom windows put in for this very problem."

"We can move him out into the sunlight, Rory," responded Quinton.

Rory waved a dismissive hand. "It's fine."

Charlie was noticeably absent from the inspection of the body. For a man living in his shoes, he was surprisingly squeamish about corpses. Instead he had chosen to walk those shoes around the scene of the incident.

At the moment, Mary was wishing she'd joined him. While she didn't share Charlie's same aversion, there was something terribly unsettling about the way the land steward's head faced the wrong way, his eyes looking at his back.

Fortunately, the shed wasn't quite large enough for all four and the corpse to fit, so Mary had graciously volunteered to wait outside.

"So what do you think?" asked Zoe.

"You said he was found at the base of the ruins of the old mansion?" Rory cocked head, squinting. "Turn him over for me, please, Quinton."

Handing his lantern to Zoe, Quinton obliged, pulling Langford up so that he rested on his side and Rory could examine the back.

"Hmm." Straightening up, Rory gestured for Quinton to return the corpse to its original position. "If he fell, I'd expect to see more trauma to the body. Bruises, broken bones, abrasions and the like. But the only noticeable sign of trauma I'm seeing is the broken neck."

"What does that mean?" Mary asked from outside the shed.

Rory pulled the sheet back over the body and stepped out, blinking at the bright sunlight. "I'd know more if I had my own equipment with me. Wish I'd brought a few things—my scalpels for one—"

"Rory!" snapped Quinton as he too joined them outside. "Just tell us your assessment."

With a dramatic sigh, Rory shook his head. "Everyone is so impatient. Fine, if you must know, I doubt this was an accidental fall—or an accident of any kind. Considering how severe the break is his neck is, it's my professional estimation that someone did this to him. Probably from behind."

"Why do you say that?" Mary suppressed the twist in her stomach.

"Lack of defensive wounds on his arms or hands. It's a small mercy, but I'm betting the poor creature never saw it coming."

A small mercy indeed. Even though he was a nasty old man,

Mary hoped he'd gone quick. No one deserved to suffer in the last moments of their life—well, almost no one.

Her thoughts drifted back to the man who had so nearly taken hers and Zoe's life. Felix Fairfax. A man who had taken multiple women's lives for nothing more than his own pleasure. He'd hung earlier that year for his sins. Mary hadn't attended the execution, but if anyone deserved to linger for a bit before shuffling off their mortal coil, it was Felix Fairfax. If there was a hell, Mary hoped he was burning in it.

Quinton sighed, running a hand through his wavy, brown hair. "Damn. I was already leaning that way, but I was hoping you'd put my unease to rest."

"You realize what this means, right?" Zoe took her husband's hand, almost as a reflex.

"Yes," he muttered darkly. "It means my family's land steward's been murdered, and the killer may still be on the estate."

The ruins were nicer than some tenements Charlie had lived in. He shook his head slowly as he surveyed the crumbling stone. Only the nobility would leave an entire building to go to waste, rotting in the countryside for no reason.

It was big too. The place where the body had been found was on the west side, where the dining room was visible through a missing wall. It had apparently been a favourite place for the land steward to spend time. He hadn't been found inside, but rather outside the foundation.

An isolated location, far enough that a loud argument wouldn't have been heard from the main house. If Charlie wanted someone dead, it wasn't a bad spot to choose for a meeting.

"Do you require anything else, sir?"

Charlie jumped; he'd forgotten the butler was still there. "No, thank you."

"Very good."

Evans still hovered. Charlie sighed—he didn't know how to dismiss him without being rude. He wasn't used to being around servants like this, without the Dovefields or Quinton to buffer.

Charlie had nothing against the profession of serving. It was a respectable career, and people did what they had to do to survive. But there was something about butlers specifically that unsettled him. They were just so . . . proud. It was as if they all took a class in how to look down their nose at people—people like Charlie, who they didn't deem worthy of being part of society. It made Charlie feel small and unimportant, which he hated.

Despite his discomfort, Charlie tried to swallow his annoyance. Evans hadn't even really done anything to him; he was just hovering. But Charlie didn't like being watched—it made him self-conscious about every action and step. As he glanced around, Charlie couldn't shake the thought that someone else's eyes were also on him, watching from somewhere beyond the tree line. Perhaps his years of looking over his shoulder were making him paranoid.

Trying to distract himself, Charlie decided to make an attempt at conversation. "Did you know Mr. Langford well?"

"Mr. Langford worked for the Colevilles for over fifty years." Evans spoke clearly. "Our paths of course crossed over the years, but we weren't friends."

Charlie was surprised at how easily Evans volunteered the information. He glanced back over at him, reevaluating the man. He was middle-aged, perhaps in his late fifties or early sixties. He stood straight, his frame slender but fit. His eyes held an intelligence Charlie hadn't expected.

"How long have you worked here, Evans?" Charlie asked, pushing his luck.

"Forty-two years, Mr. Modi. I started as a footman."

Charlie nodded. "Makes sense."

He wasn't sure what to say next, so Charlie allowed the silence to return. He studied the ground. Quinton was right—there weren't many rocks around where the land steward had been found, like one would expect if the wall had given out on the second floor. But there was still some rubble around, enough that it couldn't be ruled out. A good location if one wanted to make a murder look like an accident.

Accidents weren't Charlie's style. When he had killed men or had men killed, it was for a purpose—to send a message or eliminate a problem. Trying to disguise the fact it was murder defeated the point. But he could still understand the logic of it. The real question was why anyone would want to kill a land steward who had already resigned. It seemed like a waste, and if there was one thing Charlie couldn't abide, it was waste when it came to taking a life. Causing death wasn't a choice he took lightly, but not everyone lived by his moral compass.

"I'm told Mr. Langford frequented the ruins. Was that common knowledge?" Charlie asked his companion.

Evans paused, as if weighing his next words carefully. "It wasn't a secret." He paused again. "An accident is not unexpected, given the time he spent here. However, Mr. Langford kept to himself for the most part."

"He wasn't a very friendly sort? Didn't associate with the other staff?"

"No." Evans's tone was matter-of-fact. "But that is to be expected of a land steward."

"Oh?" Charlie frowned. "Why is that?"

"He wasn't a part of the downstairs staff."

"But aren't you all employed by the same man?"

"Yes. But there are distinctions. For example, should a governess or tutor be employed in case of children, they wouldn't typically associate socially with the maids or footmen. The same in the case of land stewards."

"Oh." Charlie felt heat on his cheeks. "I wasn't aware." Quinton's new world contained a great deal he wasn't aware of. It was going to take some getting used to.

"There's no reason you should be," responded Evans.

Charlie wasn't sure if that was the butler's way of reassuring him or poking fun at him. He glanced at the man from the corner of his eye, but Evans's expression was unreadable.

"I suppose not." Charlie sighed. "I think we've learned everything there is to learn out here. Let's head back. Hopefully the bloody Scot has had more luck."

Chapter Thirteen

Philip Coleville was the picture of elegance in his carefully tailored trousers and stiff white shirt. His cravat was tied in a series of complicated knots and his waistcoat was decorated with an elaborate embroidery.

"You've already managed to make quite a shambles of things." The words were spoken angrily, and Quinton felt his own temper rise. He opened his mouth to give an angry retort but Montgomery Coleville quickly jumped in.

"Stop it, Father. Quinton can hardly be blamed for a murder on this property when he had barely put his boots to the dirt before the unfortunate act came about."

"I wasn't talking about the death, Montgomery." Philip glared at him. "I was talking about the way the death was handled. I have been informed by my senior staff that the whole unfortunate incident could easily have been ruled accidental. What were you thinking, to demand a death be called a murder? Had you handled the situation as you should have, we could right now be sipping brandy and not having this conversation."

That dirty little rotter. The blasted butler must have ratted him out. Lesson learned.

The Coleville men had arrived within the last hour, and then learned the unfortunate details of the incident regarding Mr. Langford. Quinton had known their arrival was a given at some point during the summer, but the timing was poor.

Quinton met his grandfather's eyes unflinchingly with a steely gaze of his own. "I demanded nothing but the truth, sir. It's a failing of mine from providing my own living as an inquiry agent for a decade. Truth matters, at least to me."

To his right, Quinton heard Montgomery sigh. The man disliked the constant barbed back-and-forth between Quinton and Philip, but Quinton knew a man like his grandfather would view agreement as capitulation. Quinton felt strongly he needed to stand his ground if he ever wanted to gain Philip's respect.

The older man scoffed. "Yes, never overlook the opportunity to remind us that we somehow failed you, leaving you to grovel on the streets of London. We did not even know you existed, boy." It was plain the man would have preferred their knowledge of each other to remain unknown as well.

Taking a steadying breath, Quinton replied, "But I do exist, Grandfather, and as heir I felt I had the authority to act in the case of the death of Mr. Langford. Act I did. I make no apologies. Perhaps we can move on and discuss who might have wanted him dead."

"Do so without me." Philip stalked to the closed door and opened it. He paused in the doorframe a moment to send a final angry glance back at Quinton, then disappeared.

Montgomery sighed again, and walked to the sideboard. Dressed more casually than his father, his garb still shouted wealth, and he moved like a man used to money. Glancing back at Quinton, he reached for a bottle. "Still a whiskey man?"

Managing a smile, Quinton nodded. "I am. Also, I am sorry your father and I cannot seem to find our feet. Believe it or not, I wish we could as well."

Pouring two glasses, Montgomery shrugged. "My father is a difficult man. Few find their feet with him. I'm not sure I ever have." He handed one glass to Quinton and passed on to a roomy upholstered chair. "Interestingly, one that did was Ellis Langford. Apparently those two were thick as thieves when they were younger. Time and age widened the gap between their classes, but Father remained fond of the old land steward. His death has likely upset him more than he's willing to admit."

"Langford mentioned he knew your father since they were both boys." Quinton found a nearby oversized chair and relaxed into its depths, swirling the amber liquid in his glass. "I know the man found me disagreeable; he made that ever so clear. I guess he and your father would find that in common."

His uncle stared into his own glass before taking a healthy sip. "I've never known my father to be any other way. Even before Graham died, he was aloof and bitter. Years ago, when I was a boy, Langford told me a story about when he and my father got drunk of ale and played a prank on a neighbouring estate. Apparently they released a herd of goats into the house while the residents were entertaining a visiting Duke. Quite the spectacle. I sometimes wonder what happened to that version of Philip Coleville."

The vision wasn't one Quinton had expected: his grandfather as a young man, laughing and happy and mischievous. It was a shame that part of him had been so thoroughly stamped out— stamped out of both him and Langford.

Quinton was quiet a moment, lost in his musings of the past. But after a moment he spoke. "Tell me about your sister."

Montgomery raised an eyebrow. "How do you know about her?"

"Tapestry, in the dining room."

"Ah." Montgomery nodded. "Catriona. We don't talk about her much. I was barely out of leading strings when she ran off. But the older staff would occasionally tell me stories, as well as Graham, when I caught him in the right mood. I learned enough over the years to piece together the gist of what happened. Apparently when our mother died, Catriona became . . . unmanageable. She and my father argued constantly. Men, drink, fighting—if it was scandalous, she was involved."

"Sounds like quite the handful," said Quinton, liking her more and more as Montgomery went on.

"That's one way to put it." Montgomery shook his head. "To make matters worse, after my mother's death, my father forbade any contact with that side of the family. Catriona was quite close with them and took the loss hard."

Quinton got up to refill the glasses, glad the footmen were not present to wait upon them for once. "That would be the Scottish side of your family, yes?"

"Correct." Montgomery eyed him. "You must have really studied that tapestry."

"It was of interest, as you might imagine." Quinton retook his seat. "How did your mother die, if you don't mind me asking?"

"In childbirth—my birth." The words were spoken evenly and without emotion, but Quinton could see the weight of them was sharp. "Of course, for me, it was an easy enough loss. I never even knew the woman. But it was difficult, for the rest of them. Understandable, I suppose."

"I don't think the loss of a parent is ever easy, no matter the age," said Quinton quietly.

"Perhaps." Montgomery shrugged. "Regardless, the story of Catriona ends with one last epic argument. Then she was gone, aged just seventeen. We don't know for certain, but the most likely thing that happened is she ran off to London and never looked back." Montgomery paused and took a deep swallow of the whiskey. "I think that may have been the beginning of the end between my father and Graham. The siblings were quite close, and I don't think he ever forgave my father for driving her away."

The room was quiet as both men processed the conversation. Quinton let the silence continue, hoping Montgomery would feel compelled to fill it. But he was surprised at his uncle's next words.

"The servants believe Catriona haunts the estate."

Quinton stared at him. "I thought you said she ran off to London?"

"I said that's most likely what happened." Montgomery

continued to sip his whiskey. "But we don't know for certain. Another popular theory is that she never left the estate and is buried somewhere on the land."

"My god." Quinton couldn't quite hide his shock. "Is that what you believe?"

Montgomery laughed softly. "No. It's just a rumour spread by the gossip of maids with too much time on their hands. That being said, do I think she's still alive?" Montgomery shrugged again. "I find it hard to believe she never contacted Graham again, in all those years before he died. London is an unforgiving place, and I think any number of unmentionable things may have happened to an aristocratic girl without any real survival skills."

A harsh statement, but not unrealistic.

"So you don't think the estate is haunted?" asked Quinton.

Montgomery hesitated at that. "On principle, no. But . . . there are things I cannot explain. I don't know everything there is to know in the world. Over the years, there have been multiple accounts of a woman in white seemingly gliding through the woods. She has been spotted from the house as well, in the garden, even in the hallways of the manor."

Quinton contemplated this. "Have you ever seen her?"

"No." Montgomery shook his head. "I've always chalked it up to overactive imaginations. But there are moments when it feels as though I'm being watched, or when an object is moved that the maid swears she didn't move."

Montgomery handed the glass back over to Quinton, clearly expecting him to refill it. Some habits died hard. Quinton obliged his uncle, refilling both their glasses.

The situation was odd, he would give him that. Quinton didn't believe in ghosts on principle either, but he thought back to that first encounter at the ruins, when he had seen the figure and felt the eyes watching him. He couldn't explain that either—yet.

What a complicated web was weaved in this newfound family of his.

Chapter Fourteen

"Every family has secrets." Hugh Dovefield's response to his son-in-law's summary of the conversation with Montgomery Coleville was spoken without judgment. To Hugh, the statement was simple fact.

"Does yours?" Quinton asked, as if the sentiment surprised him.

"Of course, my boy," replied Hugh with a low laugh. "Do you really believe Simone and Zoe have shared everything with me that they saw and experienced from when they fled France all those years ago? Or that I have shared every detail of my first marriage with them?"

Hugh's first marriage wasn't something he spoke about often. He wasn't sure why he'd brought her up. He still thought about her, sometimes—poor Edwina—but it had been a long time ago and the memories were painful. It wasn't that the two were madly in love, but Hugh had been fond of her, and he thought she was of him as well. The days spent watching her slowly fade away from an illness which the physicians couldn't cure—and even worse, the days spent away as a coward, burying himself in his work, burning oil deep into the night so he wouldn't have to watch her dying—they weren't something he wished to dwell on. She had died a month short of their two-year anniversary.

Quinton said nothing in response, likely hoping the silence would encourage Hugh to share more. But Hugh was wise to the strategy and didn't feel a need to divulge more.

"Trust me, we all have things we'd rather keep to ourselves." Hugh thought of the times when Simone would wake, even now, drenched in a cold sweat and mumbling her first husband's name. He knew she wouldn't appreciate those details being shared, so he kept the memories to himself.

"I can understand that," said Quinton. "But what Simone and Zoe went through was an unusual circumstance. I doubt the Dovefields have many missing relatives or ghosts haunting their estate."

"You would be surprised," Hugh responded. "I don't think there's a noble family in all of Britain who doesn't have some scandal or another hiding in their closet."

He thought of another secret Simone had shared with him recently, regarding his sister. Losing a baby wasn't a scandal, but Theo hadn't shared the terrible heartbreak with anyone for over thirty years. It was still her secret to share or not, so Hugh didn't mention it either.

The two men continued on in silence for a while, heading toward the ruins where the body had been found.

After a bit, Hugh said, "You recall my younger brother Sebastian?"

"Of course. Zoe adores the man."

Hugh chuckled at that. "She does indeed. He is the keeper of scandals for our family, so of course she feels an affinity for him."

Quinton snorted. "That doesn't entirely surprise me."

"No, it's no great shock." Hugh sighed as he thought of his younger brother. "Nothing truly untoward, of course. Honestly I think Sebastian just enjoys being a thorn in our elder brother's side—not that I didn't do my part by marrying a French woman, with a child no less. But Sebastian takes it further. He's a third son who has never married, lives largely off his good looks and charm, yet always has the latest in fashion and is beautifully turned out. Many people have commented on his lifestyle with a wondering eye and a raised eyebrow. I'll leave it to you to infer what the truth of his secrets might be."

He stopped talking as the path opened out to the ruins. They stood there in silence, admiring the graceful lines of the structure as a whole still visible through the deterioration. The overall size of the house was smaller than the present manor but more elaborate, with spires on each side and a turret on the west, all in varying degrees of decay.

"Why would such a grand manor be abandoned and another house built?" Quinton's tone held a distinct note of astonishment. "Why not just keep this one repaired and live here?"

"Ruins like this litter the English countryside, for many reasons," replied Hugh. "As hard as it may be to believe, many wealthy landowners simply have opted for a different style of house, more in keeping with some architectural trend. Others have a period of many years where a family had no interest in their country manor so the house fell into such disrepair that the next generation simply built a new one."

Quinton shook his head. "Seems a waste to me."

"You're not wrong." Both men started down the steep path to the ruins as Hugh continued. "But I did a bit of uncovering about this land when we found proof of you being the legal heir. The Coleville family are actually not the original owners of this land, although it has been in their possession for well over a hundred years. The records are not clear that far back, but it may have been won in some sort of game of chance."

"A game of chance?" Quinton snorted. "Ironic how fate smiles on some and rains on others."

Hugh nodded at that but didn't pause, continuing to walk around the house. "In any case, it's why it was offered in the game of chance that is the real story."

Quinton raised his eyebrows questioningly and Hugh continued. "Legend has it, the previous family, generations back, held a lavish house party on the night of a full moon. The festivities went far into the wee hours of the morning, and as is true of many house parties, much drink was consumed. When the family awoke, their oldest child, who was only ten, was missing. Soon they discovered him, tragically killed, apparently having fallen from the manor roof."

Evidently entranced, Quinton stopped. "What happened?"

Hugh stopped as well. "Remember, this was over 150 years ago. Stories grow like children over time. But, according to legend, after that the house was rumored to be haunted, with a child being heard at night crying, and toys being moved from place to place. So it was then assumed the boy died that night from someone's hand, in the throes of drunkenness, and the lifeless body was thrown from the roof. As is often purported, the boy could not rest because of being murdered."

"That's a terrible tragedy."

Hugh raised his own eyebrow. "A terrible tragedy, to be sure, but more likely far more mundane. Likely, the boy was awakened by the noisy crowd and for some reason only a boy could understand, climbed onto the roof, perhaps to innocently spy on some revelers. He fell off and that was that."

"But what about the crying child?" Quinton asked sincerely.

"It never ceases to amaze me how the imagination makes real what is only supposed. If one maid heard a cat, surmised it to be a ghost child, then others would undoubtedly hear the same."

"And yet," said Quinton, "there is a ruin."

"Yes," Hugh agreed, "In time the house was considered haunted and an entire generation avoided the estate. The next generation saw the decay and saw no issue with staking it in a card game. Your family won it, and simply built Cedarbrook, allowing the old manor to become a proper ruin."

The men continued walking and came to the garden and continued to follow the game path through the tall grass to where the house itself, open to the weather, welcomed them.

Quinton picked his way to a spot he seemed to have already had in mind and gestured upward to the crumbling roof. "He was found here, and both Evans and I both first thought that he fell from there."

"Yes. "Hugh nodded. "Malcolm was telling me."

"Malcolm?" Quinton frowned. "Who is Malcolm?"

"Evans," Hugh replied. "The butler."

"Oh." Quinton laughed. "I guess I never asked him his first name."

Hugh smiled. "I like to learn each of the upper staff's full names. I find it is not just mannerly but generally results in better relations and happier staff. A personal interest never goes unnoticed. But just keep in mind not to call them by their first name to their face. It can come across as disrespectful."

This was the first time Quinton had ever had servants of his own, and Hugh wanted to offer as much advice as could be considered tactful. Fortunately his son-in-law was a man who wasn't easily offended by the offering of advice. Quinton still had so much to learn about this new life, but Hugh didn't want to undermine his confidence.

"I'll keep that in mind," said Quinton with a thoughtful expression.

Looking around, Hugh took in the comfortable little alcove where he assumed Langford would have sat, noting the chair, table, and footstool.

"I wonder why he found comfort here?" Hugh mused aloud. "He must have had a cottage nearby."

"Yes," replied Quinton. "His wife still lives there. He worked on the property for some fifty years, since before they were wed. Apparently Langford knew my grandfather from when they were but boys."

"Interesting. Hard to imagine your grandfather as a boy at all."

Quinton laughed. "That's what Montgomery said."

Laughing as well, Hugh nodded and continued his survey of

the area. He could see what Quinton meant about a cleared space with little rubble where the groundskeeper was found. Unless he had launched himself off the edge of the roof, that seemed unlikely. Although . . .

"Was Langford under duress?" asked Hugh.

Looking at him questioningly, Quinton cocked his head. "What do you mean by that?"

Hugh hesitated, but there was no delicate way to put it. "Did he seem the sort of man who might take his own life, assuming it would look like an accident?"

"Ah, I see." Quinton shook his head. "I wondered the same, though I did not say so out loud, so as not to cast aspersions upon the dead man's name. But Rory felt the blow to his neck came from behind, and yet he was found face down. A fall, on purpose or accidental, seems unlikely."

"Sound logic." Hugh turned to Quinton. "And the magistrate agreed?"

Now it was Quinton's turn to hesitate. "Well, the man seemed willing to put forth any story I wanted to concoct, but yes, he agreed it was not an accident." Quinton brought the chair over and motioned for Hugh to sit, while retrieving the footstool for himself. "What power does a magistrate yield in these country provinces anyway?"

Settling in, Hugh felt the familiar enjoyment of explaining the law warm him. "Much depends on the individual jurisdiction, but most take quite seriously maintaining law and order. This is quite a rural area, so I imagine the crimes are fairly insignificant, perhaps civil disputes and summary offenses. He does have the power to remand people in custody, impose fines. Much of his duties might be overseeing local licensing for pubs and taverns and addressing matters of public health. He probably hasn't dealt with many murders." Hugh looked at Quinton. "What was your take on the man?"

Quinton answered easily. "Easy to underestimate, but cleverer than appearance would credit him. He seemed a man I could work with. He is quietly investigating Langford's life related to the village, while we pay our attention to the people of the manor."

"A good plan." Hugh nodded to the path continuing its way past the ruins. "Perhaps we should start with paying our respects to the widow. She may have some idea who might have wanted to harm her husband."

Quinton nodded, looked at the continuing trail, but did not move. Hugh also stared at the path. It appeared the idea of dealing with the grieving widow appealed to neither of them. As one they turned back the way they had come.

"Perhaps Zoe would be a better fit," suggested Quinton at the same moment Hugh whispered, "Simone may be better equipped to handle such a delicate matter."

Both men laughed at that, then started back to Cedarbrook. Every family had secrets. They would leave it to the women in their lives to uncover the secrets of Mrs. Langford.

Chapter Fifteen

LONDON

The sound of the kitchen cabinet being slammed and of feet stomping across the room made John Smith sigh inwardly. But outwardly he stood his ground.

"I just don't think it's wise to tempt fate," he said, his tone placating. "You're doing well with the baby, and a long and arduous journey could change that."

His placating tone was for nothing. His beautiful wife Savita planted her feet in front of him, her thick black hair loose almost to her waist, and snapped, "Quinton offered to send his best carriage for us to make the trip. I am not broken, John. I am expecting. Women have been doing this for thousands of years and will keep doing it for thousands more."

Running a hand through his curly short hair, John let out a deep breath and turned to sit in the chair near the fireplace. No need for a fire now, of course, as the London summer baked on.

Savi was not done talking. "Besides which, I am past the time of concern. I am almost five months gone. The baby will not be harmed by a few bumps."

This was not the first time this argument had occurred, and John had his counter ready. "Neither of us have ever travelled that far in a carriage, or any other way for that matter, so I don't think we are experts in how bumpy things can get. I just want to protect you both." John ended with a general gesture towards all of Savi.

Savi's dark eyes flashed, and John braced for the fallout. But after a moment of tension, Savi sighed. Instead of shouting, she found her way to the other comfortable chair and lowered herself down. Silence reigned for a few minutes as the two of them waited for the other to speak, neither wanting to break the unspoken truce.

Finally with a deep breath Savi took John's hand. "I know you want to protect us, both of us. And I am grateful, truly. I know nothing means more to you than the baby and me. But we have to reach a compromise of some sort. I cannot live like someone on their sickbed. What can we agree upon? Please tell me what you are feeling."

Grasping Savi's hand tightly, John strangely felt tears well up. They had bickered so much lately, and he was tired. He didn't want to fight anymore.

Taking a steadying breath, John blinked back his tears and spoke haltingly. "You are my everything, Savita Smith. When you said you would marry me, well, I thought my heart would burst with the love I felt for you. Then we found out about the baby . . . and somehow my heart got even bigger, and my love for both of you could fit inside."

Savi managed to hold her response, squeezing his hand instead as she waited for him to continue.

"I know that I have not been as easygoing as I was before we got married. I've always been one to live in the moment and usually find the good there. But before I only had to care for myself. But with you, and now the baby, I find myself overcome constantly with fear." John's voice trailed off as he ordered his thoughts. He thought of his aunt, Mary's mother, who had suffered several miscarriages. He thought of the time when the bleeding was so bad they thought she would die. Finally he continued, "Babies die sometimes, Savi, as do mothers. And I just don't want to ever put either of you at risk."

Leaning back, Savi seemed to contemplate John's words, her expression unreadable. Despite the heaviness of the conversation, John's breath still caught in his chest as he gazed at his wife. The sunlight streaming in the window illuminated her warm brown skin and caught the shine in her thick black hair. Her stomach was just beginning to swell, showing the evidence of the child growing inside her body. In that moment, John couldn't imagine a more beautiful woman ever existing.

"I was eleven the first time I saw a baby who had died," Savi said after a few moments, apparently having contemplated long enough. "It was devastating. When your mama is a midwife, you see things. I was thirteen the first time a mother died while my mother and I desperately worked to save her. Of everyone you know, John, I am the most aware of the risk of bringing a child to this world."

Heat burned in John's cheeks at the mild chastisement. His wife wasn't wrong, and he knew she was a highly qualified, intelligent woman.

She continued. "But I've also seen plenty of babies be born healthy, with their mothers looking into their eyes for the first time and falling in love so deep all the pain of childbirth was forgotten." She paused, closing her eyes for a moment. "I do know terrible things happen. Even with the best of care, there is risk in life. I could argue that Bow Street Runners also take on a great deal of risk—more risk than average—and yet I've said nothing when you are pulled from our home all hours of the day or night to do your job. I know it is a part of who you are, and I won't change who you are."

John knew he was losing the argument, but still he persisted. "I love you, Savi. I am not trying to change you. I am trying to protect you."

"You, my darling husband, take amazing care of me. I am not

deprived in any way, of food or a clean home, or love, and for that I love you. But you want me to live my life in a cage—a beautiful cage, but a cage nonetheless—safe from all harm, but also isolated from all life." The words were spoken with passion. "I cannot find beauty and happiness and laughter inside a cage. I need some freedom to feel like me."

She was right of course. He could not control her every move and honour the free-spirited woman he married. John leaned his head back, wondering why he ever thought he could.

"I see your point," he said reluctantly. "Perhaps I have been a bit . . . overzealous . . . in my desire to protect you."

"Thank you for saying that." Savi smiled at him, and John swore his heart skipped a beat.

Standing back up, Savi went back to the kitchen and continued preparing their luncheon. "On a less serious note, this blasted heat is also taking its toll. It's as if this child is already a tiny heater inside of me. I feel as though I can barely breathe. A time spent in the much cooler country with trees and grass . . ." Savi's voice trailed off as she kept cutting carrots and potatoes into bite size pieces, allowing John to fill in the blanks.

John knew Savi was uncomfortable. Their home was cozy, but in the afternoon it felt like an oven, even to him, and he was not growing a life within him. Savi had weathered the early months of pregnancy with as much grace as a person could. But the London summer heat was enough to drive any person mad. Savi often looked drained when she came home, beads of sweat dripping from her brow and soaking through her clothes. She rarely complained, but he had seen the toll the heat was taking.

Savi spoke again, apparently growing impatient of waiting for John to fill in those blanks. "What would it take for you to feel comfortable with travel to Quinton's country home?"

After a brief pause, John sighed, knowing that the time had come. "I have days off coming, but I will need to give notice. Let's talk to your mother and see if she and Finn would ride with us.

And I will send a letter to Quinton asking for use of his carriage. Perhaps we can plan to leave on Saturday."

Savi's brilliant smile told him all he needed to know about whether he had found the right words. She carried on preparing their luncheon, and John reflected on how lucky he was to have this beautiful, clever, driven woman as his wife.

Chapter Sixteen

The land steward's cottage was nicer than Zoe had expected. Perhaps it was snobbish on her part, but she'd been expecting a proper "cottage"—something small and cramped, and maybe a bit cold and damp. But this was more like a true house, with its own garden and everything. It was smaller than the mansion, certainly, but actually quite comfortable and pleasant looking. Zoe noticed the attractive paintings on the walls, two of them excellent replicas of a sought-after local artist. She made a mental note to look further into acquiring some of their work.

She perched on the edge of the sofa, taking in the cozy sitting room. She could picture the two Langfords, sitting in their respective armchairs by the fireplace, sipping on sherry into the evening. Now the chairs sat empty, and Zoe swallowed a lump in her throat at the thought that one always would from now on. Strange how death made one so much more sympathetic to the deceased. Glancing over at Mary, Zoe wondered if she felt the same sympathy. Mary met her eyes, then rolled her own. Probably not, then.

Hugh had suggested Simone accompany her, but Mary had been eager to help, and so they came to be in Mr. Langford's sitting room with his widow. A strange nostalgia came over Zoe, reminding her of her adventures with Mary in past investigations.

The sound of china clinking against china broke Zoe out of her musings. She glanced over to see Mrs. Langford bustling in, holding a tea tray.

"I wish I had more to offer you, Lady Coleville and Miss Fletcher." The older woman placed the tray down and began pouring the tea. "I'm afraid the coffers are a little light at the moment. But I always have a few biscuits on hand."

Mrs. Langford was a plump woman well into her late sixties, wearing a day dress that befit her age and station cut in the old fashion, with white hair tied back in a proper bun. Where her late husband had had deep frown lines covering his face, the lines on her wrinkled face were laugh lines. It made Zoe wonder how well the couple got on. She supposed opposites did sometimes attract.

"It's very generous of you to offer anything at all, Mrs. Langford." Zoe accepted the cup. "Especially now."

"We are very sorry for your loss," added Mary smoothly. "It must be a terrible shock."

"Yes, a terrible shock," echoed Zoe. "I apologize that I haven't paid my respects before now. My husband also wishes to convey his grief over the loss, but he didn't want to intrude."

"Thank you for your kindness." The older woman settled in her armchair. "But there is nothing to apologize for. Lord Coleville already paid his respects, and offered to pay for the funeral arrangements."

Zoe's brow furrowed. "Quinton?"

Mrs. Langford shook her head. "No, I mean Philip. My husband worked for the Colevilles for nearly fifty years. That kind of loyalty means something."

"Of course."

Exchanging a glance with Mary, Zoe tried to hide her surprise. None of the interactions she'd had with "Philip" would have led her to believe he was capable of loyalty or kindness. To her, he seemed a bitter and snobbish old man who took perverse pleasure in putting Quinton down every chance he could. Now that she thought about it, Zoe could actually picture him and Mr. Langford getting along swimmingly.

Thinking back to her scolding of Quinton for saying these same thoughts aloud, Zoe could acknowledge she wasn't as enlightened or as forgiving as she would like to think.

Mrs. Langford looked around the sitting room, sighing. "I will miss this home. I haven't known another since I married."

"But why would you have to go elsewhere? This is your home." Zoe crossed her arms.

"No, my lady. This is the land steward's cottage, and my husband is no longer the land steward," Mrs. Langford gently corrected. "It is fine, there's no need to worry about me. My sister lives in Cork. I've written to tell her I'll be coming to stay with her shortly."

"Is that where you are from—Ireland?" asked Zoe. "I wouldn't have guessed. I'm usually quite good with accents, but yours must be very subtle."

Mrs. Langford's laugh was subdued but fit the lines on her face. "Oh, no, I'm from the village to the west. But my sister's husband is Irish." Mrs. Langford eyed Zoe over her cup. "I hope you don't think it impertinent, Lady Coleville, but I've been wondering at your accent. Is it French?"

Zoe was surprised. Years spent in England had softened her French accent to the point where it was almost imperceptible, and few made mention of it anymore. "Indeed. I came to England during the great terror, along with my mother."

Those were days Zoe tried not to think of. These days she thought less and less of it, but still at times her memories were triggered—days of blood in the streets and screams in the air—of her heartbeat pounding in her ears and hands shaking as her mother dragged her onto the boat.

Since being on the estate though, most of her reminiscences of her time before England had been of the country. That's where she had once lived as a child, in France, with her mother and father on their own grand estate. Zoe didn't remember very much from that time, but she could still picture the green rolling hills and the smell of fresh-cut grass and the sound of her father's laughter. Not a perfect man, but her father nevertheless. He was dead and buried now, his blood soaked into the same country earth, but that wasn't how Zoe remembered him. In her memories he was laughing and lifting her into the air, his face silhouetted by sunlight so she couldn't quite see his features clearly, but she knew he was smiling.

Mary and Mrs. Langford had been making small talk while Zoe got lost in her memories of the past. She cleared her throat, grounding herself back in the present.

"Mrs. Langford." Zoe set her teacup down, contemplating her next words. "I don't wish to offend your sensibilities, but are you aware of the circumstances of your husband's demise?"

"I know there was an accident out by the old ruins." Mrs. Langford tsked. "He never could stay away, no matter how I nagged him. He was just as bad with that West Wood, taking off for hours at a time."

Zoe hesitated. "Right. Well, the thing is, we don't know what exactly happened. Mr. Stewart, one of our guests, he has some experience with this sort of thing, and he doesn't believe it was an accident."

"What do you mean?" Mrs. Langford leaned forward, frowning. "What kind of experience?"

Mary was quick on her feet. "He's a surgeon, of sorts."

"Yes, that's right." Zoe turned back to the widow. "Regardless, I had a question—"

"Well, if it wasn't an accident, then what else could it have been?" Mrs. Langford looked back and forth between Zoe and Simone. "Surely you aren't suggesting that he—Ellis would never do that to me."

"No, of course not," said Zoe quickly. "The question I wanted to ask is if you know of anyone who might have held a grudge against your husband?"

A look of surprise crossed Mrs. Langford's face, then turned to something else before the widow lowered her eyes. "No, of course not."

Mrs. Langford's fingers strayed to a gold ring on her right hand, turning it round and round on her middle finger. Taking a closer look, Zoe noted it was a thick band, dotted with small red jewels—Zoe assumed faux rubies. It was quite lovely, and a contrast to the plain, thin wedding band which adorned her other hand.

"That's a beautiful piece of jewellery, Mrs. Langford." Mary glanced at Zoe, having clearly had the thought. "Was it a gift from your husband?"

Apprehension seemed to battle pride as the widow gazed at her fingers. Eventually pride won. Raising her eyes, Mrs. Langford met Mary's squarely.

"Yes, it was, Miss Fletcher. My Ellis brought it home last year. Said one of the tenant farmers owed him some money and paid with his wife's wedding ring." She paused, then caught Zoe's eye with a surprisingly hard glint in her own. "My Ellis wasn't perfect, but he always took care of me, and I'll hear no ill spoken of him now. What happened was a terrible accident." Standing, she gestured to the door, clearly signalling that the discussion was over. "Now if you don't mind, I have my packing to do."

Chapter Seventeen

Brutus looked up, happy and panting, the dirt on his face matching the hole in which he had been digging. The hole was big enough that half of Brutus's significant frame fit in it. He must want to dig clear to the other side of the blasted world, Mary thought grumpily, but she wasn't going to let that happen.

Glancing up as she grabbed his collar, she saw Oscar on the nearby wall, sitting contentedly in the role of audience. The expression of a cat was often passive, but Mary thought she detected a hint of disdain in Oscar's large eyes. Whether it was for the dog's pointless digging or Mary's pointless struggle to dissuade him, she couldn't say.

Suddenly she laughed, the absurdity of the situation as seen through the cat's eyes dawning on her. She gave up her struggle, instead glancing around for a suitable stick. Finding one, she tested its weight with a quick fake throw that immediately got Brutus's attention. Pulling her arm back, Mary launched the hefty stick across the garden and was rewarded with a view of the beast's backside as he chased after it.

Oscar gave a slight chirp and jumped from the wall to casually trot after the beast. Mary watched with mild interest, wondering if the two were finally becoming unlikely friends.

This wasn't the first hole Mary had come across, each one with enough earth moved to half bury a carriage, but it was the first where she had caught the beast with dirt on his paws. Brutus seemed quite obsessed with the new feeling of the British soil beneath his feet. It wasn't really her job to manage the beast—that would fall to Gwen—but Mary had taken it upon herself to keeps tabs on him on and off during her time at the estate.

Mary's mind wandered back to the day they had first met Brutus—the shout of the bloodthirsty crowd and the savage dogfight Brutus had lost badly. As obnoxious as his persistent damage of the garden was, Mary was pleased he was enjoying himself now, with plenty of space and greenery to roam through.

The chatter of children interrupted her musings and alerted her to the presence of Gwen and the Dovefield children racing across the grass to commandeer Brutus. The wide-open space made it difficult for Gwen to control him, and Mary suspected Gwen herself was quite distracted by the space and the smell of the dirt beneath her shoes. No doubt everyone would find their feet in this new world of theirs, given time.

She hoped the same would be true of her as well.

Mary paused to gather the flowers she had originally come down to pick. She had not expected to like this non-London world, and while the quiet was both calming and disconcerting, she couldn't deny that the feel of the air in her lungs filled her with a sense of contentment. Turning to go back to the house, Mary wondered what else had changed about herself.

She entered the home, and after putting the flowers in some water, made her way to the informal sitting room where the others had been gathering.

As she entered, Mary heard Hugh speak firmly. "You do indeed need a valet."

From the barrister's tone and Quinton's expression, she discerned that Quinton clearly felt differently, but Mary wasn't surprised by that. The trappings of this life were gilded, but confining nonetheless to the street boy who still lived not far beneath Quinton's skin.

Rory piped up, a bottle in his hand. "He's right Q. A lord needs a valet. It's not just a matter of status; it's a matter of practicality with the lifestyle you'll be living."

Mary reckoned Quinton would remain unconvinced as she walked to place her vase of flowers in the spot she'd picked out earlier.

"Not necessarily. You dress impeccably in the latest fashion, all without the aid of a valet," Quinton countered.

Rory looked surprised. "Of course I have a valet," he countered. Now everyone looked surprised. Rory continued, unperturbed. "Of a sort, just not full time. The neighbour lad comes over if I am attending a formal affair and must get the cravat just right. The sheer number of ways a cravat can be tied is enough to need an extra pair of hands. He helps me button up, and his mother presses my attire."

Quinton raised an eyebrow at that. "I would not have thought that of you."

"My lad, flawlessness doesn't just happen." Rory poured some of the amber liquid into a glass and handed it to Mary. "It is a matter of purpose."

Hugh chose to jump on Rory's momentum. "And for you, as a viscount, it matters even more that you are turned out flawlessly."

Waving his hand dismissively, Quinton rolled his eyes. "I'm not the viscount. Philip is the viscount. I'm just a distraction for the gentry which will be forgotten once the season starts again and there is other news to gossip about."

"Philip Coleville was the viscount, as his father, Kincaid

Coleville was the earl," corrected Hugh, his tone patient. "But Kincaid somewhat recently died, making Philip the earl, and you, my boy, the viscount."

Zoe scoffed at that from her seat across the room, where she had been quietly listening—or, Mary suspected, tuning out the boring conversation. "Philip Coleville's father recently died? How old was he, a hundred and ten?"

Hugh frowned at that, probably disapproving of his step-daughter's cavalier comment. "He was quite elderly, to be sure, as Philip is past seventy, and he had not been seen in public for some time. He and Philip were estranged, as I understand it."

"No surprise there," Quinton muttered.

Continuing his explanation, Hugh ignored Quinton's comment. "Therefore his death wasn't widely publicized. I'm not sure anyone outside of the *earl* himself knows the exact date."

Zoe pondered this. "So Montgomery was the viscount for a brief moment when his grandfather died, but the viscount, I mean, Philip, was the viscount before the old man's death. Unless he died after Quinton established his rights as heir, in which case Montgomery was never a viscount, but Philip is still an earl. Now Quinton is the viscount, and Montgomery is just a lord."

"Just listening to you all prattle on is giving me a headache," muttered Mary as she drank her whiskey—a particularly strong but flavourful blend. Quinton clinked his glass against hers in agreement.

Possibly emboldened by Mary's statement, Charlie decided to chime in. "Who in the name of all that is holy could possibly keep it bloody straight? And who besides you toffs even cares?" Charlie shook his head and changed the subject. "Getting back to what actually matters . . . what does everyone think of our first batch?"

"This is yours?" Mary took another sip. "It's good. It's actually quite good, if a little strong."

"No need to sound so shocked," Charlie grumbled. "Obviously a proper batch would be aged longer, but it's a good sample of the flavour profile."

As the group began to discuss the whiskey's various virtues, Mary slipped over to the large window. It looked out upon the garden she had just been in, and she wanted to see if the massive hole, compliments of Brutus, could be seen from the room. She would get the boot boy to fill it in before the gardener found it, as she had two other times since her arrival.

Fortunately, even if she peered straight down, the hole was not visible from this vantage. She glanced up to see Brutus disappearing into the western woods that bordered the garden, and the children following. She hoped they were having an enjoyable adventure in Brutus's protective presence.

Finding a comfortable chair, Mary sank into it, grateful she had chosen such a comfortable morning dress to wear. The deep purple complimented her dark complexion, and the fit was just enough to show off her curves but loose enough to allow that the summer heat had not entirely abated, even in the country. Mary swallowed more whiskey, allowing it to burn its way to her belly. She had learned the merits of good whiskey from Zoe, and though she kept this thought to herself, this wasn't yet quality. Charlie was right, it would need quite a few more years of aging.

The drink did relax her though, and she felt the long journey and surprising events start to catch up with her, and she laid her head back and started to nod off.

Suddenly an icy feeling of dread filled her and she sat bolt upright, a cold feeling of danger striking her clear to her bones. It was the same feeling she'd felt when she and Zoe had been taken by that madman. She stood quickly, looking wildly about, unsure of the source of her dread, but sure that something was terribly wrong.

Zoe was by her side in a flash. "What is it?"

Mary concentrated on her feeling, trying to see past the fear to the source. Two words sprang into her mind and then out of her mouth. "The children."

The commotion had brought Quinton and Hugh over as well. None of them questioned Mary's words.

"Where are they?" asked Quinton as he touched Mary's arm gently.

"They were with Brutus headed towards the woods." Mary took a trembling breath and shook her head in frustration. "I saw them go through that and thought nothing of it. But something is wrong. They need us—now."

Quinton walked to the window. "Where did you see them?"

Mary joined him and pointed. "There, through that break in the trees."

"That is the West Wood." His face had paled as he turned back to her. "That's where Langford said he saw the wolf."

Chapter Eighteen

The four men had rushed off, leaving the women behind to wring their hands and worry, as was the way of men. Zoe had wanted to go with them, but one look at her mother's face had convinced her that Simone needed her more.

She sat next to her mother now, holding her hand and doing nothing else other than provide a reassuring presence. Simone had said little. She was a reserved woman, and Zoe was used to not knowing what her mother was thinking. In this case though, she could see in her eyes the terror of what could happen. They were both painfully aware that bad things did happen in this world. As much as one might like to believe otherwise, sometimes children died and nothing could be done to save them.

Mary had retired to a chair across from them and had finally succumbed to the exhaustion of the journey here and the traumatic events since, her head having lolled to the side and her mouth slightly open. Zoe didn't blame her. She could feel fatigue creeping up on her too. But as long as Simone was keeping vigil, so would Zoe. They waited in silence, the only sound to be heard the ticking away of seconds from the large clock in the corner.

Two hours of seconds had passed when a knock came at the door. Zoe leapt to her feet and Mary startled awake as Evans entered. The summer sun was set low in the sky, illuminating the room in the dim light of dusk and casting an eerie look on the butler's severe features.

"The children have been safely located and are on their way back," he said simply, and suddenly the shadows no longer looked eerie.

A sob of relief escaped Zoe's lips. She clasped a hand over her mouth, instinctively trying to smother the sound, though she wasn't sure for whose benefit.

Simone let out a shaky breath and cast a look heavenward. "Thank the Lord."

"Thank you, Evans." Zoe tried to regain her composure. "Thank you for letting us know."

The butler bowed slightly and then exited the room, leaving them to experience their relief without an audience.

Zoe did so by swallowing back a generous droaght of Charlie and Rory's whiskey.

"We should meet them at the door," suggested Mary.

"Yes, of course." Simone stood, clearing her throat and dabbing with a handkerchief at the corner of her eye.

The three women hastened to the door, just in time to see it open and the search party enter. Phoebe and Walter rushed over to their mother, who gripped them tightly. Gwen hung back, Quinton having settled his large hand on her shoulder, already offering comfort.

The feeling of relief in Zoe's chest suddenly gave way to annoyance as a new thought occurred to her.

"What were you thinking?" she snapped, specifically at her brother, Walter, the oldest of the trio. "Going off into the woods and getting lost, knowing a wolf has been seen in the area? Not to mention a murderer on the loose? You're lucky nothing happened to you."

The boy blushed. "We didn't mean to wander so far. It all looks the same after a certain point."

Before Zoe could offer a scathing retort, Mary touched her

elbow. Turning to her friend, Zoe followed her gaze to where Rory stood. In his arms he held one of the girl's sweaters, something wrapped in its midst. He clasped it tightly to his chest, as if protecting its swaddled contents.

Mary gazed at the bundle pensively. "Whatever trouble the children found, they've brought it home with them."

Chapter Nineteen

Darkness had fully set in before the adults were finally together in the sitting room again. The cook had kindly sent up trays of bread and cheese and meats and pastries, since no one was in the mood for a formal dinner. The men present fell to eating with gusto while in between bites they explained what had happened. Quinton would have to wait for his meal—he was taking on the burden of explaining the day's events to the earl, separately. Hugh felt a stab of pity for the poor man, but Quinton could hold his own.

Hugh started the story. "Once we were in the woods we split up to search but stayed within earshot. Eventually I stumbled upon some broken branches of shrubbery and some paw prints in the mud which seemed like evidence of Brutus ploughing through, the blasted beast."

As Hugh paused to help himself to the tiny cakes with lemon icing, Rory took up the tale. "It took some time, as we searched for signs of their passing in the dimming light, but the beast does leave a pretty distinctive trail, so we were able to keep after them consistently."

"We actually made decent time, thanks to the bloody dog."

Charlie spoke through a piece of crusty bread, a few crumbs blowing out at the word "bloody."

Hugh took the opportunity to jump back into the conversation, still holding the remainder of the cake. "We were deep into the forest when we heard the children scream. We ran the last quarter mile or so and came upon the sight of Brutus waist deep into a large hole, and the two girls crying. Once we ascertained that the source of the crying wasn't an injury, we turned our attention to whatever Brutus had dug up to upset them."

A silence fell upon the room as Hugh considered best how to tell the ladies what they had found.

Rory apparently needed no such time to gather his thoughts. "It was bones. Brutus found bones."

"Of an animal?" asked Simone with a frown.

"No." Rory took a deep breath and removed the sweater on the table which had been concealing what they'd brought back—a tiny skull. "It was the bones of a bairn—two bairns."

Looking at the small skull, Hugh felt his stomach turn. He considered himself a man of reason and science, but there was something deeply unnatural about seeing the remains of a child so small.

"Two babies?" Zoe stood, her expression both appalled and intrigued as she stared at the skull. "Brutus found the grave of two babies?"

"Yes." Rory nodded, setting down the piece of cheese he'd been chewing on. "A grave of sorts, anyway. The recent rains had softened the ground, making it more diggable for the brute of a dog. Three rocks did the makeshift duty of headstones, and the ground had been tended. Whoever put them there laid them to rest with care and purpose. Now for what reason someone would bury them there in the woods, that I cannae say."

The room descended back into silence as the lot of them absorbed the reality of the situation. It was sobering, and Hugh knew Rory hadn't even gotten to the rest of it.

"There's more," said Rory with a sigh. "There were three headstones, but we only saw the remains of two bairns. From the size of the grave, it seems likely that someone else was also buried there . . . someone larger than the size of a bairn."

Chapter Twenty

"Every time I believe you've disappointed me to the final extent, you somehow manage to surprise me by stooping lower." Philip Coleville shook his head, turning his gaze away from his grandson as if he couldn't bear to look at him a second longer.

Quinton's first reaction was to match his grandfather's hot ire, flame for flame, but as he opened his mouth to snap a fresh retort, a wave of exhaustion came over him. It had been a long and stressful day, and he hadn't eaten anything since breakfast. Beyond that, he was tired of trying to prove his worth to a man who would never accept him. It felt like that olive branch had turned into a club.

As if reading his mind, Philip said, "I thought inviting you here would be an opportunity to lay aside our differences and for you to prove yourself, but I can see your coarse upbringing continues to influence your poor decisions."

"I fail to see how bones on your estate is my fault." Quinton's tone lacked its usual bite. He sank into a plush armchair, massaging his left temple to ward off the headache he felt coming on.

"There is no need to be vulgar," snapped the earl.

"I'm not being vulgar." Quinton sighed. "I'm stating an indisputable fact. There's a difference."

"Not when you belong to our class." Philip turning his burning gaze back to Quinton. "When you are a part of society there is only that which is appropriate and that which isn't. And dead children are *not* appropriate subjects of conversation, among ourselves or as a topic of gossip for the ton."

"And yet, they exist, whether you wish to acknowledge them or not."

The two men glared at each other for several moments, but then to Quinton's surprise, the earl sat down in the armchair across from him. He rang the bell on the small side table, the gentle ringing echoing through the quiet house.

The butler opened the door within thirty seconds. "Yes, my lord?"

"Bring us a couple of whiskeys—the good stuff, not that rotgut Master Quinton's guests brought with them."

"Of course, my lord."

They sat in silence until Evans returned with the glasses, then discreetly departed. As Quinton took a sip of his whiskey, the smooth burn instantly relaxed him—though it didn't do much for his headache.

When Philip next spoke, his volume was more moderate—though the tone was just as sharp. "The children are all accounted for?"

"Yes." Quinton was surprised at the change of subject. "They were fine. But they had the dog with them. Brutus would defend them against any wolf."

His grandfather's brow furrowed. "Wolf? What wolf?"

Quinton realized Langford had never gotten the opportunity to inform Philip of the danger. "Langford said a wolf was sighted in the West Wood."

Philip scoffed at that. "There's been no wolves in Britian for over a hundred years. He probably just said that to discourage you all from wandering and getting lost in the forest—as the children just demonstrated is so easy to do."

Quinton flushed, embarrassed that he hadn't known this information. Langford must have thought it quite funny, Quinton's request to be kept apprised of a wolf that didn't exist. Perhaps it was just a ploy to keep them out of the woods for their own safety. On the other hand . . . Quinton wondered if Langford had been trying to keep them out of the West Wood for another reason. Was it possible he had known of the graves?

A deep sigh from Philip brought Quinton back to the present conversation. "Why do you insist on testing me—on testing the limits of your station?"

Quinton let his head fall back against his chair. "That isn't my intention. I'm just trying to do the right thing."

"As am I." The earl sipped his own beverage. "As much as I would love to refute it, there's no denying you're of my blood. It's like fighting with Graham and . . ." He paused. "It's like fighting with Graham all over again. Don't you ever grow weary of digging your heels in over every disagreement?"

"Don't you?" Quinton glanced over at his grandfather, for the first time seeing the signs of age around his eyes.

"Yes," Philip answered, in a surprising turn of honesty. "But I am entrusted with our family's honour, something which you will one day also be responsible for. It isn't something to be taken lightly."

"I don't. But I do believe that the gossip of high society should come second to actual death and suffering."

"Society gossip has been the death of many a noble family," countered Philip.

"Metaphorically, perhaps." Quinton wasn't sure why he was digging his heels in on this particular point. He did believe that there were many things which trumped the scandals of the upper class, but he also understood that in this world, reputation mattered as much as money or station. That was the reason he had refused to acknowledge his feelings for Zoe for so long. As much as Quinton thought such things were foolish, he understood they carried real weight in the world he lived in now.

Quinton sighed again. "I am not trying to be dismissive, and believe it or not, this is me attempting to be discreet."

"You could have fooled me," grumbled the old man.

"What would you have me do?" Quinton was growing tired of this back and forth.

"I would have you place these remains back in their resting place and then contact the magistrate and inform him that Langford's death was a simple accident. Then we could wash our hands of this whole affair." The earl downed the rest of his drink. "Even better, send your disreputable guests home. Bad enough to have your French wife here, but also a resurrectionist? A coloured woman? And then I'm not sure what the Indian mongrel's occupation is, but I'm sure it's something sordid."

Quinton's blood ran cold.

In that moment he didn't know if he had ever been angrier. Quinton's temper had always leaned more toward a smouldering heat, like a carefully controlled fire in a hearth. But in that moment he felt nothing but a quiet, cold rage, as if he had fallen through the ice into the freezing river below, so overwhelming he couldn't breathe as it threatened to drown him in its icy clutches.

He stood stiffly. "First of all, don't ever speak that way about my wife or her family ever again. Second, my friends are non-negotiable. If you refer to them in that manner again, I will go to every newspaper in London and give them my full life story, starting with your errant son's indiscretions and ending with my actress mother's death at the hands of the most infamous killer in the last hundred years. Any hope of keeping my origins as your heir discreet will be lost, and the Colevilles will be the talk of every social circle in the country and beyond, making these few suspicious incidents seem like nothing in comparison. I will ruin your family in the press and not lose a wink of sleep over it."

The earl stared at him, his mouth slightly agape. "You would be ruining your own family in doing so. Surely even you couldn't be so dense."

"My family is in the drawing room, discussing these matters in a much more civilized light. I should be with them now, and instead I'm in here bickering with a stubborn old man who doesn't realize his time has come and gone."

Quinton knew even in the moment that he had gone too far, but he was past caring. He tossed the rest of his whiskey in the hearth, causing a blast of heat and flame. Throwing away good whiskey was the biggest insult he could think of, though it pained him to do so.

As he stalked toward the door, the earl spoke, causing Quinton to pause and look back.

"I always worried Montgomery was too soft to take over my title when the time came." Philip stared in the flames, then glanced over to the portrait of Graham. "You are many things, Quinton, but soft isn't one of them."

Quinton was too tired to spend any more time attempting to decipher the earl's words, so he didn't try. Instead he left the old man to his own thoughts, whatever those might be, and went to find his wife.

Chapter Twenty-One

When Zoe awoke the next day, the sun was already high in the sky. She blinked as a beam of light fell across her face, having slipped through the small crack in the heavy curtain that hung in her bedroom.

She rolled over toward the middle of the bed, her eyes landing on the still-sleeping Quinton. He was still wearing trousers and a loose white undershirt, with the blanket only partially covering him. Zoe herself wore only a shift rather than her usual night-gown. As the previous evening had gone on, Zoe had dismissed Louisa, feeling it was unfair to keep her up late as well, and then they had been so tired and gone to bed so late, neither had changed properly.

Quinton of course had his own bedroom prepared, but most evenings they retired together. Zoe often woke before he did, and she wondered if she would ever tire of watching his chest rise and fall, his face peaceful and still as he slept. She resisted the urge to brush his dark, wavy locks aside, not wanting to wake him. For just a moment it felt as though everything was right in the world —there were no mysterious graves on the property, or skulls in the sitting room, or dead land stewards. There was only Zoe and Quinton.

A soft knock at the door broke the spell. Quinton's eyes flashed open and he pushed himself up quickly on his elbows.

Zoe placed a gentle hand on his chest. "Go back to sleep," she said softly. "I'm sure it's just Louisa."

He did ease back into the pillow, but the stillness was already broken. "I'm awake now."

The early life which Quinton had survived still took a toll on him. Not always, but sometimes she knew the memories still haunted him. Zoe hoped that one day he would wake up and not even think about it. Maybe when that happened, she too would sleep without the memories which haunted her.

Zoe slipped out from under the covers, shivering as her feet touched the cool wood floor. As she walked over to the door, she grabbed her dressing gown and pulled it over her shift.

When she opened the door, she was glad she had. Instead of Louisa, it was the butler who stood there.

"Is something wrong?" Zoe asked. "Where is Louisa?"

Evans raised an eyebrow. "Nothing is wrong, my lady. Louisa went to run a quick errand. But a visitor is here to see you. Should I tell him to come back at a more convenient time?"

"Who is it?"

"A Mr. Alexander Dovefield."

Oh. That was unexpected. The Dovefield estate wasn't too far away, and Zoe knew her parents had planned to visit there soon. But she hadn't expected her stepcousin to show up by himself unexpectedly at such an hour.

"Are you sure he's here for me? Not my father?" she asked.

The butler frowned, as if a bit insulted at the request for clarification. "He asked for you specifically, my lady."

Even more curious.

"Very well. Show him into the sitting room and tell him I'll be down shortly."

"Understood."

As Zoe shut the door, she heard Quinton's feet hit the floor.

She turned to see him opening the wardrobe, rummaging through it. He pulled out an elaborate gown and offered it.

"Will this do?" he asked.

"No. That is a dinner gown—all I need is a day dress for now." Zoe moved past him to select a much simpler light green muslin dress. "You'll have to help me since Louisa isn't here."

Quinton's forehead scrunched in confusion, but he put the dinner gown back and complied, assisting Zoe in tightening her corset over her shift and pulling on her petticoat, then pulling the day dress up and over the layers of undergarments.

"Thank you, dear." Zoe pressed a quick kiss to Quinton's cheek as she shoved her feet into slippers. "I'm going to go down, but join when you are dressed."

"I am expected to help you dress, but you aren't going to do the same for me?" Quinton feigned distress, grabbing her wrist and pulling her back towards him. "That hardly seems fair."

"You're right." Zoe pushed herself away from his firm chest and patted his arm sympathetically. "But then again, life isn't fair. Perhaps you should invest in that valet, as has been suggested numerous times."

With that Zoe broke away and cheerfully skipped to the door. She left with one last playful glance over her shoulder before closing the door on her laughing husband and making her way down the grand staircase.

The butler was waiting for her at the bottom, and with one smooth motion opened the door to the sitting room and announced her. "Lady Zoe Coleville."

Alexander turned around with a smile from where he had been gazing out the window. "Hello, Zoe."

No one could look at her stepcousin and doubt he was a Dovefield through and through. Though his eyes were more a shade of grey than green, he shared the same blond hair and authoritative air as the rest of them. A little on the slimmer side than Hugh, but Zoe could picture her stepfather looking similar when he was the same age.

These days Zoe looked on Alexander with a more favourable light. The two had not always been friends—they had barely tolerated each other as children. But recent events had shifted their respective perspectives and now they were on better—even friendly—terms. It helped that Alexander had also grown up a great deal in the past few months. Still leaning toward arrogant, perhaps, but not so insufferable.

"Hello, Alexander." Zoe gestured for him to take a seat. "It's a bit early for tea, but would you like some coffee?"

"Yes, please."

Zoe rang the bell and ordered the coffees, then waited until they were served before venturing the real question. "Not to be rude, Alexander, but what are you doing here?"

"You've never been one to dance around the issue." Alexander shook his head, stirring the cream in his coffee. "I'll admit, I didn't plan to come here today. I was out riding and got lost in thought and just sort of wound up at the doorstep."

"Out riding?" Zoe did the mental maths in her head. "It's at least a day's journey from here to the Dovefield estate."

"By carriage," he corrected. "On horseback it's only a few hours."

"Still quite a ways to go unplanned." Zoe sipped her coffee. "Are you hungry? I can have the cook send up some cold cuts."

Alexander waved his hand. "No, I'm not hungry."

"Very well." Shaking her head, Zoe appraised him. "Still, there must be something that drew you here."

"Perhaps." He set his cup down. "Mabel and her parents are coming to visit tomorrow; I'm not sure if you're aware."

"Yes, she wrote to me." Zoe attempted to hide her smile behind another sip of coffee, though she wasn't sure how successful she was.

Mabel was one of Zoe's friends, and a recent surprising romantic interest of Alexander's—surprising only in that she was far too good for him. But after getting over the initial shock, Zoe decided it made sense, in a strange sort of way. Both Mabel and

Alexander had been irrecoverably changed by tragedy—in some ways made better, and in others made broken. But there was something bonding about understanding another person's pain in a way that only you could. Zoe felt that way about Quinton, and she suspected Alexander felt the same about Mabel.

"I thought she would." He cleared his throat. "I suppose you're aware I've been courting her for the past few months?"

Of course she was aware. What did he think she was, dense?

"It's come up a time or two, yes." Zoe resisted the urge to roll her eyes.

"Well, I am considering making the arrangement between us . . . permanent." Alexander cleared his throat and shifted in his seat.

Zoe paused, mulling over his phrasing. "Do you mean you plan to propose?"

"That's another way to say it."

"It's the normal way to say it," replied Zoe with a scoff. "And it's about time. People were starting to talk at how long you've been courting her."

Alexander frowned. "It hasn't been that long."

"It's been long enough that a decision is expected." Zoe leaned forward eagerly. "So then, you will propose during this visit?"

"I am considering it."

"What is there to consider?" Zoe stood, her hands on her hips. "You do love her, don't you?"

"Of course." Alexander also stood, matching her energy. "But love isn't the only thing required to make a marriage work."

"No. But what problems could exist between the two of you that would prevent a marriage from succeeding? Could it be your equal social status or equivalent family wealth? Or is it the fact she seems to tolerate your insufferable company?"

That struck a nerve. Crossing his arms, Alexander glanced away.

"Really? That's what's bothering you?" Zoe shook her head.

"Well, I can assure you that in my conversations with her, she's made it clear that despite usually being a very level-headed and intelligent woman, for reasons beyond my understanding, Mabel is quite taken with you. She does more than tolerate you—she loves you."

Instead of reassuring him, Zoe's admission seemed to only make Alexander more uncomfortable. He shifted from foot to foot, still not making eye contact.

"What?" she snapped. "Spit it out."

"I don't know why she likes me—or loves me, I guess."

Zoe blinked. "What is that supposed to mean?"

"I'm not good enough for her." Alexander uncrossed his arms, gesturing vaguely. "I mean, you of all people know! I'm a degenerate and a gambler and a rake. Mabel is . . . good. She's everything I'm not. She deserves better than me."

It took several moments of silence for Zoe to process Alexander's unexpected admission. She hadn't realized he'd become so self-aware. It was unnerving.

She considered her response carefully. "Why must men be so unbelievably stupid?"

"Why would you say—I'm trying to do the honourable thing," said Alexander, his tone wounded.

"Men often say that when what they mean is they want to take the coward's way out."

"That's not—"

"Sit down," barked Zoe.

Alexander blinked, clearly surprised, but he obeyed after a moment's hesitation.

Zoe let out a deep breath before also taking her seat. "The truth is, I agree," said Zoe. "You're not good enough for her. But it's not up to me, and it's certainly not up to you to decide that. If you respect Mabel at all, then you will respect her ability to make her own decisions—and for better or worse, she has chosen you."

Rubbing his hands on his trousers, Alexander slowly nodded. "You think I should go ahead and propose?"

"What the—have you been listening to me at all?" Zoe couldn't believe the audacity. "Yes, I think you should propose. And then you should live up to that proposal and Mabel's faith in you."

"Very well." Alexander stood back up. "Thank you."

Zoe stood as well. "That's it? Did you really ride all the way over here just to get me to talk you into this?"

He shrugged. "I suppose. I knew you'd be honest, even when I didn't want to hear it."

"My specialty." Zoe sighed. "Do you want to stay for luncheon? I'm sure Father would like to see you."

"No, no. I need to be getting back. My father will be wondering where I am." Alexander smiled. "You know how he gets." Indeed she did. "But I hope all of you will come out to the manor to visit while Mabel is here, despite his presence."

Baldwin Dovefield had never been a fan of his younger brother's choice of French wife and stepdaughter, and the feeling was mutual. Baldwin was a bully, to his own family as well. It was a wonder Alexander had turned out as well adjusted as he had.

"Fair enough. I'll at least have the cook make you a plate to take with you. You can't go all day without eating. It's not healthy."

"I accept," acceded Alexander. "Thank you again . . . cousin."

Zoe bid him farewell after giving the footman instructions for the cook. As she headed back up to the bedroom, she met her husband on the stairs.

"Did he leave already?" asked Quinton, his expression puzzled.

"Yes. He just needed some advice."

"On what?"

"Absolute nonsense." Zoe glanced at him from the side. "Are the others still asleep?"

Quinton returned her look. "As far as I know."

She took her husband's arm. Soon they would have to be

social and deal with the realities of the men's discovery. But right now, they still had time.

"Then perhaps we could continue this conversation in the bedroom . . . while you help me back out of these clothes."

Chapter Twenty-Two

To think, the only grave Rory had considered digging on his way to this country gathering was one for Oscar if Charlie actually murdered her. Now here he was, waist deep in another hole in the ground and pulling out the remains of a corpse, as he had so many times in life.

Carefully wrapping the last of the smaller bones in the cloth he had brought for that purpose, Rory gently laid it aside and nodded at Quinton. It felt unusual to him that he was out in the open working, instead of concealed by darkness for fear of discovery. But the bright light of the sun instead of the dim light of a lantern did make his work easier.

At his nod, Quinton joined him in the hole and began to dig again, widening the hole which Brutus had started, his waistcoat put aside and the sleeves of his white shirt rolled up. He had even managed to procure gumboots for both of them to save their own footwear. Another perk of having a new lord as a patron.

Most of the corpses Rory had encountered were on the fresher side compared to these bones. The digging up of newly dead bodies to sell to men of science was how Rory had made his not inconsiderable wealth. As the thirst for knowledge grew, so did the demand for more cadavers. Bones were not in high demand. If he had brought in the poor off the streets and ended their existence just before the hand off, the anatomists and surgeons would likely not have batted an eye. They might even have paid him more. Fortunately, Rory was not so cold blooded and mercenary as to actually do such a thing. But not every resurrectionist lived by his scruples. It was only a matter of time before a true tragedy occurred when it came to the buying and selling of bodies.

It was surprisingly pleasant to be dealing with the relative cleanliness of bones. Not that Rory was squeamish when it came to death or blood or gore. He had dissected many a corpse himself, blood up to his elbows as he sliced into a human heart, trying to puzzle out its inner workings. In another life, he would have been a proper surgeon. But still, the bones were a nice change of pace. That being said, the fact the bones belonged to children saddened him greatly.

That wasn't the only thing unsettling Rory. For some reason he couldn't shake the feeling of being watched, even though every time he looked up, nothing was there. Perhaps too much time in the city had dulled his country senses, making him paranoid of the open forest expanse. Or maybe there was something to the supposed ghost Quinton had told him about.

"I've hit something." Quinton's words nudged Rory out the world of his thoughts and into the present world. He looked over at where Quinton's shovel connected to the dirt and immediately saw what Quinton was referring to.

An adult-size bone lay partially uncovered, a humerus if Rory was not mistaken—no doubt only the first they would find. He looked up and met Quinton's eyes, seeing resignation and sadness reflected in them.

"What are your thoughts so far?" asked Quinton.

"Well, it's too early to tell much about the adult." Rory glanced toward the bundle on the ground next to them. "As for the bairns . . . I can tell you they are very small. Too small to have been viable outside of the womb."

Quinton frowned. "Do you mean the person buried here was pregnant at the time?"

Rory shrugged. "Possibly. Like I said, I'll know more once we've uncovered the rest of the body."

"Hmm." Quinton swallowed, clearly disquieted by the thought. "How long does it take for a body to turn to bone, buried like this?"

Contemplating the question, Rory leaned back against the edge of the hole to take a breather. "Well, it depends. There's a number of factors. My best guess, without a coffin, I'd say . . . at least five to ten years."

"Can you tell if it's been longer than that?"

"As stated, I'll know more once I uncover the rest. But honestly . . . "I doubt I'll be able to tell much more. Once the soft tissue has decomposed, the timeline is much broader."

Quinton nodded, his expression pensive. After a moment's consideration, he looked back to the ground. "Well, let's get back to it."

As Quinton raised his shovel, a small glint of something reflective caught Rory's eye.

"Wait!" he said, louder than he had intended.

"What?" Quinton froze, shovel poised mid-air.

"There's something next to your boot." Rory bent down and brushed away the loose dirt, exposing what lay beneath.

As his fingers found purchase on the cool, metallic texture, Rory grasped it and pulled the object out.

"Is that . . . a necklace?" asked Quinton.

"Yes, I believe it is," replied Rory as he held the jewellery up to the sunlight.

Though still covered in the grime of earth, Rory could tell it was a beautiful piece. The chain was a delicate golden herringbone, and from it hung a small heart-shaped locket, though the pictures it once held long ago had decayed. Two small garnets decorated the front, with a small empty setting between them.

"Quite lovely," said Rory. "And expensive."

"Indeed." Quinton cocked his head, his eyes narrow. "The kind of necklace you would find attached to a woman of status and wealth."

Rory met his eye and he could tell the same thought had occurred to Quinton.

The next words Quinton spoke had a bite of anger to them. "Two unborn babies and an adult with them, buried with a golden necklace . . . I think I need to have a talk with the earl about his daughter."

Chapter Twenty-Three

Quinton forced himself go to his room first and take the time to bathe and change into clean clothes before confronting his grandfather. As he struggled to button his sleeves, he thought briefly about the convenience of a valet. But he managed the small chore himself and put the matter out of his mind.

As he approached the study, Quinton saw the door was closed, and he hesitated. The thought that perhaps he should at least try to get this conversation off on the right foot popped into his head. But try as he might, he couldn't picture a world where the conversation went well, no matter what he did. So raising his hand, he rapped twice, then entered the room.

Montgomery and Philip were both present, which suited Quinton. Philip was seated comfortably behind the desk while Montgomery perused a bookshelf near the back of the room. The tones were soothing greens, dark in the furniture and lighter in the walls. The overall effect was surprisingly calming, but the calm had no chance against the look on the older man's face.

Philip stood. "This room is private, and you are welcome only by invitation."

This was going about as well as Quinton had expected.

He answered without softening the information. "Another body has been found and removed from the grave that contained the infants. It's the body of an adult, my guess the mother of the babies. What is your guess, Grandfather?"

If he understood the sarcastic question at the end, Philip didn't acknowledge it. "Removed from the grave? I thought I made it clear the course of wisdom was to put back any bones you had stumbled upon. Now you are removing more? Have you no sense at all, boy?"

"Don't you want to know whose body has been placed at rest on your land?" Quinton placed his hands on the desk and leaned forward. "Or do you already know who it is?"

This time there was no ignoring the direct question. Philip's face turned a particularly unappealing shade of red. "I don't know what you could possibly mean by that, but I resent the implication."

"If you don't know what I mean, then how could you resent the implication?" Quinton knew he was being childish, but he couldn't seem to stop himself.

"Stop it. Both of you," interceded Montgomery. "Quinton, please explain what you mean by your question."

Quinton glanced at his uncle and straightened his posture. "You said it's believed that Catriona's ghost haunts the grounds. Could there be some truth to it? Could it be that she never left the estate, and has instead been buried in the West Wood all these years?"

"The subject of the ghost is forbidden in this house." The words were angry and dismissive, but Philip sank back down in his chair, his tone notably more even.

Montgomery shook his head, ignoring his father's statement. "No, I told you, she ran away to London."

"You said that was the most likely explanation," countered Quinton. "But you also said no one knew for certain."

"Yes, but that doesn't mean—"

"It doesn't mean that just because you found some bones on

our land that they have anything to do with our Cat." The earl interrupted his son without apology. "For all you know, those bones could be a hundred years old, or even older. Your desire for scandal and vulgarity is driving you for the most salacious answer, that is all."

Quinton's hand moved to his pocket. He felt the familiar cool metal of his father's pocket watch, his favourite touchstone, but next to it he also felt the necklace Rory and he had found.

"Perhaps you're right, Grandfather. Perhaps I am just a seeker of scandal and my imagination is getting the better of me." Quinton pulled the necklace from his pocket and held it forward. "But just in case, I don't suppose you recognize this?"

The two men were silent for what felt like an eternity, but their silence confirmed what Quinton already suspected—that the necklace had belonged to his long-lost aunt.

"It is Cat's." Philip was the one to finally break the heavy tension. "Her mother gifted it to her on her fifteenth birthday. There used to be a small pearl sat between the garnets, but . . . it's the same necklace."

The feeling of victory which Quinton had been revelling in was quickly snuffed out by the look in Philip's eyes. As infuriating as his grandfather was, this was his child they were talking about —a child who was almost certainly a pile of bones being laid out in the shed by Rory at this very moment. Knowing for certain that she was dead would bring some closure, but it also eliminated any hope, no matter how farfetched.

"I am sorry." Quinton gently placed the necklace on the desk. "I don't mean to be glib about the matter. But it would help me greatly if you could tell me more of what you know of what happened to your daughter."

The earl narrowed his eyes, his composure already regained. "Fine. I will tell you what I know. But I still do not believe these bones belong to . . ." Philip trailed off, then shook his head as if to dispel the thought. "Whatever fate befell Catriona, I would bet my own mother's soul that she is not buried on our grounds."

Montgomery held up a hand. "This is not a conversation to be had sober." He walked over to the wall and pulled the chain which Quinton knew to be attached to a bell in the downstairs, alerting the servants that someone had a request in the study. A footman appeared immediately.

"A decanter of whiskey, please, Oliver," said Montgomery.

Oliver nodded, disappeared, and then reappeared within a minute with the whiskey and three glasses on a tray. Montgomery gave him leave, then poured the whiskey himself.

"You should really just keep a bottle in the room, Father. It would save us time." Handing each of them their glass, Montgomery sank into a chair and took a long swallow.

Quinton followed suit, easing into his own chair and sipping on the smooth blend, waiting for the earl to speak.

As Philip drank the whiskey, his shoulders relaxed, and Quinton could almost see some of the tension leaving his body. After a moment's pause, Philip gestured towards the end of the room, where three large portraits graced the walls. One was of the family of four, before Lady Coleville died, Philip explained. The younger Philip and Seonaid were just slightly smiling, and both Catriona and Graham had the freshness of youth. A second portrait was of a slightly older Catriona alone, her red hair in a loose bun, tendrils framing her face, her eyes alive and twinkling. The third portrait was of an adult Graham, his eyes mischievous. The earl's own eyes rested on Catriona.

"Catriona was always headstrong, even as a child. I always felt her damn Scottish blood was the cause of it, but Graham had the same blood and did not have that unrestraint. He could be stubborn, yes, but not wild." Philip sighed and took another sip before continuing. "Cat loved to paint and would wander as far as she pleased to find the perfect view that she could commit to paper." The man seemed to age as he spoke more softly. "She was talented, I'll give her that. Her mother used to say that her paintings held a . . . magic . . . of sorts, that drew a person into the painting as if they were a part of it. I never really understood what she meant, but Cat did have a unique style. She often painted a stunning scene, but then overlaid it in part with a white mist. Seonaid said if you looked closely, you could see a figure just within that mist, but I never could."

The earl shook his head and fell silent, lost in old memories and, Quinton suspected, old regrets.

Montgomery cleared his throat. "Some of her paintings are still in storage in the attic." The earl looked up in surprise, but Montgomery continued without meeting his eye. "I found them there when I was exploring as a child. We never spoke of Catriona, but she signed them, so I knew they were hers. They are quite good, actually."

"Even after she left, I could not bring myself to destroy them," said Philip. "Neither could I look at them, so in the attic they remained."

"She sounds quite remarkable," said Quinton quietly.

Philip chuffed at that. "That's one way to put it. She was a force to be sure. I did love her, in my way, but she was nothing like me. It was different, with her and Seonaid. While her mother was alive, the two were inseparable. Seo always could tame her, even when she was at her wildest. It was Seo who kept the peace, but once she died . . ."

Philip lapsed back into silence. Quinton let it hang there, not feeling like any words could be enough to fill it. He sensed his grandfather would continue when he was ready.

After a few minutes, Philip cleared his throat and took a large swallow. "After Seo died, we came apart. Cat and I quarrelled constantly, and Graham was old enough by then to take a side— hers, most often. Those two, different as they were, understood each other. So then Graham and I quarrelled as well." He sighed. "I have regrets. But regrets aren't buckets that hold water. If you try to carry them, your whole life will drip through the holes, and you will have nothing left. I made my peace with my mistakes years ago."

A pity you learned so little from those mistakes, thought Quinton. From the look on Montgomery's face, Quinton guessed similar thoughts were going through his mind. The old man might think he'd made peace, but Quinton could feel the weight of those regrets in every part of the old man's life. Relegating events to the corners of one's mind was not the same as finding peace.

"What happened, when she finally left?" asked Quinton.

"We had one last heated argument, and two days later she was gone," replied Philip. "She left a note that she was going to London and saying in no uncertain terms not to look for her."

Philip set his glass on the desk and tapped the edge, to which Montgomery responded by refilling it.

"I honoured the request for a few weeks, but when she didn't return and we didn't hear from her, I did send a man to London to check on her. He confirmed she boarded a London-bound coach, but he found no trace of her after that." Philip let out a deep breath. "That is the extent of my knowledge."

Montgomery stood up, anger flashing in his eyes. "Weeks? You waited weeks to look for her?"

His father met his gaze unflinchingly. "She brought all of her problems on herself. She's fortunate I looked at all."

Quinton watched as the emotions passed across Montgomery's face, ranging from anger to sadness and finally landing on distaste. The last part of this story must have been new to him. The two men's relationship was already hanging on by a thread, and Quinton wondered if the strain of these revelations would finally snip that thread.

Turning back to Quinton, Philip spoke with certainty. "As you can see though, I know she did not die here. As to what fate befell her in London, most likely she died shortly after she left, the harsh realities of life alone in the city not agreeing with the disposition of a wild but sheltered girl."

His grandfather was a stubborn old goat, Quinton would give him that. Pondering this, Quinton rose from his chair and placed his empty glass on the desk. "So then how do you explain the necklace?"

"I have no explanation," answered Philip. "Perhaps my daughter gave the trinket to a maid or a girl from the village. She was eccentric about wealth and was always trying to give things away. All I know for certain is wherever Cat's grave is, it's not here."

"If you don't believe the body we found is hers, how can you be so sure she died at all?" This back and forth was getting tiresome for Quinton. "It doesn't sound as if you went to great lengths to find her, after all."

"Trust me, I have my reasons," answered the old man vaguely.

Montgomery sighed. "It's the bloody ghost. He actually believes that Catriona's spirit haunts the estate."

The old man glared at his son but didn't correct him.

"Really?" Quinton turned to his grandfather in surprise. "I wouldn't have thought you were a spiritualist, grandfather."

"It's hard to deny a thing once you've seen it," grumbled Philip. "And one thing my loose-lipped son is wrong about is I don't believe she haunts the estate. I believe she haunts me, personally. It's just like that girl to be vindictive, even in death."

Quinton opened mouth to ask further questions, but Philip raised his hand. "If you don't mind, I think I've spoken quite enough about this today. Now leave me be."

It wasn't a request, and Quinton and Montgomery both exited the study. But as he left, Quinton saw his grandfather take the necklace in his hand. If he didn't know better, he also could have sworn he saw a tear well up in the old goat's eyes. Maybe he was human after all.

Chapter Twenty-Four

LONDON

The heavy heat of the London summer weighed on John as beads of sweat formed on his forehead. The thick wool of his red uniform didn't help matters, but it was expected of a Bow Street Runner.

Wiping away the sweat with the back of his hand, John looked again at the note he held.

Looking for information regarding Catriona Coleville. Believed to have run away to London in 1773. Boarded a stagecoach but has not been seen since. Please advise if possible.

Quinton

Good thing there was so much information available to go on. John sighed as he stuck the piece of paper back in his pocket. The truth was he didn't have very many contacts in the world of high society—that had always been Quinton's area. But he did know one person who might know something.

He rapped the knocker to Lady Theodosia Bexley's house, the sound echoing in the empty street. This time of year, this part of London was deserted, the influential families fleeing the summer heat for cooler weather in the country. John couldn't blame them.

The butler opened the door swiftly. Any other house on the

street likely would have refused John entry—not only was he coloured, he was a representative of the law, and therefore scandal, the nobility's greatest fear. But he had visited the Bexley house before, as a guest, so the butler showed him in without much fuss. John waited in the library, Theodosia's favourite room to receive guests in.

She arrived within a few minutes, leaning on a cane as she walked. Theo had suffered an apoplexy a few months ago, and though she had mostly recovered, the incident had taken a toll. She still carried herself with a dignified presence, but she seemed smaller now, and her shoulders held a weight that hadn't been there before, much like the cane.

"John!" Theo smiled at him. "How nice to see you. Sit, sit. Would you like some tea?"

"Lady Bexley." John inclined his head in acknowledgment. "No, thank you. I don't want to take up too much of your time."

"Ah, then you're here on official business." Theo rang the bell, disregarding John's statement. "I confess, I doubted you were here for a social call—though you and Savita are always welcome."

"Thank you, my lady."

Before John could continue, the butler reentered and Theo requested two whiskeys.

"My lady, I am on duty," protested John.

"John, I've told you to call me Theo," she responded, ignoring his half-hearted protest.

"Of course, my—" John cleared his throat. "Theo."

After the butler had been dismissed, Theo turned to him eagerly. "Tell me, what brings you to my door? I can't tell you how bored I've been these past few months. Being an invalid is not for the weak of spirit, I'll tell you that."

"Then it is good you are anything but weak of spirit." John took a seat. "I must tell you my own confession. The business I'm here on is only semi-official. I'm afraid it's more of a favour for Quinton."

"Oh?" Theo leaned back and accepted her whiskey from the tray the footmen came in holding. "And what kind of favour has my nephew-in-law asked of you?"

John took his own glass—it would be a waste of high-quality whiskey to refuse now. "He's asked for information regarding a Catriona Coleville."

"Interesting. A member of his newfound family?"

"I would assume so, but the note didn't give many more details, other than they think she ran away to London in 1773. Since you're the only person I really know in this world that's still in the city, I figured you might have heard of her or at least know someone who has."

Theo nodded thoughtfully. "The name does sound familiar, but I can't place it. And quite a number of years have passed. Be a dear, would you, John, and go fetch that book for me."

Following her pointed index finger, John quickly located the large book she was referring to—*Debrett's Peerage & Baronetage* —and brought it over to her.

"And my glasses, please," she requested.

After handing her the eyeglasses, John returned to his armchair. John sipped on the very fine whiskey as he watching her thumb through the impressive volume. What a strange thing to have a whole book dedicated to tracing not just your own family's history, but the histories of all the families who just happen to have an ancestor who was lucky and got handed a title a few hundred years ago.

"There's the Colevilles." Theo ran her finger down the page. "Ah, yes. I had forgotten Philip Coleville had three children. Montgomery, the youngest boy, then Graham, Quinton's father, and then the oldest was a girl—Catriona. Such a distinctive name; Scottish I believe. According to this, Philip's deceased wife came with a Scottish pedigree, so that makes sense, I suppose."

"That must be her." John leaned forward. "Does the book say anything else?"

"I'm afraid not. There's a birth year listed, but that's all. No marriages or children, or a death date either. Quite open-ended for a girl of her standing."

"Hmm." Leaning back, John rubbed his chin. "I don't suppose you ever ran in the same social circles?"

Theo sipped her whiskey. "No, I'm afraid not. We would have, eventually, but I'm afraid she never came out."

"Came out?"

"Yes, socially. When a young woman is presented to society for the first time. It signals her transition from childhood to adulthood, and her availability in the marriage market." A loud thump sounded as Theo closed the book and set it on the side table. "Miss Catriona Coleville was a few years younger than me. In 1773, when she supposedly ran away, she would have been seventeen, which is probably around when she would have come out. By that time, I was already married and keeping to the social circles that befit my position. Our paths didn't cross."

John nodded slowly. He was vaguely familiar with the concept of coming out, but Theo's explanation was helpful. Unfortunately that meant Catriona wouldn't have crossed paths with many people before she ran away—there wouldn't be friends in the city she might have turned to who could place her there.

"What about her running away? Wouldn't that have been quite a scandal at the time?" he asked.

Theo shrugged. "Yes, if it had gotten out, but this kind of thing happens more than you might think."

"What do you mean?"

Taking off her glasses and setting them on top of the book, Theo seemed to consider the question. Despite her age, and the toll of her illness, the sharp intelligence hadn't diminished in her green eyes. "The life of a high society girl can be quite suffocating, especially for one of naturally high spirit. Catriona certainly wouldn't have been the first to run off with an inappropriate man to a seedy inn in an act of defiance, but her family wouldn't broadcast that version of events to their peers. Fortunately for them, she wasn't out yet, so no one was expecting to see her, but other families under different circumstances might have said their daughter was visiting a distant aunt in Spain or something of the like. In the meantime, they would try to recover the girl before any elopement could occur."

The nobility certainly have perfected lying.

"What if they've already eloped, or they can't find her?" asked John.

Ringing the bell on her side table, Theo shook her head. "Whiskey first, John. Whiskey first."

As the footman returned and refilled their glasses, John contemplated this information. He didn't know if he would ever completely understand the minds of these people. The obsession with public appearance and the emphasis placed on presenting a perfect façade was pathological. As charmed as their lives seemed, John wondered that they didn't all have ulcers.

He took another drink, enjoying the cold burn on his tongue and throat. Perhaps it was worth the ulcers for the quality of whiskey.

Theo also took a long drink. "To answer your question, in that case, the girl's aunt found her a good match in Spain and she won't be returning to England any time soon."

"I see." John frowned. "Do you remember any particular story about Catriona? Even though she wasn't out yet, there must have been a few eyebrows raised when she never made an appearance at all."

"It was a long time ago, John." Theo took another sip. "I remember what happened with Quinton's father, Graham, because it was so shocking at the time. This . . . this happened quietly, whatever it was."

John sighed. This was turning out to be a dead end—informative, but not very helpful as to what to do next.

"But, now that I think on it, I do seem to recall a rumour going around that she had been married off quietly to a cousin in the Highlands or something like that." Theo chuckled. "I thought that was code for another kind of scandal."

"Which was?"

"Getting married off quickly and quietly is usually cover for one thing—a pregnancy."

Chapter Twenty-Five

LONDON

"A pregnancy?" John's brow furrowed. "As in tricking a man into raising another man's child?"

Theo chuckled. "No need to sound so scandalized, John. It may sound callous, but we both know the alternative is far worse."

John supposed that was fair, though it did seem quite cruel to him. But he also knew many an unmarried mother living on the street. It was one of the lowest social statuses a person could hold, noble or not.

"Hmm." John tapped his fingers against the arm of his chair. "That doesn't seem to be the case here. Quinton's note said the family believed she ran away. The thing about her being married off was either a deliberate lie or it really was a rumour."

"I suppose so." Theo's expression developed a thoughtful countenance. "Although it is odd the girl never resurfaced."

"Is it?"

"Quite." Theo nodded sagely. "Do you know what I learned growing up? How to paint, how to do embroidery, how to play the harpsichord, and the art of social graces. My father could be somewhat progressive for his other faults, so I also learned Latin, history, geography, and mathematics from my brother's tutor.

126

None of those are skills a young woman could use to survive on the streets, aside from needlework, perhaps. I find it hard to believe a girl from a similar background would have the grit to grind out a life as a seamstress—not coming from the kind of life-style she would've been accustomed to. Most of these girls go home once the reality of independence sinks in."

It was a good point. So then why had Catriona never gone back? Was it her choice, or had something prevented her? Was she even still alive?

"What do you think might've happened to the girl?" asked John.

"It could be a hundred things. Perhaps she eloped and did manage to build a life, although London is an odd choice for that."

"Why's that?"

"Because at her age, a parent's permission would have been required, as well as a reading of the banns. Scotland would have been the more logical choice, or Gurnsey like Graham Coleville did." Theo shrugged. "There are ways around it, but it's certainly more difficult."

"So then what else?"

Theo's sharp green eyes turned their full intensity on John. "I think you know."

John did know, he just didn't want to say it out loud. A girl that age and from that background . . . she was a predator's dream —young, pretty, and naive.

He was surprised Theo knew of such things, but he supposed he shouldn't be. Theo might have been a dowager duchess, but the more John got to know her, the more he realized that her social status had not prevented her from learning a great deal of how the world worked.

"Indeed." John cleared his throat and stood. "Well, perhaps I should be going. Thank you for your time, Lady Bex—Theo."

"Of course, anytime, John." Theo began to stand as well, with one long last glance at the book. "You know, on her mother's side, a distant cousin of mine was listed. I knew her a long time ago and I don't even know if she's still alive, but a longshot is better than no shot. If the Coleville girl did come to London, it's possible she reached out to family at some point."

"I would be grateful for any lead you can offer."

Theo nodded. "I'll write down the name and address for you."

Within a minute John had the piece of paper with in his hand, the duchess's elegant scrawl only barely readable. John didn't know why rich folk insisted on writing in such a way that it took a code breaker to decipher it, but he supposed that was just one of those things he never would understand.

"Thank you, Theo. It is very appreciated."

"It's no trouble, really." Theo smiled. "I may be getting older, but I hope I'm still good for some things."

"Wise counsel is good for a great many things." John returned her smile. "Speaking of which, thank you for the wise counsel you offered Katy and for the use of your carriage. She told me about it just as I was about to post my letter to Quinton, requesting use of his carriage. It means a great deal."

She nodded. "Wealth is worth nothing if it's not shared with one's friends."

As he left her home, John wondered at the long life of Theodosia Bexley and all the things she knew which she should not. Perhaps one day she would tell him some of the stories that made up the tapestries of her colourful life.

Chapter Twenty-Six

During his brief time in the country, Charlie had often found himself using the period before dinner was served as a time for a solitary walk about the grounds. His enjoyment of the country air and quiet lifestyle surprised him. He had built himself up as a man of the city, at home in the chaos, his hands stained by the grime and blood and sweat of scratching out a life there. But here, with the vast swathes of grass and the carefully tended gardens, memories surfaced, and with them a side to himself which he thought he'd stamped out for good.

During his boyhood in India, Charlie had lived in an English-style manor with his father and mother—smaller than the Coleville estate, but not dissimilar in its comforts. It had been an idyllic existence in many ways, carefree and pleasant compared to many other children, at least through the innocent lens of youth.

While Savi was a babe, Charlie had been left much to his own devices, entertaining himself for hours at a time. Together with a large orange tom cat he called Ravi, he had explored the country-side at will. The artful rose garden here on Quinton's estate, alive with blooms and a heavy fragrance, brought him back to a similar garden in his memory, one which had taught him that beauty could hide a great deal of pain when he had lost a ball among the thorns and sliced up his arm trying to get it back. He had cried for an hour while his mother cleaned the cuts and scolded him for his carelessness with his toys. But when his father arrived home that evening, there was no reprimand at all. He simply retrieved the ball for Charlie and the two played together until the sun was gone from the sky, all while Ravi watched carefully from the garden wall.

Those had been happy times, when the crushing weight of the future was unknown to him, before his spineless father had dragged his Indian family to English shores and then abandoned them at the first challenge. They were times Charlie didn't allow himself to think about often. Dwelling on what was lost could bring nothing but heartache—at least, that's what he told himself as he pushed the memories back to the deep recesses of his mind where they belonged.

Charlie paused near a bench, suddenly overcome by deep feelings of missing Finn. The boy had been a source of joy for Charlie in his life, and he hoped he could provide Finn with some of the stability and security which Charlie had missed out on.

It was twilight now, and Charlie listened for the coming sounds of the night—the birds and insects and scurrying animals who claimed the dark as their home. He too was a creature of the dark, and he felt an affinity for them. Much of his London life was spent in the shadows—both literally and figuratively—and he did not fear it as some did.

A quiet movement caught his eye near the short rock wall that housed the kitchen garden. A hare perhaps, seeking out the vegetables within for its own dinner. Charlie was about to turn away and head back to the house when suddenly the movement came again, but this time he could make out the distinct shape of a human-like figure. Even that he may have been willing to dismiss as the kitchen maid harvesting a few more herbs for their dinner, if it weren't for the white glow which seemed to emanate around the outline of the figure in question. Then just as quickly as it had appeared, it disappeared.

Instinctively Charlie ran towards it, while at the same time piercing the air with a loud whistle. It had been some years since the three men had been boys of the street, but Charlie hoped that wherever Quinton was that he would be able to hear the signal they used to use and would quickly bring him to his side.

Stopping at the wall where he'd seen the intruder, Charlie scanned the area, looking for any clue as to which way the figure had gone. To his annoyance, in the fading light he could see no evidence to support that a person had even stood there at all. It didn't help that he only had one good eye to look with either. He closed his eyes, listening for any foreign sounds, such as the heavy breathing or loud footfalls of someone running away. He heard nothing but the sound of crickets.

Within a minute he did hear the sound of footfalls, but they were moving toward him from the direction of the house, and Charlie knew they belonged to his reinforcements, not his quarry. Sighing, Charlie opened his eyes and turned to see Quinton moving at an impressive pace in his direction.

As he neared, Charlie held up his hand. "Careful, or else you'll trample all over any evidence which it's too dark to see."

Quinton skidded to a stop, panting heavily. "What?"

"Evidence of the ghost," replied Charlie, his expression deadpan. "Obviously."

Blinking in surprise, Quinton cocked his head. "How do you know of the ghost?"

Charlie rolled his eyes. "I talk to the staff, who are all too eager to share the dramatic details."

"Oh." Quinton ran his fingers though his hair, regaining his breath. "I didn't take you for the superstitious type."

"I'm not." Charlie glared at his friend. "If there were such a thing as ghosts, I assure you I would have a full entourage everywhere I went."

Quinton snorted at the dark humour, though Charlie wasn't kidding. "Then what is it you saw?"

Charlie hesitated, not wanting to sound like a fool. "I'm not certain, to be fair. A person, I assume, although I can't explain their appearance, or how quickly they vanished without a trace. I know it sounds mad, but—"

"I believe you." Nodding, Quinton gazed into the growing darkness of the surrounding woods. "Should we give chase, then?"

"I think at this point it would be a waste of time." Charlie sighed. "By the time we returned to the home and collected lanterns and the dog, whoever it was will be long gone."

"I agree," responded Quinton. "I'll tell the grounds and kitchen staff to steer clear of the garden for tonight, and we'll do a proper examination of the surrounding area in the morning light."

The two men turned and headed back to the house. They walked in companionable silence for a few moments, Charlie contemplating the conundrum of a ghost which he didn't believe could be real, and Quinton contemplating god only knew.

"What did the staff have to say about the supposed spirit?" asked Quinton finally, breaking the silence.

Charlie shrugged. "Several claim to have sighted it over the years. Both Oliver and Lawrence say they saw it a few years back, and you'll not find either of them sneaking out after dark." He paused, trying to think. "Or perhaps one saw it twice. I actually cannot tell those footmen apart. Regardless, a scullery maid saw it in full daylight only last spring, the apparition dressed in white and moving in and out of the trees as if floating. She was happy to relay the legend of the ruins as well. Apparently some feel the curse of that old house has come to land on this one. The murder of two upper-crust children, different eras, unable to rest."

Quinton scoffed. "That legend is what will never rest."

Ignoring the interruption, Charlie continued. "And the gardener warned me of it, telling me my nightly circuits would see me in the ghost's very grasp." Charlie chuckled at that. "I told him it was welcome to try."

"I certainly would not bet against you in a fistfight with a ghost." Quinton said the words seriously, and after a moment's pause, both men laughed at the ridiculous image.

As the laughter died away, a thought occurred to Charlie, which instantly sobered him. "You know, Q, the fact this ghost is more than just a figment of overactive, superstitious minds is cause for concern." Charlie glanced behind, the hair standing up on the back of his neck as he thought of unseen eyes watching him from the dark shadows.

"I know." Quinton's mood had also darkened. "Unless the ghost turns out to be the real undead spirit of my late aunt, which would turn my worldview on its head, it means that a very real person with flesh and blood is haunting this estate—or perhaps my grandfather, if you ask him. But either way, I cannot think of an innocent reason to do so. I fear this so-called-ghost's intentions must be nefarious."

"Nefarious?" Charlie raised an eyebrow. "That's an awful posh word."

"Knock it off," said Quinton with a light shove. "You know what I mean."

Unfortunately, Charlie did know what he meant. People didn't pretend to be ghosts to do good. Charlie would sleep with his good eye open tonight.

Chapter Twenty-Seven

The sun was barely up and the air still agreeably cool when Quinton found himself at the garden to look for whatever secrets the ground held. He had slept poorly, if at all, before finally retiring to his own quarters so Zoe would not be disturbed by his tossing and turning. He could not resist looking in on her as he'd passed her room this morning, though. He wasn't usually up before her, so he took the time to take the moment in. She slept soundly, her dark hair tousled, arm flung across the bed as if searching for him. The sight had grounded him, while also making it ever so clear what he was protecting.

As he carefully examined the earth, he thought about what Montgomery had said to him. *There are things I cannot explain. I don't know everything there is to know in the world.* While those seemed like words born from wisdom with which Quinton could agree, he still found it difficult to accept the idea of an actual spirit haunting the grounds.

He heard a noise behind him and turned to see Zoe coming to join him, her dark curly hair falling down her back and dressed only in her nightgown with her dressing gown over it, with sleep still clearly in her eyes. His chest seemed to swell with love at the sight, and Quinton greeted her with a tight embrace, grateful for her presence.

"I thought you were asleep," he said as he released her.

Trying to smother a yawn, Zoe shook her head. "I was. But I missed your presence, so I awoke. After last night's events, I knew you would want to be here as early as possible."

"Indeed." Quinton turned back to the ground. "I didn't want to take the chance an errant kitchen maid would trample over everything by mistake."

The weather was not on his side when it came to evidence. Though it had rained several days during their time at the estate, the past two days had been dry and sunny, and the ground was already hard. Quinton searched carefully in an ever-widening circle but could find no clear footprints. As he reached where the garden bordered the grass of the grounds, he did find a single imprint of a deer. Curious. The way the footprint was pointed meant the deer must have balanced precariously on a single leg while nibbling the cabbage. The damage was obvious, with one plant eaten to the ground, but only one footprint, almost as if . . .

"Did you notice the broom marks?"

Zoe's question startled him from his thoughts and he jumped slightly, then looked where she was pointing. He saw what she referred to—sweep marks made in the dry earth as if a broom had been used to level the ground. In his focus looking for footprints, he'd failed to notice the subtle disturbing of the dirt.

"I doubt those living in the spirit world need to carry a broom to cover their footprints." Tilting her head upward, Zoe paused, taking in a deep breath through the nose. "I smell coffee."

Straightening up, Quinton laughed lightly. "You are like a bloodhound when it comes to coffee."

"It's an essential, Quinton, you know that." Zoe's bright blue eyes twinkled with mischief. "I'm going to go in and change before your grandfather sees me in my dressing gown and is scandalized. After, coffee is our first priority."

"Agreed."

Wrapping his hand in hers, Quinton joined his wife in heading for the breakfast parlour. Better to discuss this newest development over warm food and hot coffee.

~

Mary followed the wandering path, complete with a basket to carry the wildflowers she plucked, enjoying her stroll towards the farms. Most of the walk was in the sunshine, with only brief parts of the path paralleling the woods. Although the day was warm, Mary found herself relishing the warmth of the sun on her back, instead of avoiding it as she did in London.

This country life agreed with her, she mused. Who would have guessed? Although despite her cheerful countenance, an unsettled feeling also lingered. She kept glancing over her shoulder, toward the tree line, feeling like there were eyes on her. But it was likely just the nerves left over from Charlie's ghost sighting last night making Mary paranoid.

As the first farm came into view, Mary straightened up and put away her idle thoughts, readying herself for the task at hand. Langford's widow had reluctantly revealed the name of the family that had been the original owners of the ruby ring, but only after Zoe had also broken all semblance of etiquette and refused to leave until she did. Later Quinton had suggested Mary pay a casual visit to the farm as a guest simply out for a stroll, and perhaps engage in some 'harmless' gossip. Mary had jumped at the chance to stretch her investigative legs, as well as her actual legs. Both activities seemed to help dissipate the unusual feeling of aimlessness she had been fighting. Smiling, she approached the home.

A woman stood outside, expertly hanging sheets on a clothesline, rhythmically plucking one from a basket, snapping it to open it, and affixing it to the line. A cheerful call from Mary broke her tempo. But the woman, Mrs. Corbyn, seemed happy for the break, and in typical country neighborliness soon had Mary on the front porch with a casual tea in front of her.

Mrs. Corbyn was in her thirties, and Mary found her to be strikingly beautiful. Her golden hair was in a simple bun, with a bonnet covering it while outside. She removed her bonnet as she served tea, and her complexion was porcelain, with just a sprinkle of freckles over her nose, which simply added to the charm. Her blue eyes were the color of the summer sky, without the depths of color that Zoe's eyes held. She smiled cheerfully at Mary as she served the tea, complete with a thick slice of bread and fresh butter, in which Mary happily indulged.

Mary had explained who she was, a guest of the new lord, out for an amble, and Mrs. Corbyn was clearly willing to chat to gain her own tidbit or two about the manor house inhabitants that she could pass on to other farmers' wives. Mary obliged for a bit, dropping some harmless tidbits about Zoe and Quinton before subtly inquiring about the farm wife's own life.

"A lovely home you have here, Mrs. Corbyn. You and Mr. Corbyn must both be hard workers."

The woman's blue eyes sparkled as she answered. "That we are, Miss Fletcher, that we are. Edgar had this farm before we wed, and we have made it our own to be sure."

Mary saw no animosity towards her husband as they continued to talk, so she changed her approach, after a second helping of the bread and butter.

"Terrible what happened to the old land steward at Cedarbrook," she said. "Poor Mr. Langford."

The change was instant, and Mrs. Corbyn made no attempt to hide her disdain. "Don't waste your time feeling sorry for that poor excuse of a man, Miss Fletcher. Whatever he got, he had it coming."

Surprised by her candor, Mary cocked her head and spoke thoughtfully. "Sounds like you know that from experience." She hoped by now the woman would feel a certain camaraderie, and answer honestly.

Mary watched as Mrs. Corbyn absentmindedly reached for her finger, almost exactly as Mrs. Langford had, but this finger was empty of rings. After a moment, she answered. "Folk make mistakes, don't they? Sometimes a person gets to thinking about all they don't got, and forgets about all they actually do."

Mary spoke quietly. "Your husband?"

The woman's blue eyes glanced up and met Mary's eyes before casting her own around the view from the porch. "Edgar and I weren't blessed with children, though not for want of trying. I let that lack fill me up." She smiled sadly. "The mistakes were mine, not Edgar's, and the cost was mine to pay, something my mother had gifted me from her own. But the scandal would have ruined not just us, but . . . someone else. So when that old louse demanded payment for silence, I paid."

Mary saw the anger in the blue eyes fade, and surprisingly a twinkle replaced it. Mrs. Corbyn smiled. "I hope Langford rots in hell for what he took from me, but it made Edgar and I look each other in the eye and decide what we wanted. Turns out, that was each other. We built back what we lost, and we are richer now than before, in here." She pushed her hand against her chest and continued. "And we got our name out in the church for when a child needs a home. In God's time, we will have a family yet."

On the walk home, Mary shifted the now-laden basket Mrs. Corbyn had filled from one hip to the other. The farmer's wife had insisted she take the remainder of the loaf of bread, and jars of preserves, as well as fresh vegetables for the kitchen. Mary did appreciate the gesture. The bread was quite good. And Mrs. Corbyn had impressed her by more than her baking skills. Clearly the woman had no love for Langford, but just as clearly she had resolved the situation and was at peace. Mary was quite certain no one in that household had done harm to the man.

Setting a more direct route, Mary hastened her paste. She had something of note to share and was eager to tell the others.

Chapter Twenty-Eight

Zoe had been kind to tell him how she was sorry his time here, earmarked for relaxation, was to be spent in his work. But speaking for the dead gave Rory purpose, and his recent experiences demanded he use his mind for purpose, lest he fall back into the bleakness that had marked last year. In truth, he was grateful for the opportunity to use his skills to tell this story.

Though this story was hidden under decades of quiet and decay and secrecy. Finding the truth was not going to be easy, but Rory had ascertained at least one thing for certain. The discovery had surprised him, and he was eager to tell the rest of them.

After washing up, Rory found his friends together, eating, as usual. Though luncheon was not far gone, tea and cakes were available lest hunger overcome any of them. Though he knew this was simply the way of things and he had other things on his mind, Rory found the surplus of food a sad contrast with what he saw daily on the streets of London. He wondered briefly what became of the uneaten remnants.

Quinton was mid-conversation. "We need a replacement. I'm just not sure how to even start a search for a land steward candidate."

"Perhaps your uncle or grandfather will know of someone," replied Zoe. "It's really your grandfather's job anyway, isn't it?"

Scoffing at that, Quinton wisely said nothing more, reaching for a cake instead.

Spotting Rory, Mary made her way across the room and enthusiastically showed him a lavender cake shaped like the flower. "Simone hired a French pastry chef to start after Quinton and Zoe returned, as a wedding present. Today is his first day."

Rory accepted the lavender cake. After all, his not partaking wouldn't make the poor any less hungry, and he had skipped luncheon in favour of his work.

"He is an artist." Mary sighed dramatically. "Try the cherry tart too. He added elderberry flavouring. I've never tasted anything like it."

She wasn't wrong. Rory quickly scarfed both treats, washing them down with a cup of hot coffee. Even the coffee tasted amazing here. Though his life was certainly quite comfortable by most standards, it hardly compared to the amount of wealth on evident at Cedarbrook. Perhaps everything just tasted better surrounded by luxury and beauty.

The Dovefields breezed in and helped themselves as well. Rory could see the look of satisfaction on Simone's face as she ate a lemon cake. That woman did love a French cook.

Having restored the equilibrium of his body by eating, Rory cleared his throat. "I have some news about the bodies we found."

Every eye turned to him.

"What have you found?" Zoe asked.

"My best guess from the size of the bones, the bairns were formed about seven months in the womb. Both female, with no obvious deformities."

"So the mother was still pregnant when she was buried?" asked Quinton.

Rory shook his head. "No, actually. I can say definitively that was not the case. Most likely the bairns were stillborn, which is not so unusual when a woman is carrying twins."

Charlie frowned. "Now I know we accept a great deal of what you say at face value, but how can you possibly know that?"

Normally the question would annoy Rory, but he turned with satisfaction to Charlie because he had such a good answer. "Because, my good man, the body buried with the bairns was male. So unless a miracle occurred and he carried them in his own body without a womb, I think we can safely say the poor souls exited their mother before they were buried."

A stunned silence followed his statement. Rory leaned back and took another sip of his coffee, allowing the revelation to sink in.

Mary was the first to recover. "How can you tell with just bones?"

"A good question, lass. As it happens, the pelvic bone is a dead giveaway. A woman's pelvis has adapted to accommodate childbirth, which is obvious in the size and shape. There are other indicators in the skull and length of the longer bones, but besides all that, this body was close to two meters tall, and had a broadness typical of a grown man as well."

Charlie frowned and grumbled, "You do love to be the smartest person in the room, don't you?"

"Well, when something comes naturally—"

"Alright, you two." Quinton held up a hand. "Rory, can you tell cause of death for the man?"

Rory dropped his good-natured ribbing of Charlie and turned back to Quinton. "One can't know for certain with a skeleton like this, but I can tell you his neck was fractured. Whether that was the result of an accident or not, it's impossible to tell."

Everyone was quiet for a moment and Mary took advantage of the pause to help herself to another cake, this one chocolate. Charlie too found his plate and added to it. Rory was glad his friends did not have delicate stomachs.

Quinton cleared his throat after everyone had settled back down. "The question becomes what relationship the man had to the babies. They must have died around the same time to have been buried together."

There was an obvious answer that Rory suspected they were all thinking, and Zoe was the one to say it.

"Perhaps he was the father," she said quietly.

"It's a distinct possibility," affirmed Rory. "But I don't know that we will ever know without the mother's input."

"Then we must find the mother." It was the first Simone had contributed to the conversation. "Has the grave been searched thoroughly, past the bones themselves? If it were me in her place, I might leave something of myself with my children and their father —something personal, with value to me, to keep them company and keep me connected to them."

Her eyes met Rory's and he thought he knew what she was thinking of. Over the past two years, Rory had become particularly good friends with Theo, someone whom Simone was also close to. It wasn't common knowledge with the group, but Theo had told Rory of how she had lost a daughter she'd named Catherine, early in her marriage. The poor soul had died shortly after birth, and Theo's husband had refused to acknowledge the child. Theo was left to grieve the loss alone, but one thing Rory remembered was that Theo had left a memento with her daughter. Rory couldn't recall what it was, but he knew it was something sentimental, which had been gifted to her by her own mother. Forty years past, and Theo had still teared up telling him the tale.

Rory glanced at Quinton, waiting for him to tell them what had been found in the grave. He didn't have to wait long.

"It's funny you say that, Simone." Quinton sighed and leaned forward. "We did find something else in the grave—a necklace, which my grandfather confirmed belonged to my great-aunt, Catriona. She disappeared nearly forty years ago, but the necklace in the grave confirms a connection to the bodies, at least in my mind. Before Rory's report, I would have put money on it being her in ground, but now . . ."

Hugh rubbed his chin, chiming in for the first time as well. "Where is this necklace?"

"I left it with my grandfather."

"If Catriona isn't buried in the grave, do we have any idea where she might be?" asked Mary, already onto her third cake.

Quinton and Zoe exchanged a look before he answered. "It's possible she went to London. I have John looking into it."

Chapter Twenty-Nine

As interesting as the conversation with Rory had been, Simone decided to leave the young people to their graves and ghosts while she turned her attention to more domestic matters. There was little glory to be found in balancing accounts or tallying expenditures, but it was a necessary part of running a house—or an estate. The task usually fell to the lady of the house. Cedarbrook had been without a lady for years, so Philip had entrusted the work to his housekeeper, a woman by the name of Mrs. Temperance Fox. So far Simone had found her to live up to both namesakes.

But since Zoe would one day become the countess of Cedarbrook, Simone had taken it upon herself to make sure that everything was in order. There was also the matter of hiring a new land steward, which the current earl seemed reluctant to do, and Quinton and Zoe seemed too preoccupied to set aside time for. Besides which, there was another position which Simone had decided had gone unfilled long enough.

"Mrs. Fox, what time is it?" Simone glanced up from the paperwork spread out on the desk in front of her. "The first applicant should be here soon."

"Yes, milady." Mrs. Fox glanced at the wall where a clock was placed. From Simone's position the face was obscured. "It's ten till two o'clock."

"Very good, he'll be here shortly." Simone picked up the letter she had received from the candidate. "And you're certain one of the footmen couldn't be trained? I'm concerned that this one may be a bit overqualified. He really doesn't need anything exceptionally difficult."

Mrs. Fox shook her head, her lips pinched. "No. The footmen are a pair, and it would be a waste to break up the set."

Simone sighed. "Very well. Could you please have the kitchen prepare a light tea spread?"

"Of course, milady." With a displeased sniff, Mrs. Fox disappeared, off to terrify the poor kitchen maid no doubt.

Simone's intrusion into Mrs. Fox's domain had not been taken well. While her protests were silent, the woman still knew how to make her discontentment strongly felt. Simone didn't really blame her—after all, Simone was in the woman's work space going through all her records with a fine-tooth comb. But Simone still thought it better than having Mrs. Fox haul all the paperwork upstairs. She supposed it was a situation in which neither was destined to be completely happy.

"What is going on in here?"

Simone looked up to see the butler standing in the doorway. His face paled as he recognized her.

"I apologize, my lady," he said, his posture stiff. "I mistook you for Mrs. Fox for a moment."

"It's quite alright." Simone hesitated, trying to remember his name, but for some reason it escaped her at the moment. "I am interviewing a new valet for Quinton—Lord Coleville."

"Ah, very good. Do you wish myself or Mrs. Fox to sit in on the interview?"

For a household servant or an estate employee, Simone would have allowed one of them to sit in and offer input, but this wasn't a household matter.

She shook her head. "That won't be necessary at this time,

thank you." Simone wished she could remember his name. "But I am interviewing a new land steward later this afternoon, if you would like to come back."

His brow furrowed. "A land steward? Forgive me, my lady, but isn't that a task better left to Lord Philip?"

"I've spoken to him and he has given me permission to handle the matter on his behalf."

That wasn't entirely true, but Simone planned on discussing it with him after she had chosen a candidate, and she was sure she could bring him around. The timing of the conversation was just semantics.

The butler raised an eyebrow but didn't say anything more. Giving a slight bow, he excused himself, just in time.

The tea was brought in shortly after, and then Mrs. Fox entered, a man following close behind. Simone could not fault the candidate for his dress. His white shirt was pressed, and a cravat neatly tied at the throat. His waistcoat was cream, contrasting nicely with his dark-coloured tailcoat. His trousers fit perfectly, and even his ankle boots were polished to a shine.

A promising start.

"Mr. Justin Darrow, I presume." Simone smiled and gestured for him to take a seat. "That will be all, thank you, Mrs. Fox."

After the housekeeper had closed the door behind her, Simone began pouring the tea. "Mr. Darrow, you mentioned in your letter that you've served as a valet for sixteen years. Were all of those under the same employer?"

"I see you're a lady who gets straight to business. I appreciate that." He accepted his cup from her. "In answer to your question, yes, Lady Dovefield. My employer was the late Marquess Westerfield. He passed two months ago."

"I was sorry to hear about that," said Simone. She wasn't personally familiar with the Marquess, but she'd read about his death in the newspaper. "How did you come by that position?"

"I was trained up in the household and eventually promoted to valet. At the time Lord Westerfield hadn't inherited the title yet

146

and was still quite young, so he didn't yet require an excessively experienced valet."

Simone nodded. "I understand. And I assume you have references?"

"Yes, indeed." He handed the papers across to her with a quick smile. "I think you'll find everything in order."

As she skimmed the references, Simone eyed the man sitting across from her. He was not particularly tall, or particularly short. His build was average but athletic. She guessed him to be somewhere in his mid-thirties. His blond hair was neatly trimmed, and his brown eyes hinted at an honest and open soul, if not a deep one. He gave the impression of a likable man, which worked in his favour, but Simone didn't rely merely on a man's ability to charm when it came to judging his worth and competency.

The papers said what was expected—that Darrow was a hard worker and a man of excellent reputation. It was all fairly standard, so Simone quickly set them aside on the small desk.

"You're correct, everything does seem to be in order," said Simone. "But I do have a question, Mr. Darrow. You're clearly quite experienced and qualified—some might even say too qualified. Are you certain you wish to serve a viscount, after your long years in service to a marquess? It is a drop in prestige, is it not?"

"I am not interested in prestige, merely earning an honest living," Darrow replied without hesitation.

"Perhaps." Simone took a sip of her tea. "But surely someone with your skills and qualifications could obtain a position with a higher-ranking noble. Why apply here?"

Darrow smiled. "If I may speak honestly, milady? There are not as many high-ranking nobles in search of valets as you might think. Besides, the viscount will be an earl one day, will he not?"

"Yes, he will." Simone returned his smile, but she wasn't done asking questions yet. "Tell me, what was your late employer's temperament like?"

"His temperament?" Darrow's brow furrowed. "Forgive me,

TAYLOR PREISLER & SANDRA PREISLER

milady, but I fail to see how that is relevant. Even though he has passed, Lord Westerfield is still entitled to my discretion."

That was a good answer, Simone had to give him that.

Simone inclined her head. "Of course. I hope that same discretion will extend to my son-in-law, should you accept the position."

Darrow leaned forward. "Are you offering me the position?"

"I believe I am, at least on a trial basis."

She liked the valet. He was earnest and quick-witted, and Simone thought Quinton would like him too. But even better, Darrow had a backbone, which meant Quinton wouldn't be able to bully him.

But she would be remiss if she didn't warn Darrow of what he was getting into. "However," Simone started, holding up a hand before Darrow could respond. "There are a few things you should know before you accept. My son-in-law—Viscount Coleville—is not like other nobles you've encountered. You may have heard of his . . . unconventional . . . start as the heir to the Coleville title. The reason I ask about your former employer's temperament is that Quinton's is unusual by the standards of society."

Darrow cocked his head, considering. "I am aware of the proclivities the upper class may be inclined towards. I doubt anything would shock me."

Simone resisted the urge to smirk. "You'd be surprised. He did not grow up in such circles, and as such does not share all of the same values or sensitives. He can be reckless, and he is prone to finding himself in the middle of unconventional situations— some of them dangerous and nearly all of them scandalous, should they come to light. Will that be a problem for you?"

There was a momentary pause. Simone studied the man as he contemplated her statement. She would not blame him if he wished to apply for other positions. A scandal could taint a servant as much as a noble, and servants lived and died by their reputations.

"No, my lady, I don't believe that will be a problem for me," he said finally.

"Very good." Simone stood. "I'll introduce you to Lord Coleville. I assume you can start in the near future?"

Darrow nodded. "I need to collect a few belongings from the village inn, but I can start this evening if that's acceptable."

"That will be very acceptable, thank you, Mr. Darrow."

Chapter Thirty

"This is completely unacceptable." Quinton shook his head as he contemplated his mother-in-law, astounded at her behaviour. "You had no right to make this decision without my input."

Simone did not have the decency to appear cowed at his objections. "What is completely unacceptable is for a gentleman of your status to still be without a valet. You are clearly much too busy to handle the task of hiring one, as you have strenuously made clear, so I have done it for you. The correct response is 'thank you.'"

Quinton blinked, opening his mouth to respond, but then promptly snapped it shut again, at a loss for words. He looked to his wife for her support. Though she had the audacity to look more amused than indignant, Zoe did understand his signal for assistance.

"Mr. Darrow, would you mind giving us a few minutes," she said smoothly.

"Of course—"

"Hugh, arrange for the coachman to take Mr. Darrow into the village to collect his belongings," interrupted Simone. "He'll need to be back by seven o'clock to dress Quinton for dinner."

There was a pause, the tension stretching as each member of the conversation sized up the others, but after only a brief hesitation, Hugh stood. "Of course, darling. Come with me, my good man." As they stepped out into the hallway, Quinton could hear Hugh still talking before the door shut behind them. "I haven't had a chance to try the pub in the village yet. Perhaps we'll stop for a pint, aye?"

Leave it to Hugh to cozy up to the interloper. Quinton didn't really blame the valet, of course. He was just a man in search of a job. No, Quinton's ire was directed at the source of the problem —Simone.

"What is wrong with you?" Quinton knew his tone was sharp, but he was frustrated, and growing more so as Simone continued to sit there, as unbothered and unapologetic as a cat who'd brought home a dead mouse.

"There's no need to snap, Quinton. Perhaps you should take a glass of whiskey to calm your nerves," replied Simone, still completely placid.

"Maman, you must admit you've overstepped a bit," interjected Zoe, saving Quinton from saying something he couldn't take back. "Quinton has been adamant he doesn't want a valet. Where you or I agree or not is beside the point."

"And my mother was always adamant that a *lutin* was living in the attic and stealing her silverware," Simone responded. "It doesn't make either one right."

"You are being ridiculous." Quinton was nearing the end of his tolerance. "I don't want a valet and I don't need a valet. You'll have to dismiss him."

Simone stared at him as though he was a petulant child throwing a fit. "He's your valet. If you wish to dismiss him, then you shall have to do so. But before you do, perhaps you should take some time to reflect on why you're so resistant to the idea of having a valet."

"I don't need to reflect on anything." Quinton winced, fully aware of how childish he still sounded. "I am a grown man, and I can dress myself. It's a waste of time and resources for me to have one."

"You have been able to dress yourself, up until now," corrected Simone. "But you haven't even begun to associate with the levels of society which you will be expected to in the coming months and years. With the upcoming season will be countless balls and operas and dinners to attend, some with the highest-ranking members of British society. Have you thought about what you'll be wearing when you meet Prince Frederick or Princess Mary, or even Queen Charlotte or the Prince Regent himself? What about when you take your place in the House of Lords, when the other lords are snickering behind your back because you don't know the difference between black tie and white tie? When they won't take you or your ideas seriously because you still dress like a shopkeeper from the West End?"

The words landed like a load of bricks on Quinton's head. Was that really how people perceived him? He already felt like such an imposter in this world, he supposed he shouldn't be surprised that others saw him the same way. But it still stung to hear it from Simone's own mouth

"A shopkeeper, really Maman?" Zoe frowned, her expression no longer amused, and crossed her arms. "That isn't fair, and you know it."

"I didn't say that's the way I saw it, but you must accept the reality that what you wear and how you present yourself do matter—especially to society." Simone's tone had softened, but she did not take back what she had said.

"I suppose you may have a point," replied Quinton after a moment's consideration. "I shall give Mr. Darrow a trial run, but I make no promises."

Simone brightened visibility. "Excellent. That just leaves the matter of the land steward."

Quinton blinked. It was something he'd been meaning to get around to but hadn't found the time. When he asked Philip about it, he'd been brushed off, and so the menial task had fallen to the wayside.

"Land steward?" he asked lamely, feeling woefully inadequate.

"Yes, of course. The estate can't go on without one in the long term." Simone nodded, smoothing the fabric of the front of her gown. "I've already selected a candidate and cleared it with the earl."

"Well, you've certainly been busy, Maman," said Zoe with a raised eyebrow.

"You have things you do to keep busy and so do I," Simone replied. "One day you will be mistress of Cedarbrook and I want it well maintained for your future."

Quinton sighed. He knew she was right. He wasn't lord of the manor yet, but he would be one day, and Quinton needed to take responsibility for the decisions made here, both good and bad, and the effects they would have on the other people in his life.

"I'm glad we have you on our side, Simone." Quinton knew when he was outmatched by his opponent, and with Simone he was often outmatched. "Who did you hire?"

"You'll find out tonight." Simone still had that same self-satisfied look on her face. "He's joining us for dinner."

Chapter Thirty-One
LONDON

The address Theo had given John was that of a home nestled between brownstones on Temple Street, with only a whisper of space between the structures. The house was attractive-looking—or rather, John thought it likely had been attractive at one point. Now if one looked closer, one would see the cracks in the plaster and the paint flaking off the sconces.

The neighbourhood, which at one time had been considered quite respectable, had changed over the past couple of decades. Now it was a mix of people from all kinds of backgrounds, from immigrants to merchants to fallen members of society. Not a slum by any means, but also not the kind of place John would expect to find an acquaintance of Theo's.

He knocked on the door, but when the door opened, the person who answered was no butler. Instead a middle-aged woman stood there, drying her hands on a stained rag.

"Can I help you, constable?" she asked, looking his red uniform up and down. "Is there a problem?"

"No, there's no problem, ma'am." John hesitated. "Is this still the residence of a Lady Imogene Powderfell?"

"I'm afraid you've missed her by about twelve years. She's

passed." The woman threw the rag across her shoulder. "I'm her daughter, Mrs. Langley."

"Ah. I'm sorry for your loss." John tried to hide his disappointment.

She cocked her head, her expression quizzical. "May I ask what business you wished to discuss with my mother?"

"I wanted to inquire after a relation of hers about an incident from several years ago, but it's nothing for you to concern yourself with, Mrs. Langley." John tipped his cap. "Thank you for your time."

As John turned to walk away, Mrs. Langley cleared her throat. "Sir, may I ask to what incident and relation you're referring to?"

John hesitated for a moment, but he couldn't think of any reason she shouldn't know.

"It's in regard to a Lady Catriona Coleville. I believe she would be a distant cousin to you, on your mother's side."

Mrs. Langley frowned. "Hmm. I don't recall any Colevilles, but my family hasn't had much to do with society in many years."

"Yes, the relation would be with Lady Catriona's mother, the Gordons."

"Ah, yes. I haven't thought of the Gordons in an age." Mrs. Langley paused, as if considering something and then finally coming to a decision. "Would you like to come inside for a cup of tea, Constable . . . ?"

"Oh, I apologize for not introducing myself. Bow Street Officer John Smith, ma'am," said John with a slight incline of his head.

John considered the offer. He wanted to get home to Savita before it got dark, and he doubted Mrs. Langley had much to offer in terms of information. Doing the math based on John's guess of her age, he doubted she could have been older than ten at the time of Catriona's disappearance. More likely she was just lonely and middle-aged and seeking company. But on the other hand, John didn't want to be rude, and he did have a few minutes.

"That would be very kind, Mrs. Langley, thank you."

Following her inside, John took in the house. It was full of many fine things—mahogany furniture and elaborately embroidered curtains and fine paintings, but upon closer inspection, John could see all of it was old and worn by time. When they reached the sitting room, Mrs. Langley gestured for him to take a seat before bustling off to the kitchen. She was gone for several minutes before reappearing with a small tray containing tea and a few scones.

No servants then, John mentally noted.

She poured the tea into his cup and handed it to him. "May I ask how you came to be at my door?"

"I was given your address by Lady Theodosia Bexley."

"Ah." Mrs. Langley nodded as she sipped from her cup. "That is a name I'm familiar with, though I haven't seen her since I was a girl."

"Quite." John was curious as to the downfall of this family from society, but he didn't want to be rude by asking.

Seeming to sense his curiosity, Mrs. Langley smiled sadly. "You are wondering why my mother's acquaintanceship with the duchess lapsed?"

John cleared his throat. "I don't wish to pry into your family's private affairs."

She waved a hand dismissively. "It's fine. It's been so long, the sting has long since faded. I was barely out when it happened anyway. It's hard to miss society when you never really belonged. My mother had a harder time with it than I did, but then the situation was of her own doing, so she had no one else to blame."

"What happened?" John couldn't resist asking, since she seemed so keen to share.

"She fell in love."

"Ah." John's brow furrowed. "Was he unsuitable?"

"Not in station." Her eyes twinkled with mischief. "But the fact both parties were married to other people at the time was an issue."

"Oh." A flush crept over John's cheeks. "That will do it."

"Once the affair was discovered, we lost everything. My father didn't wish to divorce my mother, but he couldn't forgive her either. He left for his estate in the country and never looked back. I could have gone with him, but I didn't wish to abandon my mother. Her lover also turned his back, trying to salvage his own standing as best he could. The two of us were left to rot here, without society or family to support us. I never saw Theodosia Bexley after that, though I don't blame her for trying to protect her own status."

"I'm sorry to hear it." John shifted in his seat, unsure what to say. "I've heard high society can be quite harsh once it's cast judgment, but I wouldn't know personally."

She chuckled at that. "You should count your blessings."

John wasn't sure what he should say in response. He wasn't used to people being so open, not just about sensitive personal matters, but also with officers of the law. Usually getting information out of people was like pulling teeth.

He glanced around the room, taking in once again the moth-eaten cushions and curtains and the wallpaper peeling from the ceiling corners, in contrast to the expensive vases and artwork decorating the shelves and walls.

"You're wondering why a house crumbling at the foundation is still filled to the brim with expensive artifacts that serve no other purpose than to decorate?"

For being what looked like an ordinary middle-aged woman, Mrs. Langley seemed quite adept at reading John's mind.

His flush deepened. "I apologize, Mrs. Langley. I don't mean to be rude. It's none of my business."

She shrugged. "There's nothing to apologize for, Mr. Smith. It's a fair question. While my mother was alive, she couldn't bear to let any of it go. Now it just seems disrespectful to her memory to sell it. Irrational, I suppose. But my husband has always been able to support our needs, so it never seemed very urgent. I'll leave it for the next generation to sort out."

"As I said, it's really none of my business." John attempted to swallow a dry scone, praying he didn't crack a tooth on the rough-ground wheat.

"No, but I would wonder in your place." Mrs. Langley paused, eyeing him up and down. "This matter regarding Catriona Coleville . . . what happened?"

John hesitated.

"Come on, Mr. Smith. I told you mine—it's only fair if you tell me yours."

Hard to argue with that logic. Besides, John couldn't see any real harm in it.

"My information is limited, but I know Miss Coleville left her family estate in the year 1773. Apparently the running theory was that she ran away to London, but she's never turned up since." John hesitated, unsure how to explain Quinton's interest. "There are members of the family now interested in locating her current residence and renewing ties, if possible," he finally decided on. "Lady Bexley suggested that since your family was related, Miss Coleville might have come here, at least for a bit, and that your mother may know where she went from there."

"Hmm." Mrs. Langley's expression was contemplative. "1773 you said? I was only eight at the time, but I do have a vague recollection of someone coming to stay with us around that time. I always thought her name was Katherine because I used to call her Kat."

John sat up straight. "Really? Do you remember anything else about her?"

"Not really. I remember she was pretty, and from my perspective seemed quite fascinating and worldly wise, but when you're that young it's hard to know what's true and what's just your perception. My mother seemed fond of her."

"Do you know where she went after she left?"

Mrs. Langley tapped her fingers against the arm of her chair, as if deep in thought. "No, I don't think so. She didn't stay long —maybe a month—and then I never saw her again."

"Did she ever have any visitors while she was staying here?"

"Not that I recall, but I was so young that I wouldn't have been allowed to be present even if she had."

It wasn't much, but it was a start. John couldn't be completely certain Kat was Catriona, but the timeline and the nickname fit. If he was a gambling man, he'd feel safe wagering it was the same girl.

"Well, thank you very much for your time, Mrs. Langley." John stood up, placing his half-drunk tea and half-eaten scone down on the table. "You've been very helpful."

"Of course, Mr. Smith. I am happy to have been of service." Mrs. Langley also rose and escorted him to the door. As she was about to close it behind him, she paused. "Actually, I do remember one other thing about her."

"Oh?" John glanced at the sky, noting that it was later than he'd realized. "What was that?"

"She tried to hide it, but I remember seeing her looking out the window one time and crying. Kat never told me why—why would she tell a child anything about something like that—but I could tell there was a deep sadness about her." Mrs Langley offered one last smile. "I don't know if that is helpful, but I didn't want to let you go without mentioning it."

"I don't know either, but I appreciate you telling me regardless." John tipped his cap to the woman. "You have a good evening, Mrs. Langley."

As he hurried down to the street and raised a hand to hail a hackney, John began to mentally compile his report for Quinton. He and Savita would be headed for the estate early tomorrow morning, so he would be able to tell him of his findings in person. It wasn't much to go on, but at least he had a few more details than Quinton had deigned to put in his note.

Chapter Thirty-Two

Walking into the dining room, Mary surveyed the scene quickly. The higher-ups always insisted on having designated seating for every person at the dinner. In a perfect world there would be an even number of men and women alternating seats, but that wasn't the case with the group staying at the estate. Nevertheless, they still insisted on alternating the arrangement each evening so that members of the party could carry on conversation with a different neighbour. Not a bad idea in theory, but the practical application left much to be desired, especially that time when Mary had been forced to make conversation with Montgomery. She didn't have anything against the man personally, but what a bore.

This time was different though. When she came to her seat, the one beside it was not empty, and she didn't recognize its occupant.

Standing up when he saw her approach, the stranger pulled her chair out for her. "Lady Mary Fletcher, I presume?"

"It's just Mary Fletcher, actually." Clearing her throat, Mary took the offered chair and allowed him to push it in after her. "And you, sir?"

"Renard. Renard Baptiste," he replied with a light French

accent and a smile. "I've been hired on by Lady Dovefield as the new land steward."

Now it made more sense. Renard Baptiste wasn't the type of man Mary was used to seeing at a nobleman's table. He was well groomed with nicely tailored clothes—not overly lavish, but still nice—and quite handsome, but the thing that stuck out the most to Mary was his complexion. She wasn't used to seeing people who looked like her sitting at the table.

Granted, she knew the Dovefields were more eccentric than most noblemen in their tolerance of the unusual. They were the exception to the norm, since John was also of African ancestry, though not as dark skinned as Mary, and Charlie was Indian, and they both were invited to social gatherings. But she had never seen someone outside of her circle enjoy such privilege.

"Oh?" Mary glanced away, realizing she'd been staring. "How much experience do you have?"

He laughed. "Is this part of the interview?"

Mary blushed and took a sip of her wine. "No, of course not. I only meant you look quite young to have much experience—not that you look that young. But I'm sure Simone—Lady Dovefield —did her due diligence."

"You're not entirely wrong," Renard responded. "I am perhaps a bit younger than the usual candidate who would manage an estate this size. I am turning thirty years of age next month. But I assure you, I do have experience. I grew up on a plantation in Martinique. My situation was somewhat . . . unique . . . so instead of working in the fields, my early years were spent in a study, immersed in the paperwork of running the operation. Later, my situation—how shall we say—changed, and I ended up in a more hands-on role. While an estate such as this is not the same as a plantation, there are enough similarities when it comes to managing large swathes of land to ensure that I am well qualified."

As she listened to the explanation, Mary realized what he was implying. "I see. You were born a . . . slave?"

"Yes." He smiled. "I take it from your reaction that you were not?"

Mary shook her head. "No. My father was born a freeman, and my mother escaped a plantation when she was a child alongside her own mother. I grew up in London."

"That's wonderful, to be born a freewoman."

"Yes, I know I've been quite fortunate."

It was true, not that Mary had never encountered difficulty. Life as a servant was still harsh, but she knew it didn't compare to slavery. Her community in London was a mix of born freemen and escaped slaves, and she had heard the stories—rape, beatings, whippings, and families torn apart forever, all while being worked down to the bone. She didn't always see eye to eye with her parents, but Mary was grateful for the life they had been able to give her, and for the opportunities she had been able to take advantage of in London because of that life.

"How is it you came to be a freeman yourself?" Mary asked.

Renard's face darkened, just for a moment. "It's a long story. But I'm more interested in how is it you came to be sitting at an earl's dining table as a guest? Lady Dovefield mentioned you used to be her daughter's companion?"

Mary hesitated. "It's also a bit of a long story."

His eyes crinkled as he smiled again. "Well, perhaps we can both share our long stories another time."

Their conversation was interrupted by a footman offering his platter of food. Mary took a quail—which did look quite appetizing—and then he moved on to Renard. It was all a carefully choreographed dance in social etiquette, one which had taken Mary some time to learn, but which she felt confident in now . . . most of the time.

On her other side sat Charlie, a man who went out of his way to reject social etiquette, as he did now by leaning over and speaking in a low voice. "Who's the newest guest?"

"The new land steward, apparently." Mary cut off and took a

bite of her quail, and it tasted as good as it looked. "Renard Baptiste."

"Hmm." He raised an eyebrow, his expression unconvinced. "He doesn't look very French."

"Well, you don't look very English, and yet here you sit," snapped Mary, keeping her voice low enough that no one else could hear.

She wasn't sure why she felt so defensive of the stranger. She didn't owe him anything, and in truth she didn't know anything about him.

Fortunately, Charlie didn't seem offended. He merely shrugged and went back to his own dinner. Charlie had been quite infamous for his temper, and while it did still occasionally rear its head, Mary saw it less and less these days. Besides, even at his worst, Charlie had rarely turned his ire towards her.

They'd been friends a long time, she and Charlie. He was John's friend first, of course, but Mary had known him for as long as she'd been alive. Her earliest memories of her cousin included his two friends standing at his sides, causing mischief and wreaking havoc. All she'd wanted then was to get their attention and be included in their schemes, but as a child, a ten-year age gap was insurmountable. When she was old enough to finally scramble after them, they were adults, starting on their own paths, who no longer had time for childish games.

Now they were all adults, and ten years didn't seem like such a chasm between them. They were equals, and Mary was finally able to be included in their lives as a peer and a friend. She knew she shouldn't care so much, but the feeling still brought her satisfaction.

For a moment, during the events of the past few months, Mary had wondered if the easy friendship between her and Charlie had blossomed into something . . . else. While Zoe and Quinton's and John and Savita's relationships had been developing and growing, Mary and Charlie had been the two odd men left out. It was hard to not let the thick air of romance influence you when it was shoved in your face every day, and Charlie and Mary did get on quite well. She felt comfortable being honest with him and putting him in his place when he needed it. And when she needed help, Mary always knew she could rely on Charlie to provide it. On the other hand, he had always been heavily involved in the criminal underworld, a man of violence and grey morality—not exactly the best foundation upon which to build a life together.

But things had changed recently, and now Charlie was coming into his own—opening the distillery with Rory and taking on the young boy Finn as a ward. Mary would be lying if she said the possibility of a relationship with Charlie had never occurred to her, and she suspected he had wondered something similar.

Fortunately the fantasy had been fleeting and neither party had acted on it. The reality was that Mary looked at Charlie as family, and a part of him would always see her as John's baby cousin. They still loved one another, but as friends, not as lovers, and Mary was content with that.

"What do you think of the quail?"

"What?" Mary struggled to process the simple question, being brought back to the present abruptly.

"The quail?" Renard pointed with his fork. "What do you think?"

"Oh, right. It's quite delectable, don't you agree?"

"Yes, indeed. Although no one cooks poultry as well as my mother," said Renard with a crooked smile. He lowered his voice. "Sometimes I believe the British are allergic to spices—ironic for an empire who has profited off them so much."

Mary snorted, trying to cover her laugh with a cough. She glanced to her right and Charlie caught her eye, a mischievous twinkle in his eye. She glared at him, warning him to keep whatever thoughts he might have to himself.

The dinner went on uneventfully from that point on, with Zoe and Quinton, along with his uncle and grandfather, disappearing into the parlour as soon as was socially acceptable. Mary knew they would be discussing the latest developments and how they related to Quinton's sister, Catriona. She didn't have much right, but a pang of jealousy still twinged between her ribs watching them leave without her. At one time, it would have been the three of them, and her presence would have been indispensable, but now the couple was married and no longer in need of a chaperon or a companion, nor a lady's maid, which was what Mary had been when she first met Zoe. It was irrational and unfair, but a part of her felt as though she'd been demoted.

It made her wonder what her purpose in Zoe's life was now.

Chapter Thirty-Three

The tones of the parlour were much more to Zoe's liking than the other rooms in the house. Someone had chosen a pale yellow for the walls, and the east windows heightened the sense of morning light. Gratefully the furniture was practical, comfortable while still being tasteful, and the colourful floral patterns of the cushions paired well with the walls. The wood of the furniture was light as well, and even the artwork was cheerful, as if not taking itself too seriously. Leather-bound classics filled two shelves at the end of the room, but another shelf to the side had well-worn books, obviously loved. She wondered if the late Seonaid Coleville had been the one to decorate it, with appropriate updates simply carrying her choices forward.

Quinton had arranged this meeting here instead of the study due to her preference, Zoe was sure. She had briefly explored the study, but the family portraits had unnerved her more than she cared to admit. The portrait of Catriona showed a spitting image of their mother. But the portrait of Graham, so closely resembling her Quinton, sent a chill down her spine, though Zoe wasn't sure why. It felt in a way like looking at her own husband's funeral portrait, even though she knew it wasn't him. The eyes were different, set closer together and coloured lighter, and the man in the portrait was younger than Quinton was now.

Irrational though it was, looking up at them looking back down at her, Zoe felt as though they were watching and judging her from the other side. She didn't need to spend too much time in their gaze.

As much as she felt at ease in the parlour, Montgomery and Philip seemed to feel equally ill at ease. They both sat stiffly on the edge of their chairs, clearly wishing they were anywhere but here. Quinton poured a glass of port for his uncle and his grandfather, and a glass of whiskey for himself and Zoe. She hoped the libation would help the gentlemen relax.

As he passed out the refreshments, Zoe took a sip and waited for her husband to speak. Quinton was more deliberate in his words, particularly when they carried weight, preferring to take time to organize his thoughts before voicing them aloud. It was not Zoe's way, but he had told her on their honeymoon that he found it frustrating to be carefully formulating an important thought only to be abruptly interrupted as Zoe rushed ahead. Patience had never been her forte, but she knew how much this conversation meant to Quinton, so she let him take his time.

Her patience turned out to be for nothing, as Philip decided to be the impatient one this time.

"What is it you wished to discuss?" Philip downed most of his port in one go. "I don't want to be kept here all night listening to your fanciful nonsense."

Quinton sighed, and Zoe felt a stab of sympathy that all his careful thought was for naught.

"Trust, Lord Philip, that we don't wish to be kept here any longer than necessary with you either," snapped Zoe. "Perhaps you would do well to listen for once."

His eyes snapped to hers with sharp surprise, but Philip said nothing more.

"What is it you wanted to tell us?" asked Montgomery in a softer tone.

TAYLOR PREISLER & SANDRA PREISLER

Quinton sat next to his wife and took her hand in his own. "I have news, of the body we found."

Philip rolled his eyes. "I knew it was going to be about this. I've told you before—"

"I know," Quinton interrupted. "It's not Catriona."

That caught the earl off guard. He blinked in surprise, then sat back in his chair. "And how have you come to this conclusion?"

"My friend, Mr. Stewart, has identified the adult body as that of a male. So you were right, grandfather. It can't be Catriona."

Despite his earlier adamance about the identity of the body, the news seemed to take the wind out of Philip's sails. His shoulders sagged, and for the first time he appeared truly old in Zoe's eyes.

The effect was only momentary though, and Philip quickly straightened back up. "Right, well, I did tell you as much. Now can we put this whole business behind us?"

"Not necessarily." Quinton exchanged a glance with Zoe. "There is still the matter of the dead man's identity, as well as how he was connected to your daughter."

"I'm not sure what you mean by that," said Philip stubbornly.

Now it was Zoe's turn to roll her eyes. The man couldn't be that dense, he had to be deliberately avoiding the reality.

"Surely you can't believe that the necklace was placed in the grave by accident?" she asked incredulously, unable to help herself. "Along with two stillborn babes?"

Quinton gave her another look—clearly not how he would have introduced the subject, but Zoe just shook her head. It didn't matter how well he phrased it, this old man was determined to be difficult.

"Stillborn?" questioned Montgomery.

"Yes." Quinton turned his head away from Zoe with a sigh. "Based on the size of the bones, Mr. Stewart believes they were around seven months along. Girls, both of them."

168

"I see." Montgomery leaned back, appearing pensive.

Philip was not so easily moved. "I fail to see what you could be implying."

"Grandfather, surely you must see the connection—" started Quinton.

"I see no such connection, and I find it offensive—" Philip interrupted.

Quinton was losing his patience. "Well, I find your unwilling-ness to even consider the possibility—"

"Once again, you show yourself impertinent—"

"And once again, you show yourself to be a stubborn, old—"

"Enough!"

Everyone turned to stare at the unlikely source of the outburst. Zoe had yet to see Montgomery truly stand up to his father, but now with his stony expression and clenched jaw, she saw a glimpse of the man who would've been the heir—the man who had spent his life preparing for the role, despite living in the shadow of his dead brother and hobbled by his distant father. She hadn't realized he had it in him, but there was a solid backbone after all.

"I have had enough of you two." Montgomery emphasized his point by slicing through the air with his hand. "The discovery of Graham's son being legitimate was a shock to all of us. Do you think I wanted to give up my title and my inheritance to a man who slept in doorways most of his childhood?" He took a deep breath, as if trying to calm himself. "But he is the legal heir, and I have made my peace. And despite all his reasons to hate us, Quinton has also been more than generous."

Montgomery wasn't done, turning to his father before anyone else had the chance to speak. "You have made all of this far harder than it had to be with your damned closed-mindedness. It is what it is, but you have fought against it in every way possible, kicking against the goads at every turn. It is exhausting at this point, and I. Have. Had. Enough." Each of the last four words were spoken with specific emphasis. He glared, alternately his gaze between each man. "Both of you, start acting like responsible adults, put away your blasted egos, and let's work together as a family. Because like it or not, that is what we are. We are family."

There was a weighted silence as the four members of the party exchanged glances. The outburst had been unexpected, but Zoe could see that the words had an effect on Philip and Quinton. Sometimes men just needed to be put in their places. Of course, no one seemed to appreciate when Zoe did it . . .

"Very well," said Philip reluctantly. "I will attempt to be more . . . open-minded."

Quinton nodded. "And I will attempt to put away my . . . blasted ego."

"Good." Montgomery leaned back with a satisfied look. "So then, Quinton, you believe the necklace connects my sister to the inhabitants of the grave? I understand the logic, but I find it hard to believe that she could have hidden a seven-month pregnancy without anyone noticing."

It was a fair point. Zoe studied Philip's face—he was the only one around who would have actually set eyes on Catriona in such a condition. But his expression remained inscrutable, even to her prying eyes.

"I understand what you're saying. But you must admit the necklace is a rather large coincidence," countered Quinton.

"True." Montgomery glanced at his father. "Do you still have the necklace in question, father?"

After a moment's hesitation, Philip nodded. "Yes."

He reached into his pocket and retrieved the jewellery. As he held it out in his hand, Zoe was struck once again by how beautiful the piece was. She also noted it was significantly cleaner than when Quinton had first showed it to her. Philip must have polished it.

"It's in good condition, considering," said Montgomery, taking it in his own hand and holding it up to the light.

"Not so unusual, really." Zoe did not consider herself an

expert in many things, but she did know her jewellery. "Gold doesn't tarnish like silver, which is one reason it is so valuable. Even now this locket could be polished and restored to its original lustre, as gold is quite impervious to corrosion."

The men blinked, but then nodded, accepting her word as fact. Zoe said nothing about the source of her knowledge. Her memories of her mother taking the gold jewellery from their home in France before they fled in the Great Terror would remain her own. The ensuing journey included a treacherous and stormy crossing of the Channel, and, for a time, sleeping in the wet of London's streets. Simone's choices had kept them from starvation in those early years on British soil, and Zoe still appreciated the durability of gold.

"You are certain this necklace belonged to Catriona?" Zoe asked.

"Yes." Philip spoke as if someone was pulling his teeth out. "I am certain it belonged to her, but as I told your husband, Catriona was quite eccentric. She was always giving away things. Its presence in the grave proves nothing."

"Perhaps not." Quinton spoke with a level tone. "But you must admit it's a rather large coincidence."

Philip admitted nothing. Zoe thought if he did, he might suffer an apoplexy as Theo had.

"There is also the matter of the man." Zoe decided it was time to change the subject. "His neck was broken, much in the same manner as Mr. Langford. Do you happen to remember any other unusual events happening around the same time as Catriona disappeared, perhaps involving a man?"

Philip paused, seeming to actually contemplate his answer.

"No," he said finally. A true poet.

Zoe glanced at her husband. She suspected they wouldn't get much more from Philip tonight. She could see Quinton was thinking, no doubt forming a plan in his head. She decided to hold her tongue and see what he would come up with.

"We need to know more about what was happening during

that time." Quinton returned her glance, then turned back to his grandfather. "Tell me what servants have been here since before Catriona disappeared."

Chapter Thirty-Four

Quinton slumped into the chair in his room, suddenly exhausted. Most nights he would be in with Zoe, but when he had peeked in on her just a few minutes ago, her maid had already undressed her and Zoe was sleeping soundly. Quinton didn't want to wake her, so he had decided to retire to his own bedroom tonight. He absentmindedly tugged at the cravat around his neck, but he couldn't seem to get it looser. The knot was ridiculously complicated—why would anyone need a knot tied like this? It was like having a noose around his neck.

A knock at the door startled him from his slight dozing off, and Quinton sat up suddenly, shaking his head to try and wake himself up.

"Come in," he said.

It took Quinton a moment to place the face of the person who stepped inside his room, but then it came to him—Darrow. He didn't know how he could have forgotten, he'd seen the man only a few hours ago when Darrow had dressed him. He was the one who had tied these stupid knots in his cravat.

"Good evening, my lord." Darrow inclined his head respectfully. "If you stand up, I'll start undressing you."

"Right. Of course." Quinton swallowed hard. Somehow getting undressed by someone as a grown man was more humiliating than getting dressed. "If you could just untie the cravat, I can handle the rest of it."

"With all due respect, this is my job, my lord." Darrow smiled. "I assure you, I am more than capable."

Quinton sighed, but he couldn't think of a way to weasel out of it without sounding like a petulant child once again, so he simply stood and allowed Darrow to begin loosening the cravat. The silence stretched out, the tension unbearable—or maybe it was just unbearable to Quinton—until he finally broke and said something.

"Tell me about yourself, Darrow." Quinton glanced at him. "I'm sure you already mentioned some of the finer points to my mother-in-law, but to me you're practically a stranger."

Darrow paused, just for a moment. "I suppose that's true. What is it you would like to know, my lord?"

"I don't know . . . where are you from?"

There was another pause as Darrow seemed to collect his thoughts. Quinton took the opportunity to study the man properly. Darrow was older than him, maybe in his late thirties or early forties. Quinton could tell from the way he styled his hair and tailored his clothes that Darrow cared deeply about his own personal appearance—probably a good quality in a valet. There was something about the way he carried himself though . . . it wasn't the air of a servant. He didn't avoid eye contact the way Hugh's valet or Zoe's lady's maid did. It wasn't that he was confrontational or disrespectful, he just wasn't as deferential as Quinton expected.

"I actually grew up relatively close to here, in a small village. But I went into service quite young and I've spent most of my adult life in London and then in Lord Westerfield's employ." Darrow shrugged as he finally freed Quinton's neck from the oppressive fabric. "There's not much else interesting to tell."

"Did you like working for him?"

"Hmm?"

"Lord Westerfield?"

Darrow nodded, unbuttoning Quinton's waistcoat and pulling it off from behind. "It had its moments, both pleasant and not so pleasant."

He was answering the questions, but without actually revealing anything personal. Quinton was impressed at the skill. Darrow was obviously practiced in polite but impersonal conversation. Quinton supposed a servant with as much experience as Darrow had would have to be pretty good at it. It was something Quinton would have to get better at.

"I suppose every job does."

As Darrow began to pull the white muslin shirt over Quinton's head, Quinton scrambled to come up with another topic of conversation, but his mind remained frustratingly blank. The whiskey he'd stayed up drinking with his uncle after Zoe and his grandfather had retired didn't help.

"What about you, my lord?" asked Darrow, perhaps taking pity on Quinton's discomfort.

"What?"

"Did you enjoy your job, when you had one?"

It was a forward question, but Quinton was too grateful to care.

"Yes." That was the simplest answer. "I did enjoy it."

Quinton considered explaining further, but how could he articulate the feeling of prowling down a dark alley in the middle of the night, tailing a thief to their lair, or of catching a killer in a lie—the moment you both knew the game was up—or even of just sitting in his office and tabulating the income and expenses of his latest case? For Quinton it was second nature, but he knew it would sound mad to a person who had never lived in that world.

"I take it Lady Dovefield mentioned my more unorthodox past to you?"

"She did." Darrow began to carefully fold the clothes he had removed, which Quinton didn't understand since they were just going to be laundered anyway. "But your rise in society is not exactly a secret. Haven't you heard that the servants' gossip circle is faster than the royal messenger service?"

A smile quirked at the edge of Quinton's lips. "I've heard something along those lines, but I try not to put too much stock in rumour or gossip."

"Then you're a stronger man than most." Darrow stepped back, holding the discarded clothing across his arm. "I'll let you handle your own trousers, for tonight. I've laid out a night shirt and a dressing gown on the bed."

Quinton cleared his throat. "Thank you. I suppose the whole . . . valet thing will take me a while to get used to."

Darrow smiled. "I suspected as much. Goodnight, my lord."

"Goodnight, Darrow." Quinton watched the man walk across the room and open the door. "One more thing."

"Yes?" said the valet as he turned slightly.

"Call me Quinton, please."

He didn't smile, but Quinton thought he saw a glimmer of humour in his eyes. "That would never do in public, my lord." Darrow paused. "In private, I'll consider it. Goodnight."

As soon as the door closed, Quinton stumbled over to the bed. He held up the nightshirt, but the idea of undoing his trousers and then pulling the shirt over his head just seemed like so much work. He ended up letting the shirt fall the floor and crawling into the bed, letting the soft sheets take him.

Maybe there was something to this whole valet thing after all.

Chapter Thirty-Five

The happy sounds of children's chatter floated up the stairs as Mary and Charlie descended. They had been tasked with talking to the older staff to see if anyone remembered anything of note. It had been agreed that she and Charlie would be less intimidating, as they held no position. Rory had volunteered, but though no one had said so outright, some definitely found him off-putting. Not everyone appreciated his ghoulish talents.

The stairs opened to a large kitchen, with the central hearth as the focal point of the room. Wooden tables complimented the hearth, with several kitchen maids preparing vegetables for the upcoming luncheon. Two separate ovens flagged the hearth, with shelves and cupboards available for food storage. A short balding man with an apron was busy at his own table at the far end, a cheerful whistle emanating from his lips. Watching him roll out the thin dough and then fold it over itself, Mary realized this must be the infamous pastry chef. She wished him nothing but good fortune.

The three children sat at a separate table, set up for the staff to dine, and as the three faces turned towards them, Mary could not help but notice the evidence of sticky jam on every face, making her smile.

"We found an empty stall in the stables for Brutus," Gwen said hurriedly. "I was just in here for a quick snack."

Mary heard the uncertainty in her voice and immediately related. Gwen was in a unique place, starting as a servant with a specific responsibility but somehow morphing into almost a peer of the Dovefield children.

"That was clever, to find a place that could keep the beast contained," Mary replied reassuringly.

It wasn't long before all three children raced out the open kitchen door to the yard, disappearing from view. Walter seemed somehow younger here. He had shed the cape of adulthood he had started to adopt and was a boy again. Good for him. He would have to pick the cape back up soon enough.

Charlie had gone over to Mrs. Foster's side, less interested in the three young ones than Mary. Mary watched him chat easily with the cook as she stirred a large pot. and suddenly they both laughed. It was surprising to Mary how quickly Charlie had seemed to adapt to these surroundings. She had never known him to be one to embrace change, but something had shifted in him in recent months.

The older woman turned to the kitchen staff and spoke loudly. "I'm going to take a cup of tea with these fine folk, so keep at your tasks."

The pastry chef met the cook's eyes briefly, then nodded. Mary hoped fervently the silent communication would result in cakes. Delicious cakes. She followed Mrs. Foster and Charlie out an alcove to a smaller room with a table and four chairs.

"This is where the senior staff take our tea," explained the cook. "It's nice to 'ave a minute of peace now and again."

A few moments later a scullery maid brought in a pot of tea, milk and honey, and three teacups. With a quick bow, she then retreated.

As the tea steeped, Mrs. Foster looked at the two of them carefully, her broad face earnest. She was not much past fifty, and Mary concluded she could not have been the cook while Catriona was at the manor. That position would take some years of lesser work to attain.

Charlie spoke first. "The reason we wanted to speak with you, Mrs. Foster, is that we thought you might have some insight on the ins and outs of this place from when Lady Catriona was a girl. Lord Coleville said you were working here at the time."

Mrs. Foster sat a little straighter, her eyes surprisingly sharp. "Does this have something to do with the hole that Scot was digging in the woods? Oliver told me bones were found. Is it Catriona?"

Mary and Charlie exchanged a glance, and she could see they were of the same mind. They could share a few of the facts, but there was no need to go into every detail. It wouldn't be long before the story spread, and they needed to limit the damage if they could.

"It wasn't Catriona," said Mary. "But whatever happened, we believe it may have taken place around the same time as she disappeared. We just need to know a bit more about that time."

"Hmm." Mrs Foster leaned back, clearly pleased to be considered a source of insight. "It's a shame you didn't find the poor girl, God bless her. She needs to be laid to rest, or else her soul will never find peace."

"Yes, we've heard about the ghost." Mary hadn't seen it yet, but she knew Charlie had, and she was decidedly jealous. She had always wanted to encounter a ghost of some kind, but thus far had not been lucky enough. "Are you sure it's Lady Catriona?"

"Oh, yes." Mrs. Foster nodded sagely. "I've seen her myself. Not up close, mind you, but it's definitely her. Same hair, red as fire and wild as the earth itself. No mistakin' it."

"You do remember her?" asked Charlie, steering the conversation back to their purpose with a scolding look at Mary.

Spoilsport.

"Of course. My mama, God rest her soul, was the cook here at the manor for many years. She had me starting as a scullery maid like anyone else, but when she couldn't work any more I was set to take her place. Miss Catriona was older than me by a few years, but I remember her well, poor lass."

Charlie leaned forward conspiratorially. "Tell us how it happened that she disappeared."

The older lady poured the tea and each added the sugar and milk they wanted. Mary noted this home did not abide by the sugar boycott like the Dovefields and Theo did to protest the use of slaves to harvest the product. She made a mental note to address it with Zoe.

"I was young, but all of us remember when Lady Seonaid died birthin' Master Montgomery," continued Mrs. Foster with a sad sigh. "That lady was a beautiful soul, and she smoothed over Miss Catriona and the lordship's rough edges. When she died, it was like a light went out in the 'ouse."

"That must have been difficult for Lady Catriona," Mary offered with feeling.

"She never were the same. She and her father always was like chalk and cheese, but after that the shouting was louder, and not just behind closed doors. Poor lass were mad with grief, that's a fact. I suppose Lord Philip was too, in his own way." She leaned forward and lowered her voice. "Between you, me, and the mice in the wall, my mama thought she blamed her father for what happened."

"How's that?" asked Charlie.

"It were a difficult birth, and when the time came that a decision had to be made, his lordship told the physician to save the babe." Mrs. Foster shook her head. "They had to cut the poor woman open. She didn't linger long after that, and Miss Catriona never forgave her father."

Mary's blood ran cold at the thought. It was a choice many a family faced, with the final decision often left to the father by the male physician. If she were here in Catriona's shoes, she did not know if she would be able to forgive either.

"What about the week she disappeared?" Charlie had already moved on. "Do you remember anything about that? Was anyone else missing during that time?"

Mrs. Foster's brow furrowed as she thought. "Now the you mention it, there was one thing, but I don't think it's what you're looking for. I remember Mama fussin' about a footman who left, but he went home to 'elp his kin. I only remember because Mama was telling me how I should always give notice in a big house if I had to move along, as that would allow me a good reference. She were right perturbed this footman left with only a day's notice. But all that was overshadowed by Miss Catriona running off a few days afore. Her father and her had one last fight—a screaming match, really—and that was that."

Mrs. Foster shook herself as if to physically dislodge the memory, then took a fortifying sip of tea. She reached for the pot to refill her cup just as a kitchen maid appeared with a tray of varied cookies.

"Frenchy is at it again. Feel as if Napoleon himself 'as invaded my kitchen," grumbled Mrs. Foster, as if the look between the two cooks had never taken place, but Mary noticed the older woman's haste in sampling one from the plate. "Can't beat a well-made pan of ginger biscuits as far as I'm concerned."

Mary herself had no issue with ginger biscuits and had never in her memory passed up an opportunity to partake. But as a sugar cookie melted in her mouth, she couldn't deny that this was a delicacy beyond the common. She closed her eyes, sighing in contentment.

When she opened her eyes, both Charlie and Mrs. Foster were reaching for a second helping. Maybe it was worth putting up with "Napoleon" for such treats.

Catching her eye, Charlie stood quickly and shoved a few more cookies in his pockets. "You have been so helpful. I know it was a long time ago, but do you happen to remember the name of that footman?"

Her nose scrunched up as Mrs. Foster thought. "No, I'm afraid I don't. As I said, Mr. Charlie, I was but a slip of girl."

"No matter." Mary followed Charlie's example and lifted a few more cookies. "We have the names of the other staff that are still here from that time, but do you know where anyone might be that has retired or left?"

Mrs. Foster shook her head, taking time to finish her mouthful of jam cookie before replying. "Well, there was Mr. Pearson, the tutor Lord Philip hired for Master Graham. He quit a year or two after Miss Catriona disappeared. He lives down by the shore, in Hartlemond, last I heard. It's only a few hours' carriage ride away. Everyone else be done and gone, I'm afraid, like Mama." Eyeing the offending plate of cookies, which held far fewer than when it was brought in, she lifted her chin and stated without a hint of irony, "At least Mama knew the value of really good ginger biscuits."

Chapter Thirty-Six

They'd entrusted Charlie and Mary with interviewing the senior staff, but somehow Evans had managed to evade them, caught up in some essential task every time they came close to cornering him.

"Leave it with me," Quinton had told them. So now the responsibility rested with him.

When he asked Mrs. Fox, she directed him to the wine cellar. But when Quinton arrived, he found the cool stone room empty, though the butler's previous presence could be seen by the selections for dinner which had been placed on a silver platter by the door.

He flagged down a passing footman—Lawrence . . . or was it Oliver?

"Have you seen Evans?" Quinton asked, avoiding saying the young man's name.

"I think he's outside," replied the footman.

Quinton waited a moment, but no further information was volunteered.

"Do you have any idea where I might find him outside?" he finally asked.

The footman hesitated. "I believe he said he was going to the chicken coop."

"The chicken coop?" Quinton frowned. "What for?"

"To butcher the chickens for dinner." The young man said it as though this was an obvious conclusion. When Quinton didn't respond immediately, he continued, "It's usually Oliver's job, but Evans didn't realize the time and had sent him to the village before Oliver could do the butchering. My lord." The last part was tacked on awkwardly, and Quinton could tell Lawrence wanted this interaction to end as much as Quinton did.

"Right, of course." Quinton dismissed the footman with a quick gesture. "That'll be all."

As the young man scurried off to attend to his other duties, Quinton made his way up the stairs and out into the soft light of the fading afternoon sun. It was the hottest part of the day, but without the direct sunlight it didn't feel so bad. He stripped off his jacket and cravat and hung them up on a hook outside the servants' door, exposing his white undershirt and waistcoat. In the new world of society this was considered "half-dress," meaning not to be worn in mixed or formal company, but Quinton didn't think the chickens would mind.

As he walked along the grounds toward where the few livestock were kept, Quinton took a deep breath of fresh air and glanced around the garden. It really was beautiful. He could understand why someone might live out here full time, sequestered from the world and all of its troubles. It felt like something out of a fairy tale. But maybe if someone lived their whole life in a place like this, growing up and getting married and then raising children of their own, it lost some of its magic. He supposed anything became ordinary if one looked at it long enough.

Within a few minutes, the chicken coop came into view, and sure enough, there was Evans. He was also in a state of half-dress, even more so than Quinton, with his sleeves rolled up to his elbows and his waistcoat unbuttoned. There was something deeply disconcerting about seeing Evans in such an informal setting, like seeing a dog riding a horse or a cat eating at the dinner table.

Even more unsettling, Evans looked very . . . natural . . . standing there with an axe in one hand and a headless chicken in the other. He was always so stuffy and proper—maybe not the same as other butlers Quinton had met, but in his own way. But in that moment, even with the grey hair and lines of age on his face, Quinton felt like he was seeing into the past—catching a glimpse of a handsome, younger man completely at ease in his element.

"Evans!" Quinton called out once he was close enough.

Caught up in his own world, the butler jumped at the sound of Quinton's voice, clearly not expecting the company of someone else.

"My lord," he said, recovering smoothly. "What can I do for you?"

"Well, I just had a few questions. I'm sure you heard my friends were talking to some of the senior staff." Quinton's gaze fell to the decapitated chicken. "Do you often take care of the butchering personally? Seems a bit beneath your role."

"Not always, but it's Oliver's day off and I don't trust Lawrence to handle it correctly. I grew up on a farm, so it's a skill I still occasionally employ." Evans embedded the axe into the bloody stump and laid the chicken down out of sight. He picked up a rag and began to wipe the blood off his hands. "Yes, I heard of their quest, but I'm afraid I'm far too busy to be playing games with your friends."

"It's not a game," Quinton countered, already irritated.

Evans inclined his head. "Of course not, my lord."

The words were deferential, but there was no mistaking the patronizing tone and dismissive body language. Quinton was getting tired of the man's attitude.

"You would never speak to Lord Philip in this manner, Evans. If you have something to say, just say it," snapped Quinton.

There was a long silence as Evans stared at him, and Quinton couldn't help but feel he was being sized up.

"It's not my place, my lord," said Evans finally. "I apologize if I've come across as unwelcoming. I shall strive to do better in the future."

"Oh, come down off the cross, Evans. Just spit it out." Quinton threw his hands up in the air. "In that house, things maybe have to be different, but out here, just the two of us, we're equals. Just say what you have to say."

There was a long pause, the two men staring at each other silently, the tension thick enough to cut with knife. Finally it grew too much to bear, and Evans was the first to break.

"Fine." Evans threw the rag down on the ground, his normally unreadable expression clouded by anger. "I think a man is dead. He may not have been a very good or a very nice man, but he was a person nonetheless, and you and your little band of friends are treating his death very much like a game—something to relieve your boredom or take up your time. And now you're digging into the past, reopening old wounds, for the same selfish reasons, and I simply don't have time to indulge your childish fantasies."

Quinton was taken aback by the forthrightness of Evans's words. He knew he'd asked for his honest opinion, but part of him hadn't actually expected the butler to give it.

"I don't think this is a game." Quinton knew his tone was more defensive than he would like. "I think a man is dead and we as the living have a responsibility to him. I think three other souls are also dead, buried on my family's land, which is a fact whether you like it or not, and we have a responsibility to them as well."

"What are you talking about?" Evans shook his head, as if he'd never heard anything so ridiculous. "You barely knew Langford, and you never knew them three in the grave. You don't owe them anything. Any other lord would have put this whole thing to bed by now, but not you. You and your wife aren't doing this for them —you're doing it for yourselves."

186

He stopped then, as if he knew he'd gone too far. His frustration was evident in the slip in his diction, as if seeing the spectre of a younger, less refined Evans, before he had taken on the role he held now. Evans took a deep breath, as if composing himself. The two men stared at each other, the tension thick between them. As shocked as Quinton was by the words, a small part of him wondered . . . if Evans was right.

Growing up there had been opportunities for a different life. Quinton could have been dockworker or street sweeper or even an actor—he'd spent his formative years in a theatre after all. But he'd chosen to make his living in the shadows, living in between worlds and chasing down lost things of varying values and fixing problems and solving mysteries, both minor and major. Being an inquiry agent was something Quinton had been good at, for better or worse. Helping people was rewarding, but if he was being honest, that wasn't the only reason Quinton did it. He liked the puzzle of it, turning it over in his mind and putting the pieces together until the picture became clear. He liked the adrenaline rush that came from a brush with danger. Did that make him a bad person? Or, at the very least, an exploitative one? Was that the real reason he was pushing forward so hard on this, because he missed that rush?

"You're right that I'm not like other lords," said Quinton finally, shoving his doubts aside for now. "I didn't grow up in this world. But like it or not, I am here now."

Evans glared, but said nothing, returning to his state of silence.

"Look, just tell me what you remember about when Catriona disappeared. We know you were a member of staff at the time. Tell me, and I'll leave you alone."

After a long pause Evans relented. "Fine. I remember her, of course. But she was the daughter of the house and I was a footman, so our paths rarely crossed other than what was required."

"And what was required?"

"The usual duties of a footman—pouring her wine and serving food at dinner, holding the door open, that sort of thing."

Quinton nodded. "Right. And what was your impression when she disappeared?"

Evans snorted. "Disappeared? She didn't disappear—she left. That girl may have been born a lady, but she was ill-suited for the role. She was wild and her father couldn't control her. No one around here was surprised when she took off. Probably eloped with some rake and never looked back."

"I see."

At least the butler was being honest, if a little harsh.

Crossing his arms, Quinton pondered how to phrase his next question. "As to the rake she supposedly ran off with, do you have any idea who that might have been? We have been told there was a footman and a tutor who took off around that same time."

Scowling as if Quinton had just personally insulted his mother, Evans mirrored his crossed arms. "Servants come and go—there was nothing unusual about either of their departures. Besides, they both left after Lady Catriona. Now can I go back to my duties, Lord Coleville?"

There was no mistaking the sarcasm placed on the word lord. Quinton doubted he would get anything more from the butler, but there was one more thing he couldn't resist asking.

"You don't think the three bodies in the woods are related to Catriona's disappearance?" Quinton studied his face carefully. "Or to the recent death of Langford?"

"I told you, she didn't disappear, she *left*." Evans shook his head, as if he couldn't comprehend being forced to participate in a conversation with someone so stupid that they couldn't remember such a simple fact. "And to answer your question, no, I don't think it's related, but perhaps I'm not bored enough to reach such imaginative deductions."

He hesitated, as if he had something else to say, and Quinton waited, his own frustration simmering, hoping Evans would add something, but the butler snapped his jaw shut and said nothing more. Quinton sensed the conversation had reached the end of productivity.

"Very well," said Quinton, the words clipped. He inclined his head. "Thank you for taking the time. I'll let you get back to your chickens."

Evans said nothing else, just bent over to pick up his decapitated chicken and went back to the task from which he'd been interrupted. Quinton backed away, feeling like a child who'd been scolded. More than anything, though, he was annoyed with himself. He'd underestimated the butler and allowed the man to get under his skin.

Before the wedding, while they were waiting for Theo to recover, Montgomery had taken Quinton falcon hunting. It wasn't an experience Quinton felt a need to repeat, but in this moment, he felt like the rabbit. Evans had picked at his insecurities like a falcon tearing bits of meat from the bones of its prey: efficient, methodical, and ruthless. It made Quinton feel small and he didn't like it.

There was only one thing to do for it. He needed to speak with his wife.

Chapter Thirty-Seven

aving arrived the night prior with Savi, Katy, Finn, and Lady Bexley, John had been thrust into the role of investigator without any time for reprieve. The choice was his own, though. Having heard the magistrate was going to speak with the tutor, John had volunteered his services.

But just because he was offering his services did not mean he was doing so in an official capacity. John found it freeing to wear normal clothes, his Bow Street woollens left at home. Here the magistrate was the authority, and John was just accompanying him, leaving the bulk of the risk and reward to the older local man.

He had to admit, it was a nice change of pace.

The journey from London had proved more comfortable than he'd expected, and both Savi and Theo had travelled well, thanks to Theo's excellently crafted carriage. If anything, Savi had had more energy than he had by the time they arrived. Remembering his conversation with his wife, John was working diligently on not hovering. Finding a task to keep himself busy helped with that effort, and he knew his wife would be well cared for at the estate.

For their short journey to visit the tutor, the magistrate had offered the use of his personal carriage, and John was grateful. The trip would be less than two hours on horseback, but having lived his whole life in the city and without access to a stable, John had never learned to ride. That was for the rich, or for those who worked with the beasts, and neither applied to John.

The time passed quickly, with John finding Medley Dandridge to be an easy traveling companion and a competent conversationalist. Upon arrival, they left the driver to care for the horse while John and Mr. Dandridge walked the main road through the quaint seaside village of Hartlemond. A smattering of shops dotted the road; the general store and fishmonger's next to each other and the bookstore and tailor nearby. The tavern was their first stop, and after ascertaining directions and grabbing a quick pint, the two walked by way of the side streets until they reached their destination: a smattering of cottages on the cliffside by the sea.

The first thing John noticed was how the salt hung heavy in the air, along with a distinct scent he couldn't place. As they crested the hill, they were rewarded with their first glimpse of the ocean. Gazing out at the vast expanse, John was momentarily overwhelmed by the crashing of the waves and the sight of the endless water. He had never seen the sea before, and the sight of so much vast emptiness filled him with equal parts awe and dread.

Forcing himself to tear his eyes away from the scene, John swallowed hard and tried to focus on the task at hand, walking faster to catch up with the magistrate who hadn't even missed a beat. He didn't want to appear like some small-minded rube from the city, easily taken by every sight and sound that came his way. He was a Bow Street Officer, a respected professional, and he would act like it.

The tavern owner had known the number of a Mr. James Pearson's cottage and had given it without reservation, indicating to John the former tutor had little to hide. The home itself was solid and cozy, with a white front porch decorated with colourful bowls of shells that blended with the surprising pale orange of the house. It exuded a certain cheerfulness that stood in contrast the other seaside cottages, all of them painted a clean white and trimmed in more white.

Mr. Dandridge knocked, and after only a few moments the door was opened wide, revealing the cottage's occupant. Although he would guess the man to be somewhere in his early sixties, John's first impression of Mr. Pearson was ease, both in movement and attitude. He wore a pair of spectacles, accentuating his angular features. His tall frame was still slender, and he moved with the grace of a younger man, though his dark blond hair was streaked with grey, betraying his age.

He seemed not at all disconcerted by two strangers at his door, and greeted them cheerfully, his brown eyes watchful but unconcerned. "Good afternoon! And what brings you two men to my door on this fine day?" Before Mr. Dandridge could answer, the former tutor continued. "Would you like to come in?"

Mr. Dandridge looked surprised, but after a moment replied with an equally cheerful, "Don't mind if we do!"

The two were quickly bustled from the porch to the living area and were soon ensconced in chairs. The sea breeze kept a gentle draft through the house by two open windows, and John felt a peace in this home.

Mr. Pearson perched on the edge of his seat, waiting expectantly for them to make their business known.

After making quick introductions, Mr. Dandridge got right down to business. John noticed he included that he himself was a magistrate but did not mention John was a Bow Street Runner.

"There's been a bit of excitement up at Cedarbrook House, Mr. Pearson, where you used to tutor Graham Coleville. A grave was discovered, with three bodies inside."

Mr. Pearson's eyes flew open in surprise, and but John couldn't tell if the shock was real or an act.

"Really? How terrible." Mr. Pearson clasped his hands together and shook his head. "I'm shocked, of course, but if I might ask, what brings you to my door? I haven't set foot on the property in over thirty-six years."

John answered. "We are just looking for insight as to that time frame of when you were employed there. We believe the graves date back that far. People who lived there at the time are not so common all these years later, as you might imagine."

"Yes, I'm sure." Mr. Pearson's expression turned thoughtful. "Of course, I would be happy to help in any way I can, but I doubt I'll be of much assistance. I mostly kept to myself during my time there. The only person I interacted with regularly was young Graham, and occasionally Lord Coleville."

"Sometimes details you didn't think were important at the time can be very helpful." John phrased the next question casually, but kept a close eye on Mr. Pearson's reaction. "Do you remember when the daughter, Catriona Coleville, ran off?"

"Cat—I mean, Lady Catriona?" Mr. Pearson frowned. "I haven't thought of that time for many years." He stood suddenly, still moving like a much younger man. "Tea or whiskey, men?"

Dandridge answered unhesitatingly. "Whiskey."

At John's nod Mr. Pearson disappeared past an open door into a hall that no doubt led to the kitchen and carefully pulled the door shut behind him. John glanced at the magistrate as the man settled his burly frame a bit deeper into the chair. To the untrained eye he might have appeared complacent, lazy even, but John saw how his eyes carefully scanned the room, taking in the details.

John did the same, noting the pencil drawings of children in the waves on the windowsills, and oil paintings of seashells dotting the walls. A variety of plants hung drying from the ceiling in two corners of the room, giving the tangy salt air a pleasant aroma, perhaps of fennel and sage. Living plants spilled from pots on shelves, framing stacks of well-read books with more shells. The room itself carried the orange colour inside, with three walls painted the unusual colour as a light wash over a stark white. The fourth wall and an alcove were painted a dark orange, which even to John's uneducated eye made the paintings on those walls stand out. There was something unique about those paintings, but John wasn't able to study them further before Mr. Pearson bustled back in with a tray, three glasses, and a half bottle of whiskey.

John and Dandridge gratefully accepted the glasses and allowed Mr. Pearson to pour a generous measure.

As each settled back, Mr. Pearson spoke. "You were asking about Lady Catriona. It's been many years, but, yes, I do remember the day she left. Lord Coleville was in rare form, storming about, having the grounds and home searched from top to bottom. They even ransacked my quarters, though I had just gotten back from visiting my parents and had barely spoken two words to the young lady in all the time I worked there."

"You didn't know the girl well then?" asked Dandridge.

"No, I didn't know her at all." Mr. Pearson said the statement emphatically. "It wouldn't have been appropriate if I had, her being a young, unmarried girl and me being a single bachelor at the time. I do remember she fought with Lord Coleville often, but that was common knowledge for anyone living within those walls."

John latched on to the last sentence. "Yes, we've heard she was quite wilful."

He waited, hoping the older man would fill in the blank, and he was not disappointed.

"Aye, she could be wilful, I suppose," Mr. Pearson affirmed before taking a sip of his whiskey. "But I never got a sense of maliciousness, if that's what you're implying."

It had not been what John was implying, but he found it interesting where Mr. Pearson's mind went.

John pondered his words while Mr. Dandridge shifted the conversation. "One of the remains found in the grave was an adult male. Do you know of any man who went missing or left abruptly around that time?"

Mr. Pearson stared into his glass and swirled the amber

contents. "I'm sorry, I'm trying to think, it's just been so many years. In truth, my focus was on Graham at the time. He was quite distraught when his sister left. It was my third year as his tutor, and we had become quite close."

He paused again, still swirling his whiskey. John appreciated how the magistrate made no comment, letting the silence extend so that Mr. Pearson might feel compelled to fill it with his own words.

"As I think on it, I do seem to recall something about a foot-man." Mr. Pearson nodded slowly, as if trying to coax the memory to the front of his mind. "I think a footman quit about that that same time. I don't remember why, but it was abrupt."

"Do you recall his name?" asked John.

"No. I think his brother also was a member of staff, but I don't know if he still is." Mr. Pearson sighed. "I'm sorry I'm not more help."

"No need to apologize, Mr. Pearson, we appreciate you taking the time." Dandridge smiled pleasantly. "May I just ask under what circumstances you left the Coleville's employ, seeing as how close you were with the boy?"

It was a good question. John watched Mr. Pearson carefully, but once again he saw no indicators of deception.

"Lord Coleville decided it was time for Graham to go to boarding school, and so my services were no long needed." Mr. Pearson shrugged. "A regular occurrence in my former trade."

"Of course, of course." Mr. Dandridge nodded, as if nothing could make more sense in the world. He glanced around their surroundings appreciatively. "You know, this really is a beautiful home, Mr. Pearson. That view must never get old. What brought you here, if I might ask? Do you have family in the area?"

The question seemed casual, but John felt there might be more to it. John felt his impression of the man was correct. The magistrate was sharper than he liked to let on.

But Mr. Pearson answered easily. "I met a woman who loved the sea. This was where she wanted to be, and I wanted to be with her. Raised our children in this home, and welcome our grand-children back when they visit."

The words were simple but John could see they came from his heart. Here was a happy man, at peace with the life he had built. Leaning back, John let the magistrate finish with the small talk while he enjoyed the luxury of his drink. By evening he would be back with Savi, and he found he felt the same feeling of this home wash over him.

He was at peace with his own life and wanted to get back to it.

Chapter Thirty-Eight

The tea was poured and tiny cakes selected as the women gathered in the sitting room. Zoe was enjoying this afternoon, with the men of the house busy with their own pursuits. The conversation was eclectic, bouncing easily from subject to subject, matching the equally eclectic women themselves. It began with preferences in tea blends, broached by Theo, then easily flowed into the merits of a sugar boycott to protest slavery, a subject close to Simone's heart, then continuing into a helpful discussion on the best herbs to benefit a woman's monthly needs, a question posed by Mary. That somehow led to a more technical consideration of techniques to stem blood loss, with Katy and Savi leading that discussion to include both wounds and childbirth.

Zoe was listening intently when a footman appeared at her arm, startling her.

"I apologize for interrupting your tea, my lady, but a message just came for you," Oliver said in a low voice.

"Thank you." Zoe took the held-out piece of paper, and Oliver took his leave, obviously desperate to get out of the room.

She opened the note, reading the elegant scrawl quickly, grinning in satisfaction.

"What does it say, dear?" asked Simone from the other side of the room.

"It's from Alexander." Zoe stood and walked over to her mother, handing the paper to her so she could read it as well. "Apparently, he is getting engaged."

Mary smirked, reaching out to take another scone with cream. "Mabel Anderson, right? I knew he was smitten."

"That is wonderful news. Naturally, we assumed after he visited—" started Simone.

"Yes, of course, after that ball at the end of the season. Right before the wedding—my wedding that is," Zoe interrupted. "You remember, Mary? He couldn't take his eyes off Mabel."

Zoe realized she had never told Mary that Alexander had visited, asking for advice. She had meant to tell her—to discuss the conversation and all the possible implications—but she must have forgotten with everything else going on. A slight wave of guilt came over her. Zoe needed to make sure she didn't neglect her dear friend.

"Right, I remember." Mary squinted at her, but didn't say anything further.

"You said he's getting engaged? He hasn't actually asked the girl yet?" asked Theo, who was sitting next to Simone on the sofa.

"No, not yet." Simone passed the note to Theo. "Apparently this is an invitation to his engagement party, to be held at the Dovefield estate, where he will then ask her."

Savita laughed at that. "Why would someone invite people to an engagement party when the engagement hasn't even taken place yet?"

"Don't try to understand it, Savi," replied Mary before anyone else could respond. "It's high society nonsense."

"I would hardly say it's nonsense for young people to want their friends and family there when taking such a huge step forward in their lives," Simone scolded. "It's not uncommon among society circles."

This sparked a lively debate about the benefits and disadvantages of planning a garden party for an upcoming engagement, and for a moment Zoe kept her thoughts to herself, allowing the others to discuss the topic. She smiled as she watched Katy and Savita shake their heads, clearly unimpressed, and Mary egg on Theo and Simone.

"Well, I still find it absurd," said Mary with a sniff.

"Perhaps it is, but nevertheless, we are invited." Zoe took a sip of her tea. "The date is a week from now."

"I assume my mother and I are not invited, though?" asked Savita.

"Ah, well—"

Savita held up a hand. "It's fine. He doesn't even know who we are, even if we weren't so far outside his social circle. I wouldn't expect an invitation; I just wanted to clarify."

"Well, still, I'm sure I could ask Alexander to make an exception." Zoe meant that, although she wasn't sure how his father, Balwin, would take it. Not that she cared much for Balwin's opinion on anything.

"No, no." Katy shook her head. "This is a time for family and true friends. Savita and I will be fine entertaining ourselves for an afternoon."

Mary cleared her throat. "I'm sure you meant 'Savita, Mary, and I.' And yes, we will be just fine."

"Actually, my dear, you are included in the invitation," said Theo with a soft smile. "As you should be. Who knows where Alexander would be without your assistance? You deserve as much credit as Quinton or the rest of them."

"Oh." Mary cocked her head. "I didn't expect that."

"Theo is correct, Alexander owes you a debt." Simone patted her hand. "And even if that wasn't true, you're family."

A blush bloomed across Mary's face at that, so Zoe quickly changed the subject. "Savita, you are looking beautiful," she said. "How are you feeling?"

It was true—Savita was practically glowing. To be fair, Savita was almost always the most beautiful woman in the room, with her golden-brown skin and thick black hair and perfect, delicate features. The pregnancy just accentuated the beauty she already possessed. Then on top of all of it, she also happened to be a lovely person. Zoe hoped John was grateful every day that a woman like Savita had even looked at him.

"I'm feeling fine at this stage." Savita placed a hand on her stomach, her face glowing. "But ask me again in four months."

In the loose dress she was wearing, one could hardly tell she was with child at all. Zoe wondered if once she started to show more prominently Savita would sequester herself. That's what women of Zoe's class did. She always thought it was odd that the sight of a pregnant stomach was so taboo, since bearing heirs was supposed to be one of a lady's main purposes, but something about it made the upper class very uncomfortable. She supposed it was the implication of how the woman came to be pregnant that made them uncomfortable.

But Savita wasn't like the women Zoe had grown up with. She was a midwife and working woman. The judgment of others seemed to hold little sway over her.

"Are you still working?" asked Zoe.

"I was, but I've turned most of my cases over to another midwife while we're here," replied Savita. "But I was talking to Mrs. Fox and it seems one of her nieces is near to giving birth. I told her I would stop by later this afternoon, just to check everything is moving in the right direction."

Zoe shook her head. "You do manage to keep busy."

Savita shrugged. "I know my passions."

Katy smiled at her daughter, her pride clearly beaming from her face. "It won't be long before your son expands our own family."

Savita rolled her eyes. "You don't know that it will be a son, Maan."

"Just you wait and see," retorted Katy. "Perhaps you don't recognize the signs, but for a midwife with my experience, there's no mistaking the way he's sitting in your body—"

"Maan!" Savita blushed. "You're going to scandalize the ladies."

Theo laughed at that. "No one is a stranger to pregnancy in this room. We may not all have children ourselves, but how many siblings do you have, Mary?"

Mary snorted. "Too many to count."

They all laughed then, but Zoe didn't miss the faint glimmer of sadness in Theo's eyes, or the way Simone lightly squeezed her hand. Zoe didn't know the full story, but from what Simone had hinted to her, Theo understood the grief that came from planning an entire future, seeing all of it laid out in front of her, and then having it cruelly snatched away.

Turning to her, Katy raised a good-natured eyebrow. "And what about you, my dear? Any news to share?"

Zoe nearly choked on her tea, sputtering brown droplets across the skirt of her light-coloured gown.

"Um, well, no, not as of yet." Zoe wiped her mouth with a white napkin before attempting to dab up some of the rapidly growing brown stains which were now scattered across her lap.

"Maan!" exclaimed Savita once again. "You can't just ask someone that!"

"Why not?" responded Katy defensively. "She will be with child before long, won't she? Why be embarrassed about it?"

"It's fine, Katy." Zoe gave up on the stains—she would have to apologize to Louisa for the inconvenience. "I just swallowed wrong is all."

It was a lie, but Zoe didn't want Katy to feel embarrassed. The question had caught her off guard, but the midwife wasn't wrong. Having children was the natural next step in Zoe's life. Quinton and she hadn't discussed it in so many words, but it would happen eventually. Wouldn't it? After all, children were a natural, normal part of building a family. And Quinton was titled now—he would be expecting an heir, maybe not this minute, but soon enough.

So why did the idea of her stomach swelling with a baby make

Zoe break out into a cold sweat? Zoe's early memories of her life once her mother had married Hugh were of her mother's pregnancies with Walter and Phoebe. Neither had been easy. The state of childbearing didn't suit Simone. She had been deathly ill while pregnant and then confined to her bed for months afterward each time. What if the same thing happened to Zoe? What if she never recovered?

Or what if something even worse happened? It was common for women to die in childbirth. Both noblemen and working-class men often took a second or even a third wife when their first died young, often due to the process of bringing their progeny into the world.

The chances for the child weren't much better. Babies died all the time, either shortly before birth or afterward from a weakness they were born with or a disease they contracted. Zoe wasn't as strong as Theo. Would she be able to survive the loss of her child? Or would she be forever broken by the event, forged into a shadow of her former self by the tragedy?

Glancing at her daughter, Simone seemed to sense that a change in conversation was needed. "We shall have to send a note back accepting the invitation."

"Quite right." Theo nodded sagely. "I should really take a carriage over regardless. It's been quite some time since Baldwin and I had a proper chat. I wonder how he's taking the whole thing."

Mary snorted. "Probably just glad Alexander is choosing a bride in his social bracket."

The words were glib, but Zoe knew how smitten Alexander had become with a serving girl over the winter months prior. If it weren't for her untimely death, and the fact she was involved in a scam to steal his wealth, who knew how far it might have gone.

"Mabel is a respectable girl from a good family," said Simone. "But she also seems to have a good head on her shoulders, which is vital when running a household. She's an excellent match for him."

"Which makes it even harder to understand what she sees in him," said Mary with a light laugh.

"Now, Alexander has grown up a great deal—" started Theo.

"I know, Theo, I'm only teasing."

Zoe cleared her throat to hide her own laugh. Theo had always had a soft spot for Alexander, even when he was a rogue. Zoe supposed they all had their own blind spots when it came to love.

Chapter Thirty-Nine

Savita stood at the threshold of the doorway, unsure how to proceed. It had just now occurred to her that there would be no hackneys for her to hail. The village wasn't far and normally she would walk, but as much as Savita didn't want to admit it to John, she was nearing the part of her pregnancy were fatigue was taking a toll and she didn't want to put undue strain on her body. Despite what her husband thought, she did have some sense.

As she contemplated asking Theo for use of her carriage, Savita sensed a presence come up alongside her.

"Can I help you, miss?"

She turned, expecting to see the butler or one of the footmen, but was surprised to see the earl standing there instead.

"Good afternoon, my lord." Savita extended her head toward him. "I was going to go look in on Mrs. Fox's niece, Virginia, but I forgot to ask Theo—Lady Bexley—for use of her carriage."

"I see." Lord Coleville raised his eyebrow, his expression sceptical. "And are you familiar with Miss Virginia then? I wouldn't have thought you'd know many people in the area, considering where you're from."

It was a reaction Savi had come to expect, but that didn't mean it didn't annoy her nonetheless.

"Are you referring to India or London, my lord?" Savita liked to think of herself as kind and even-tempered most of the time, but she wasn't someone to be walked on, no matter what title the lord held. "And to answer your question, no, I am not personally familiar with her, but I am a trained midwife, and I offered my services." She inclined her head again. "If you'll excuse me, I need to find Theo."

As she turned to take her leave, Lord Coleville spoke. "Wait."

Savi paused, waiting to see what he would say. He was silent for a long minute, staring out the open door at the garden beyond. "I apologize if I offended you, Mrs...?" he said finally.

"Smith," she responded.

"Of course. The Bow Street Runner's wife."

It was a simple and accurate statement, but he somehow managed to make it, too, sound insulting. Savita held her tongue, wondering what else the earl would say. She took the time to properly study his features. It was subtle, but Savi could see the hints of Quinton in his face—the set of his jaw, and the prominence of his cheekbones, and the colour of his eyes. Even at his advancing age and with his hair greying at the temples, there was still an apparition remaining of the handsome young man Savita imagined he'd once been.

After another lengthy pause, her patience was rewarded.

"Tell me, how is it you came to be a midwife, Mrs. Smith?" asked the lord.

It wasn't the question Savi had been expecting. She blinked. "My mother taught me, as her mother did her."

"I see." He didn't sound surprised. "My wife considered herself something of a healer—not a midwife—but she came from what she imagined to be the Scottish wilds, even though it was actually an estate finer than this one, and had a knowledge of plants and herbs and their uses. She liked to go around to the tenant farmers and offer her concoctions for whatever ailments they were suffering from."

"She sounds quite kind," offered Savi.

"She was—far kinder than I, at any rate." He sighed. "She passed some of that knowledge on to my daughter, who was even worse when it came to her imaginings, but instead of her mother's kindness all she got was my stubbornness. Always roaming the countryside in search of some rare root or another, ignoring any sense of propriety or good sense." Shaking his head, the lord sighed again. "There are times, though, when I almost miss the wildness."

Savi wasn't sure what to say in response to his admission. It seemed like something private which Lord Coleville should be confiding in a personal friend, not a stranger on his doorstep. But then Savita supposed a man like him didn't have many friends. Maybe it was easier sometimes to share things with strangers.

Fortunately, it seemed a response wasn't expected.

"You may take my carriage, Mrs. Smith," He turned away from the door, heading back into the house. "I'll inform Evans, and he'll have it brought around. And I will cover your fee."

"Oh." Savita must not have hidden her surprise very well, because he chuckled in response, the smile softening the severity of his features.

"I'm not quite as cruel as some make me out to be. I take care of my staff and their families." He leaned closer, as if telling a secret. "And besides which, I am quite fond of Mrs. Fox. Virgina is the closest thing she has to a daughter, and I know she's been anxious about her expecting."

Savi laughed. "Well, I appreciate it. But I am not charging anything."

"Of course you're not." Lord Coleville shook his head, softly muttering to himself as he walked away, leaving Savi to wonder at the strange but not unpleasant interaction.

Chapter Forty

G etting dressed for dinner had to be one of the biggest wastes of time the nobility had come up with yet. Charlie had begrudgingly agreed to change into clean clothes, but he wouldn't be convinced to participate in formal dress. As far as the actual dinner went, even he had to admit there was a certain charm in simply appearing and being served a feast. A man could easily get used to such a lifestyle, and Charlie regularly reminded himself that he was a guest in this world, not a part of it.

Gratefully tonight the earl was taking his meal in his study, and Quinton's uncle had chosen to join him. With all the blasted bodies showing up, perhaps they could actually get a handle on where this whole thing was headed without the old geezer weighing in with his nay saying. It made Charlie wonder what the earl had to hide.

Charlie took his seat next to Savi, with John on her other side and Quinton and Zoe across from him. The rest of the eclectic clan filled out the table. The group was small enough tonight that all could speak comfortably while the meal was served in courses, the first being an excellent consommé rich with herbs.

While the footmen served, Charlie glanced at the corner

where the seemingly ever-present butler often lurked, but tonight he was absent. While Charlie had made inroads with the other servants, Evans still remained aloof. The older man moved silently, often startling Charlie by appearing out of nowhere when Charlie was exploring the manor. He knew it was irrational, but he found the man irritating, so he wasn't disappointed to see that he was occupied elsewhere.

Evans wasn't needed in the dining room anyway. The two footmen were more than competent. Indeed, both tall and broad, the two served flawlessly. They were perfectly composed and moving in unison to do their jobs while attempting to remain invisible. Charlie still could not tell them apart.

"So how was your visit with the tutor?" asked Zoe after the course was served to everyone, her question directed at John.

"The carriage ride itself was uneventful, but I am not certain whether the journey was wasted or not." John quickly filled them in on his conversation with the tutor.

"Hmm." Charlie laid his spoon down, indicating he was done with his bowl, which was then swiftly removed. "From what you found in London, John, it does seem the girl made it that far. But it's been so many years, I fear we may never know the rest of her story."

Quinton pushed his own empty bowl aside as well, and it was removed just as quickly. "You're not wrong. Cat remains a mystery, but we can pursue what we do know."

Zoe nodded. "Agreed. The footman who left abruptly was mentioned twice. It may be nothing, but I find it noteworthy. Perhaps we should try and track him down, or at least find his family and pursue what happened to him."

"Neither the cook nor the tutor remembered his name, so I don't know how we would go about finding him." Mary said the words absentmindedly as she kept her eyes on the door, no doubt anticipating the second course.

"I've been going through Mrs. Fox's records, and she keeps

meticulous notes, including from her predecessor," offered Simone. "She may have a record of his hiring. I'll look."

"An excellent idea." Hugh beamed at his beloved wife. "If we can locate his name, I'm sure we could track down whatever family may be in the area. I could go with Dandridge. I wanted to chat with the man anyway on some interesting nuances of country law."

"While you're at it, perhaps ask if he's found at anything else about Langford himself," said Quinton with a sigh. "With Mary's conversation with Mrs. Corbyn being a dead end, we're still at loose ends on who would want him dead."

As the fish course was brought in, conversation died down. Charlie eyed the offending dish distastefully. He had never been a fan of fish, unless it was masked by the strong flavour of a curry. The British, of course, didn't believe in strong flavours of any kind, so he was forced to choke it down as it was. As far was fish went, it wasn't terrible.

A few minutes passed amiably with the only sound to be heard the clinking of silverware against dishware and the noise of mouths chewing.

Eventually, Theo spoke up. "Unrelated, Mr. Stewart and I are headed to the village on the morrow. Apparently a traveling theatre troupe is putting on Hamlet in the village square."

"Mm, yes, indeed." Rory swallowed, washing down his last bite with a large swallow of white wine. He evidently had no hang-ups when it came to fish and had tucked in enthusiastically. "We leave after lunch, if anyone else wants to accompany us. Apparently there is also a village market we could explore as well."

Charlie had to hand it to the Scot. He moved seamlessly between his own world of graves and dissection and the world of the upper crust. Rory was equally comfortable discussing what he found in the depths of a desecrated corpse with Quinton and having an animated discussion with the old lady toff about the merits of the latest London play. It was a quality which both annoyed and impressed Charlie.

For most of his adult life, Charlie had been happy with his life lived in the darker grey spaces. What Charlie had done, he had done as much for his mother and Savita as for himself, to give them a home and a sense of security. His conscience had never been bothered by doing what he considered necessary for their survival. But things had changed recently. Now Finn relied on him, not just for a full belly and a warm bed, but for an example to aspire to. Charlie didn't want the boy to walk the same path he had. It was a painful realization, but he knew he needed to find a comfortable place in the light to raise Finn. Finn wasn't his blood, but he wanted to be a better father to the orphan than his own father had been to him

Not a high bar, Charlie thought, as he finally was able to push aside the picked-at fish course in favour of the third course.

Charlie pulled himself back into the conversation as Hugh said, "That explains the large market cross we passed on our way here."

Mary frowned. "Don't most of the villages have markets?"

"Actually, market rights are a legality obtained by a village to host a regular market," responded Hugh, clearly excited to share his knowledge with another victim. "There cannot be another market town within a day's travel."

Charlie had long since learned to not ask follow-up questions, for fear of lengthy legal explanations. He just took the barrister at his word now.

"The large cross in the village square advertises the coming market?" John had evidently not learned this lesson. "Clever, I would say."

"Yes, yes." Hugh nodded. "It should be a lively event. I suspect you will all have quite a fine time."

Well, at least the rest of the meal wasn't taken up with legal babble. As for his own next step here, the ghost awaited Charlie. He had his own plans for the supposed spectre.

"I'll stay here tomorrow." Charlie turned to his mother. "If you want to take Finn, I'm sure he would love the outing."

"I'll help keep an eye on the boy as well," volunteered Rory. "I have taken it upon myself to teach him the finer points of Shakespeare."

Lord, that's all Finn needed, to be indoctrinated by the Scot. But Charlie refrained from saying as much.

"Perhaps the other children would enjoy it as well," Zoe joined in. She looked at her mother. "And you might find a day out invigorating as well, Maman."

Simone smiled. "It sounds like fun. I'll arrange a second carriage for the children and you and I. That way Theo and Savi can enjoy the smoother ride with Rory."

Charlie leaned back, comfortably full even without the complete fish course. He knew dessert was next, and could see Mary's impatience, but his mind was already on the next day.

The house would be practically empty, save the staff. A perfect opportunity to stalk a ghost.

Chapter Forty-One

I t wasn't until much later that night, approaching the early
hours of the morning, that Zoe and her husband had
anytime to just themselves. Zoe collapsed onto the chaise in
their room, having already been undressed by her maid, then
redressed in her nightgown and a dressing gown.

"I feel as if I can breathe again," said Zoe, stretching out.
"Sometimes I swear that corset is trying to suffocate me."

Quinton shrugged, tugging at the collar of the nightshirt
Darrow had insisted he put on. "Then don't wear it."

Zoe snorted. "You clearly don't understand the need for
support when it comes to a woman's upper body."

His brow crinkled. "What?"

"Never mind." Zoe glanced over at her husband, noting not
for the first time his well-formed forearms and strong hands, her
thoughts turning to other activities they could be participating in.
But the expression on his face dissuaded her. Something was
clearly on his mind, hanging over him like a dark cloud.

She sat back up. "What's wrong?"

"Hmm?" Quinton cleared his throat, as if he had been lost in
thought. "Oh, it's nothing important. Just something Evans said

earlier that got under my skin. It's foolish of me to let it bother me so."

Zoe frowned. It wasn't like Quinton to be so out of sorts about a few misspoken words. "What did he say?"

"Nothing, it doesn't matter."

"Just tell me." Zoe moved to sit next to him on the bed, her fatigue momentarily forgotten. "What happened?"

Quinton sighed, apparently sensing that he would lose this battle. "I went to ask him about his time here, when Catriona disappeared."

"And did he say anything helpful?"

"On that front, no, he was not helpful." Quinton paused. "But he did make his negative feelings about me very clear. He thinks I'm just a bored noble who uses the tragedy of others to entertain myself."

"Really?" Zoe's frown deepened. "That's unacceptable. I'll speak to him tomorrow, and you should speak to your grandfather about his dismissal."

"No, don't." Quinton placed his large hand over her own. "I asked him to tell me his thoughts honestly, and I'll not punish a man for that."

"Fine. He insulted you, so it's your decision." Zoe was less forgiving than Quinton, but she would respect his wishes in this.

This was one of the things Zoe loved most about Quinton— that he was steady when she wasn't. His steadiness gave Zoe the freedom to express herself, while still giving her a safe space to come back to should things burn too hot.

The irony of that sentiment didn't escape Zoe. When they had first met, the two had bickered constantly, the sparks of attraction mixed with the cold water of irritation. As time went on, the same things which had once been so irritating were the things they had learned to love about the other. They still bickered, but there was trust and affection now to soften the sharp edges.

"Since you do not intend to seek retribution, what is it that is still bothering you?" Zoe asked.

Quinton didn't answer immediately, staring off into the distance, perhaps studying a particular patch of wallpaper.

"I don't know if I belong here," he said finally.

Zoe blinked. "Here as in the estate, or here as in . . ." She let the thought trail off, unsure what to say.

"I really want to make this work," he replied, not answering the question. "I want to be a good husband to you, and a good heir for my grandfather, and a good friend to my friends, and a good noble for my position. But sometimes it feels like I'm being pulled apart—like I'm not good enough for any of it. Like I'm just pretending."

"You are good enough." Zoe grabbed his arm. "You've always been good enough."

"What if I'm not though?" asked Quinton, not making eye contact. "What if I've never been a good man?"

Taking a deep breath, Zoe tried not to give in to her instinct to tell her husband how utterly stupid he sounded right now. "Of course you're good enough. I would never have married you otherwise, you foolish man," Zoe bumped his shoulder playfully. "You know I'm an excellent judge of character."

Quinton chuckled at that. "I know you *think* you are."

She laughed as well. "I am! It's not my fault you never listen to me."

"I listen to you all the time, woman." Quinton shook his head. "You're the one who never listens."

A fair criticism, but Zoe wasn't going to give him the satisfaction of admitting it. Besides, men said a great many things. One couldn't listen to everything.

"Mm." Zoe leaned her head on his shoulder. "Now what did Evans really say that's got you all wound up?"

"He said that I—we—are only investigating Langford's death and looking into those three bodies because we're—I'm—bored.

That I don't owe them anything and I'm only doing this for myself."

"So you said." Zoe leaned backed to look at him again. "But why does that bother you so much? Men have said worse."

Quinton suddenly stood, his arms crossed. "Because what if he's right? What if I am just doing this because I'm bored and selfish and I don't actually care that a man is dead at all?"

"I don't think trying to get justice for a dead man makes you selfish." Zoe sighed, confused. "Quite the opposite, in fact."

He waved a hand in a vague, dismissive gesture. "You don't understand."

That familiar feeling of irritation was beginning to come back.

Zoe stood as well. "You're right, I don't. What is the matter with you? Why are you acting this way?"

"Because I *am* bored!"

The snapped words hung in the air, their admission shocking both of them.

"Because I am bored," Quinton repeated, this time quieter. "I miss being an agent. I miss the excitement of that life—the struggle of making a living and having a purpose. Langford's death and the grave and the history with Catriona . . . it all gave me an excuse to have a taste of that again, and I jumped at it. And maybe that makes me a bad person, but it's the truth."

There was a long pause as they both processed what he'd said. After a moment, Zoe stood as well, moving to stand next to Quinton. "Being bored doesn't make you a bad person. Finding joy or purpose in your work doesn't either." Zoe brushed some of his hair back out of his dark eyes. "You've given up a great deal for me, but some things you've turned your back on that I never asked you to. I never expected you to give up your work completely, or to sever ties with your old life. It is a part of you, and I love all of you."

"I know," admitted Quinton. "But I don't know if I can keep that side of myself and be a good noble."

"Then you will be a bad noble," said Zoe simply. "But you will be a good man who is true to himself."

Quinton relaxed, as if her words were what he'd been waiting to hear. "I knew there was a reason I married you."

"Oh?" Zoe smiled. "I thought it was for my charm and wit."

There was no reply to that. Instead, his left hand gripped the back of her neck as Quinton pulled her close and leaned down, pressing his warm lips against her own. Zoe, in turn, leaned into him, her fingers tangling in his hair as she returned the kiss. It was passionate and deep—the kiss of two people reassuring each other of their love, no matter what happened.

Quinton suddenly pulled away. "Zoe, it means a great deal to me—"

"Be quiet and kiss me again."

And he did.

∾

Much later that night, Zoe lay awake in Quinton's arms, feeling his even breathing as he slept. She knew Quinton was still finding his way, but she also knew him to be a man of depth and integrity. As a man, and now a rich noble, he had a variety of options at his disposal. In the end, his wealth and status would make any path he chose acceptable. His real battle was accepting that.

Zoe felt a similar struggle, but without those options. Of course wealth was hers, and she did know that was a privilege. In a way it made her mind even more unsettled, as she should appreciate that gift. Instead, as a woman, and as a nobleman's wife, her role seemed to have little flexibility.

She too wanted to be good at this new role, a good wife, a welcome addition to the estate and village. She needed to find her own path in this world, one that fulfilled those desires but one where she did not lose herself.

Quinton shifted in his sleep and drew her closer. Exhaustion trumped her uneasiness, and she felt herself drifting into a deep sleep, her last thought gratefully not of concern, but of how safe she felt in her husband's arms.

Chapter Forty-Two

Reining in his mount, Hugh waited for Mr. Dandridge to catch up. The horseflesh here at Cedarbrook was exceptional. He made a mental note that he must ask the earl where he found such bonnie steeds. His was a gelding, strong in spirit but still eager to please, while Dandridge had chosen a sweet-tempered, but somewhat plodding, mare.

Dandridge finally came up beside him, his face flushed and his breathing heavy, but with a pleasant gleam in his eyes. Hugh suspected that the man didn't spend much of his recreational time on horseback.

"Do you enjoy, riding, Mr. Dandridge?" Hugh asked.

"Oh, yes, indeed." Dandridge took a moment to catch his breath. "I am simply out of practice. It has been far too long since I have had the pleasure of a fine ride on a good horse."

The gelding whinnied, as if in agreement, and pranced ahead, wanting to run. A thought suddenly occurred to Hugh.

"Forgive me if this seems boyish." Hugh pointed to a knobby outcrop some distance ahead. "But care to race to the topmost tree ahead? Loser buys the first pint in the village?"

The glint in the magistrate's eye alerted Hugh his wager was accepted a moment before the man let go of his hold on the mare and urged her forward with his heels. His cheating gave Dandridge a split-second head start, but Hugh hardly had to encourage his horse. He pointed him towards the disappearing tail of Dandridge's mount, loosened his hold on the reins, and nothing else needed to be done.

He beat the magistrate by a half a length.

There were no hard feelings between the men. The magistrate laughed in delight, and Hugh easily joined in. He felt like a boy again, eager to find speed and the winning length. Both men, still smiling, turned their mounts towards the village and rode side by side.

After some more amiable silence had passed, Hugh spoke. "Mr. Langford has been returned to his family? I hope they understood the need for an autopsy."

"Yes." Dandridge nodded. "He is buried now, next to his father and mother. I did not see a need to tell his wife about the . . . details involving the resurrectionist."

"Buried? They already had the funeral?" Hugh was surprised. "I know Zoe and Quinton wished to attend."

"I was unaware you hadn't been informed." The magistrate shifted his considerable weight in the saddle. "The earl attended."

"Oh?" Hugh could understand the earl's attendance—he had heard of Philip's childhood friendship with the man—but he was surprised Philip had chosen not to share those details with Quinton.

Upon further reflection, maybe he wasn't so surprised at all.

Dandridge continued, perhaps feeling awkward at Hugh's lack of reaction. "Lord Coleville's presence was no surprise. The earl has a reputation of fairness when it comes to his staff and the tenants who rely on him."

Hugh raised an eyebrow at that. "I must admit, I wouldn't have expected that. I do not know him well, but that is a side of him I have yet to see."

"He is not an easy man, that I will give you," admitted Dandridge. "I've known him since I was young, so my view of him is likely more generous than yours. I grew up near here, and my family have lineage—though no land, to speak of—and so we would occasionally mix socially. I remember his wedding to the late Lady Seonaid. A happier time for him, though even then I wouldn't say he was a soft man."

It hadn't crossed Hugh's mind that Dandridge might know Philip personally, but it made sense. Though, Dandridge's words were hard to accept; Hugh couldn't picture Philip Coleville with an emotion even close to resembling happiness.

"I suppose most men aren't born bitter." Hugh shifted in his saddle, his legs beginning to fall asleep.

"No, I don't suppose so." Dandridge paused at the top of a gentle hill as the village came into view below. "But losing a wife and a son will change a man, besides that whole business with the daughter."

"A fair point," conceded Hugh.

Dandridge gestured toward the village. "All I know is that here, despite his personal loses, it is not uncommon for him to pay for a funeral, or arrange medical care, or even help a widow find suitable lodgings so she is not destitute. And for that, he has my respect."

Hugh was quiet as they descended the hill. Not for the first time, Hugh reflected that every person was a conundrum, both good and evil, both kind and harsh. The percentages might vary, but most lives held both. He found it interesting that Earl Coleville's animosity seemed to be in his personal life, while the public facing figure had gained a reputation for good deeds. The two were hard to reconcile.

Guiding his horse around a felled tree, Hugh changed the subject. "And what of Mr. Langford? How was he viewed in the village?"

The magistrate scoffed slightly. "Mr. Langford is a different horse altogether. I'd met the man, a time or two, but I didn't know him well. I've made inquiries, naturally, since his death. He grew up in a neighbouring village, the only son of a vicar. His father was a decent man, respected. Not Ellis. His reputation leaned more towards . . . unseemly."

"Unseemly?" Hugh questioned. "How so?"

"Well, when he was young, he was known as a bit of a mischief maker—mostly pranks and overindulgences. But evidently those habits lost their charm as he grew into adulthood, turning from childish ignorance to something darker." Dandridge rode silently for a moment, adjusted his hat briefly.

Hugh waited. He suspected the magistrate would speak his mind soon enough.

"Ellis made people uncomfortable. He never quite broke any laws, as far as I was made aware, and I don't get the impression he was a monster by any means. But he rubbed people the wrong way, not just because of his poor attitude. Folks seemed to think he always came out just a bit better than the rest of them."

Hugh frowned. "For example?"

"For instance, several people claimed Ellis's family was always given the best cuts of meat at the butchers, for a greatly reduced price. But when I asked the butcher about it, the man grew angry and refused to say anything about it."

"Interesting." Hugh pondered this. "And the two weren't friends?"

"I'd say not." Dandridge snorted. "The only thing he would say was that Ellis Langford was a blasted bounder."

Hugh slowed his horse to step over a narrow part of the trail. "I take it from your tone this wasn't an isolated incident."

"No." Dandridge followed Hugh's example, allowing his mare to pick her own way across a trail. "None of these people ever said as much, but if I were to make an educated guess . . . blackmail would be it."

That would be Hugh's as well. Vicars were the gatekeepers of a village's secrets, and if one's son was so inclined, it wasn't much of a leap to believe that he could gain access to some of those secrets. The kind of thing a youth might do out of curiosity or lack of proper boundaries, but then with the wrong temperament could grow into something malicious and twisted.

"I did ask around in the village for any recent interactions with the man," continued Dandridge. "Unfortunately, nothing much came up. He only came into the village for necessities; no one was sorry he was dead. I think Lord Coleville might have been the closest thing the sorry bastard had for a friend."

"What a depressing state," said Hugh, almost feeling sorry for the man despite himself.

They continued through the village to a small farm a few miles outside the town—their destination. Simone had indeed managed to find the records regarding the footman. The page was damaged, so all that could be made out was the name "Maxwell" and "Grimsley Farm." It hadn't taken long for Dandridge to ask around the village and locate said farm.

Looking around as they rode up, the two men stopped their horses and waited.

An older man came from the small outbuilding behind the cottage, leading a cow. He ambled up to the men, the content cow following. Both man and cow seemed well fed, and the home was neat and maintained.

The man looked inquiringly at the two visitors. "We don't get many visitors around here. What can I do for you?"

At the sound of his voice, an older woman came from the home. She was slightly stooped, with her grey hair tied back in a tight bun. She was wiping her hands on a clean towel and came to stand near her husband, looking inquiringly at the two men.

Hugh and Dandridge dismounted, and the magistrate spoke first. "I am Medley Dandridge, magistrate of these parts. My companion is Hugh Dovefield, a visitor at Cedarbrook. We came to visit with the Grimsley family. It's about their son Maxwell."

The man stilled at the name. "I'm George Grimsley. He was my sister's boy, but we raised him up from when he was in leading strings. Why you askin' after him?"

A loaded question, but Dandridge answered smoothly. "The

housekeeper was going through some old records and realized Maxwell never received his final pay. The earl wished us to deliver it, though we know it's a bit late."

"You came all this way to offer a few shillings to a servant who hasn't been in the Coleville's employ for nearly forty years?" Mrs. Grimsley asked sceptically.

"The earl is quite meticulous about these things," replied Dandridge.

The old woman didn't look convinced, but if Mr. Grimsley thought the explanation a bit weak, he refrained from saying so. "Well, we haven't seen the lad since that time either, so good look with yer search."

Hugh had to temper his excitement. "What do you mean?" he asked.

"He took off to London to find his way as an actor and we never heard from him again." The wife spoke, and Hugh could see the bitterness in her eyes. "He did not even have the decency to tell us hisself—left his brother to do the dirty deed."

Dandridge and Hugh exchanged a glance. A coincidence or something more?

"Was his leaving like that out of character, if you don't mind me asking?" Dandridge asked the question casually, but Hugh understood the weight behind it.

"Aye, I wouldn't have thought so." Mrs. Grimsley shook her head. "Max was always a bit of a dreamer, but he wasn't a cruel or stupid sort—at least, we thought he wasn't. But I guess you never really know a person, even your own kin."

Hugh mulled this over in his mind. "How old was Maxwell when he left for London?"

"Max left in '73, just after he turned twenty. Had that good job at the manor and everything. Damn fool boy he was." Mr. Grimsley sounded more disappointed than bitter. Hugh could well imagine the excitement at the opportunity given with the position at the manor, and the astonishment when Maxwell had thrown that away.

"Have you heard from him since he left?" asked Dandridge.

It was a good question, and the only one that really mattered.

"We get a letter, from time to time, and a little money." Mr. Grimsley shook her head. "Not enough to make up for the fact he left his brother here to do all the hard work."

"But no visits in all that time?" Hugh knew he sounded a little overeager, but he needed to confirm they hadn't seen him in those years.

Mr. Grimsley looked offended at Hugh's lack of tact, but he still answered. "No, he's never come home."

That was what they needed to know. Hugh glanced at Dandridge and could see he was thinking the same thing.

Dandridge pulled his hat. "Thank you for taking this time to talk to us, and I will relay this to the earl."

Hugh started to mount the gelding, but feeling a bit guilty about his abrupt manner, felt compelled to say something more. "This is a beautiful plot of land, if I may say so, Mr. and Mrs. Grimsley. You do a fine job of keeping up on it."

The praise worked. Mr. Grimsley's face lightened. "I do what I can, but I can't do what I used to. We would be lost without our boy Mac. He comes and helps out every chance he gets, making sure the place stays kept up. We never could have any children of our own, and now he's all we have left." He paused and looked around. "Thank God for Mac. Max had his head in the clouds, but Mac was always firmly planted in the dirt. Always knew where he was going and how he was going to get there. Good head on his shoulders."

Mrs. Grimsley smiled sadly. "Their mama said it was the same when they was inside of her, may she rest in peace. One sleeping, and one kicking."

Hugh stopped mid-air as he was mounting his horse and stepped back to the ground. "What did you say?"

"One sleeping and one kicking in the womb," she responded. "You know how twins is."

Chapter Forty-Three

I t was a festive group that arrived at the stables just after luncheon, the children especially filling the air with happy chattering. Zoe was grateful to see that Finn, younger than Gwen and Phoebe by a few years, held his own, bantering cheerfully. Walter seemed to relax as well, though at sixteen he was more conscious of being perceived as silly. The girls were still masters of silly, though Gwen looked more like a young lady daily. Even Phoebe, a late bloomer, was beginning to show the features of a young woman.

"I locked Brutus in a stall for now, on account of him maybe following us," Gwen assured Zoe. "The stable boy says he'll give him some air after we're gone. He's right fond of Brutus."

The last was said with a hint of wariness, and Zoe wondered if Gwen was just a bit jealous of Brutus's affection for the stable boy. Since her marriage, Brutus was another one Zoe felt as though she had neglected a bit. He had saved her life once, and she ought to make more time for him, even though she needed his protection less now. He was a good dog, despite his incessant digging.

Zoe nodded to Gwen, and all the children piled into a carriage with Simone, while Savi, Katy, and Rory boarded Theo's more luxurious carriage. Mary hesitated briefly, glancing between the two, but then made her decision and walked over to Theo's side as well. Zoe could respect the move. She would have been riding with them as well, if Simone hadn't requested her help with the children.

Not only had her aunt had the carriage modified for a smoother ride, along with the ability for the seats to recline should anyone need a rest, but it was also outfitted with a place for food, and two flasks kept permanent company in a special compartment in the wall, in case anyone needed some brandy for fortification. The carriage and its many fine trappings had all been provided for at a generous rate by a very grateful Mr. Chedrose, whose son had been saved from the noose last year by a group effort that loosely included Theo. She was happy to take the discount on services though. Mr. Chedrose was one of the best carriage makers in England.

The village was only half an hour away by carriage. They travelled first through the home farm, which provided produce for the manor—not just for the family, but for all the staff, both inside and out. Several farm hands working in a small field rose from their work, keeping a watchful eye on them as the carriages went by. Zoe thought of the symbiotic relationship with the manor. The goal of the Colevilles, and any noble family lucky enough to own land, should be to be good stewards—to offer jobs for staff, and fair rent for the farmer tenants, and to support the village's tradesmen. Some landowners did this well, and others did not. Zoe wondered where the family she had married into fell in the range. This would be her estate one day, and she wanted to be good in the role.

But she felt very much like a stranger. She was hoping the day in the village might make her feel more of a bond with the people here. Perhaps she just needed to spend a bit of time among them.

Zoe's thoughts turned outward as they approached the village, eventually stopping near the town square. The market was in full swing, and as the drivers pulled away to await their ride home, the rest of the group looked around excitedly.

"Finn and I and Lady Bexley plan on attending the play at the town theatre. It begins at five, so we will make our way there a bit earlier." Rory offered his arm to Aunt Theo as he finished, and Zoe was grateful he was there to support the older woman. Zoe still worried about her aunt, thinking she was doing too much and would have a serious setback. But she had to admit, Theo looked strong again, and frankly exhilarated at the moment.

Katy decided to accompany the theatregoers, and Zoe saw her offer Theo a small vial as they walked, which Theo drank quickly. Katy would also take care of her as well.

That left Mary and her mother with Zoe and the children, aside from Finn. Such a serious little boy, so eager to please Rory by partaking in his love of Shakespeare. He seemed to be finding his footing fine with the other children, but Zoe didn't think she'd ever seen a ten-year-old so determined to impress an adult. She wondered if he felt like he needed to gain their approval in order to be accepted. Or perhaps she was reading too much into nothing, and the boy was just a literary savant.

The three remaining youths hurried to the market stalls. Zoe had passed out a few coins to each to spend on whatever trinkets they chose while she, Mary, and Simone walked more leisurely into the fray of the market.

The local shops each had stalls, the butcher displaying cuts of beef and the grocer with colourful displays of beans, lentils, and spices. Even the bookshop had a small booth, with books visible for those with discerning tastes and an ability to read. Zoe saw Gwen in an earnest discussion with the bookshop woman, who pulled several small books out to show her. Zoe was heartened to see Gwen have such a love for reading, though she was still not completely skilled. But whatever book she purchased, Zoe had no doubt it would be read many times when the skills grew. Walter was entranced by the cutler, who was cheerfully showing the boy a variety of knives for sale. The knife he was inspecting had mother-of-pearl in the handle and a sheath to store it—rather nicer than what he could afford with what Zoe had given him. She wondered if his father had also lined the children's pockets with some spending money. Clever of them to not mention it if they had, cheeky devils.

By the time the whole group had come together as one, the rest had decided to join the theatregoers at the play and so headed for the small theatre. Once arrived, all of them had bought something, and they all gathered around, driven by the human need to show off their new treasures. Aunt Theo brandished a new scarf, purchased from a hawker who had proclaimed it came from the Far East. It certainly was soft as silk, with colours like a swirling oil painting, so perhaps it had. Rory had also visited the cutler and proudly demonstrated the tiny catch that enabled the knife he bought to fold unto itself. All of the children had purchased a variety of baked goods, with crumbs still adorning their faces. Zoe and Mary had been entranced by the potter, who had pieces of varying sizes, beautifully formed, fired, and colourfully painted. Zoe had purchased a small bowl to store her jewellery in at night, and Mary had chosen a colourful vase for fresh flowers.

"Hello, Lady Coleville," said a voice from behind.

Zoe turned to see her maid, Louisa, along with a familiar face, though it took her a moment to recall his name. "Mr. Darrow, what a surprise. Are you here for the market?"

"Indeed," he responded with a smile. "Miss Parsons and some of the other servants who had a few hours of free time during the day thought the weather was quite nice for a stroll through the stalls, and they kindly invited me along."

From the blush creeping up Louisa's neck, Zoe could deduce where the invitation had originated from. She couldn't really hold it against her maid—Darrow was a handsome man, in his own way. There was something familiar about him to her, something in the nose and the set of the eyes that reminded her of someone, but she couldn't quite place it. She supposed he must just have one of those faces.

"Is that so?" Zoe returned his smile. "That's lovely. Are you enjoying it so far?"

"Yes." Darrow glanced around the various vendors. "It's quite a charming affair."

"I suppose this must all seem rather quaint to you, after having spent so many years in London," said Zoe.

"I actually grew up in a village very much like this." Darrow cocked his head at her. "What about you, my lady? Didn't you spend much of your childhood in London?" Zoe must have looked taken aback by this knowledge because he quickly corrected himself. "Your husband mentioned it."

"Of course," said Zoe, brushing past the familiarity which had surprised her. "You're correct, I did spend much of my formative years in London. But I was born on an estate in France. I remember my father taking me to the village for the market and for festivals when I was very young. This reminds me of that."

She wasn't sure why she was sharing details of her childhood with the valet, but then again, why shouldn't she?

"Justin, we should get back to the others," Louisa said. "We don't want them to walk back without us."

"Oh, did you walk here?" It was a stupid question; Louisa had just clearly stated that they had. How else would they have gotten there? "Would you like to take the carriage back to the estate? They can come back for us."

"No, thank you, my lady." Darrow smiled again. "It's too nice of a day not to enjoy."

Zoe nodded. "Very well. A good rest of the afternoon then, to you both."

"And to you as well, my lady," muttered Louisa quietly.

Darrow tipped his cap as he guided Louisa back into the crowd, and Zoe turned her attention back to the people she had come with.

The cheerful group made their way to the theatre and enjoyed the play immensely. The family troupe was small, but the enjoyment of their craft was evident in every line. They were travellers, so the sets were constructed to bend or divide to serve a second or third backdrop, also making them easier to pack up and carry. All in all, it was a delightful performance, and Theo and Rory were especially generous when the hat was passed. The man collecting the money was elderly, balding and still amazingly spry. He paused as the hat made it to Zoe, and cocked his head in a thank you when she threw in some coins.

"Thank you, m'lady," he said happily, and passed the hat to those behind them. He paused a moment to chat. "From Cedarbrook, m'lady?" he asked, his eyes keenly following the hat. "I 'eard tell of the changes yonder."

Zoe was surprised, but nodded. "We are. Word must travel fast for a traveling troupe to be aware of the family here."

The man stepped back as the hat was passed back and took it firmly. "We're from around 'ere, m'lady. We do travel, but these parts be home." His eyes crinkled as he smiled, evidently pleased with the monetary offerings. "We always do well here. Appreciative folk 'round these parts."

"Yes, we have found them to be quite welcoming." That wasn't entirely true, but Zoe wasn't going to tell this stranger that.

He nodded, like he knew it all along. Zoe found his accent difficult to comprehend, but when he slowed his speech down, she could understand. Shifting the conversation, he said, "I know a few geezers at the manor. When we swing back 'round a time or two a year, I always 'ave a pint or two with Mac and Bernie, and we three had a time last night. Got the lowdown, 'oos marrying on and 'oos carrying on, what's what at the big house." He gestured positively to the men already packing up, and Zoe could see the interest from the troupe in the amount of money the man had gathered. The man saw it too, and he spoke more quickly, moving towards the stage, making Zoe strain to keep up.

"Bernie says leave things be, but Evans is in a right flap over the changes. When he was younger he was chuffed just to have a bit of coin, now he struts like it's all owed to him. Anyways, have a good day m'lady." With a final smile the man turned away and Zoe, her mind still translating, turned back to her group.

She had enjoyed the fair and the day out. The weather was perfect and she had her tribe here. But the conversation with the actor simply added to her inner struggle. She did not dislike these people, but she did not feel any tie to them either. She barely understood them, in fact. She felt more of a bond with the new valet than she did the villagers. How could she properly take on a role as mistress of the manor when she still felt so very apart from the people of the land?

Chapter Forty-Four

Quinton had lived a life of relative solitude before the recent events changed everything. He was grateful, he really was, for his dramatic change of circumstance, even though he doubted his own merits at times. But at times he missed the quiet contemplation which came with a more solitary existence.

Evenings had often been him and Oscar sharing the fire, with room for thoughts and time to order them. A decent whiskey, Oscar's purr, and his old chair constituted a peaceful end to any long day. He loved Zoe more than life itself, but life with her was rarely quiet.

Which was why this moment held weight. Most of the rest of the household were off to the festival, while Hugh went off on his errand with Dandridge, and Charlie was god only knew where, but John had stayed back to spend time with Quinton. Although that meant he was not completely alone, since neither man needed to fill space with words, they simply sipped their whiskey and enjoyed the view of the gardens.

Oscar leaped softly into his lap, purring contentedly as she turned in a circle and finally lay down. Quinton felt himself following suit, finally relaxing into the plush chair, feeling the tension in his shoulders ease away.

"I hope I am not disturbing you." Montgomery Coleville suddenly appeared beside his chair, causing Quinton to jump. "Evans said you were here, but I did not realize your friend would also be present."

There was no way to dismiss his uncle without being rude, so Quinton forced himself to lean back again and gestured to the decanter. "Help yourself."

As Montgomery helped himself to a generous pour and seated himself, Quinton wondered what his uncle thought of Quinton's eclectic company. His grandfather had made his dislike clear, but Montgomery had yet to comment. Quinton wasn't sure if that was because he was more tolerant or simply more polite.

As he mused on his thoughts, Quinton noted a tiredness in Montgomery's eyes.

"Don't know if you are aware, but your grandfather is a bit of an arse." Montgomery paused briefly, then giggled, much to Quinton's surprise.

"Well, he's not the most personable man around, I suppose," replied Quinton nonchalantly.

"No, not at all." Montgomery emphasized his statement with a strong hand motion that he evidently miscalculated, slamming his arm down on the table and causing his whiskey to slosh.

Using his extensive powers of deduction, Quinton put together what was happening. He exchanged a glance with John, who was struggling to hide the amusement on his face.

"Not your first drink this afternoon, Montgomery?" Quinton asked as he took a sip of his own beverage.

"Heavens, no, nephew. I have been in with my father discussing family matters. Nothing drives a man to drink like family matters." Montgomery sighed heavily. "Nothing is easy with my father. Have I mentioned he is an arse?"

This time John choked, having taken a long sip of his whiskey at the same time as he laughed. Quinton could not think of a diplomatic reply, so he said nothing. Fortunately, Montgomery happily filled the silence, too far in his cups to be embarrassed by his behaviour. His uncle gave a deep sigh and turned towards him, hiccupping gently. "Speaking of family, I am sorry, Quinton. Was a sorry idea all the way around, but it seemed like a perfect way through."

Quinton said nothing for a long moment, searching fruitlessly for some way to understand what on earth Montgomery was talking about. It was just long enough for the man to let the whiskey keep talking. "Ivy wasn't a fan either, just so you know." Montgomery leaned back and whispered conspiratorially to Quinton, "My daughter is your cousin, you know."

Hearing John laugh out loud, Quinton ignored his friend and drily replied, "I am aware, sir."

Montgomery leaned back, satisfied. "Just wanted to let you know her mother said we should apologize. So I apologize."

Ah, of course. The attempted entrapment. Had they succeeded Quinton would be wed to said cousin, and the inheritance would be intact for his uncle's family. He had not thought of that for months, but apparently his uncle and his wife had not forgotten. And though the man was clearly drunk, Quinton could feel his sincerity. Truthfully, an apology felt good.

He replied equally sincere. "Montgomery, I hold nothing against your family. It was a confusing time for all of us. And things have worked out in the end."

. . .

The older man stared at him briefly, then, to Quinton's horror, sniffed loudly and wiped a tear from his eye. "Thank you, my boy. That means a lot. Ivy refused to even come here, she was so embarrassed. Deborah and the rest of the family are staying at her family's estate for the summer, to avoid being here."

Quinton supposed it should have crossed his mind why Montgomery's family was not in tow when he arrived, but the question hadn't actually occurred to him. Hopefully they could all put this behind them and, if it were up to Quinton, never speak of it again.

Montgomery did seem satisfied with the conversation and leaned back in his chair. After a few moments of silence, Quinton thought the man had drifted off when he spoke again, subject changed.

"The thing is, they are beautiful," he said, as if all three of them had the same amount of context, even though Quinton and John once again had no idea what he was talking about. But Quinton suspected perhaps he had circled back around to the conversation with Philip, the arse himself. "They should be on display for all to see, not hidden away under an old moth-eaten sheet. The old man thinks if he can't see it, it doesn't exist. But they are still here even if she isn't."

It was frustrating trying to continue engaging with a person this drunk, but Quinton was curious. "What exactly are hidden away?"

Montgomery rolled his eyes. "The paintings, obviously. What else could I possibly be talking about?" He slumped back in his chair with a dramatic sighed. "They're beautiful. Bloody shame."

Paintings . . . Quinton had to think for a moment to place the conversation about paintings. The discussion with his grandfather, about Catriona. She was a skilled artist. There were paintings of hers in the attic.

"That's it!" Montgomery leapt to his feet, once again startling Quinton. "The paintings deserve to be seen, even if the old bastard won't display them." He stood for a moment, slightly swaying, and Quinton feared the man might throw up. But the moment passed, and Montgomery started for the door, glass in hand and held in the air as if to toast. "To the attic, men!"

Watching him disappear into the hallway, Quinton stood reluctantly, unsure what to do next. He was too sober to be dealing with someone this drunk.

"Better follow your uncle to the attic, Q, or he'll break his bloody neck getting there." John gestured toward the door but made no effort to come along.

"Oh no." Quinton shook his head. "I'm not going to take this on alone. If I have to explore the depths of the Coleville attic, so do you."

John gave a groan, but he allowed Quinton to lead him out of the room.

"Come on," said Quinton. "Maybe it'll be fun, you don't know."

"Fine, but you owe me one. And we better not happen upon the bloody ghost, or I'll definitely leave you behind to save myself."

"You've followed me into worse places than an attic." Quinton quickened his pace. "You'll be fine."

Montgomery was no longer in sight, but a muffled curse followed shortly by a mild thud made it easy to catch up. His uncle came into sight glaring rather angrily at a small standing bookshelf. The smattering of books on the floor indicated a collision.

"Where did that thing come from?" Montgomery asked no one in particular, speaking to the air around him. Quinton stepped up and took his uncle's arm, guiding him up the stairs, leaving the fallen books to be taken care of another time.

The broad staircase led to the attic, and when the three entered, the sight made Quinton pause. The attic itself spread across the top of the highest floor, with furniture and crates dotting the space. An actual piano was pushed against one wall, and ornate trunks lined another. A small writing desk sat surrounded by crates of books and documents, pushed into an eave, and several other crates were filled with wooden toys and games.

The sight took Quinton aback. Sometimes it still struck a nerve with him just how much stuff and space the wealthy wasted. From John's curled lip and wrinkled nose, Quinton guessed he was thinking something much the same.

Montgomery walked slowly, keeping exaggerated margins around the furniture he passed, apparently remembering the poorly behaved bookshelf. Arriving upright at his destination, he reached down to move a covering sheet, revealing a jumbled pile of rolled canvases.

He selected one and held it aloft. "Behold, men. My sister's work," he said, only hiccupping slightly.

Losing his balance at the sudden movement, Montgomery tripped and nearly toppled over, but Quinton caught his arm in time to steady him.

"Why don't we find you someplace to sit for a moment, uncle?"

Failing to locate a chair within arm's reach, Quinton instead assisted his uncle in making his way to the floor, leaning him up against the wall and taking his now mostly empty glass away from him. Within a few seconds, the man was dozing off, the drink finally catching up with him.

As he straightened up, Quinton gently took the rolled canvas and opened it.

His uncle was right. The painting was not large and could be held easily by an arm's width, but it was remarkable nonetheless. The scene itself was of a moor, sweeping into the distance, dotted with grasses and moss that looked real enough to touch. The sky was cloudy with a hint of colour where the sun fought to shine through. But the magic was in the foreground, where a mist had rolled in. The scene within was still visible, just softer. At the corner of the painting, softened by the mist, was a girl with flame-red hair, looking just barely behind her. She was obscured enough by the mist that Quinton felt drawn to peer closer. Yards away from her, a man was striding through the moors, caught mid-stride, face obscured but still radiating anger.

Quinton found himself caught in the emotion of the painting immediately. He wanted to reach in and grab the girl, saving her before the man could reach her, a man Quinton somehow knew would do her harm.

Beside him he heard John take a sharp breath. "I've seen this before."

"What do you mean?" Quinton turned to him, trying to shake off the eeriness of the portrait. "This painting has clearly rested her for decades."

"Yes, that much I do know, thank you for clarifying." John rolled his eyes and reached down for another canvas.

This one was a similar moor painting, but a different man was behind the red-haired girl. Where the other one evoked fear and anger, Quinton immediately felt safety and love when he looked at this one.

"I mean I've seen this style before. It's unmistakable." John carefully rolled the painting up again before returning it to its place in the pile. "I saw paintings just like this at James Pearson's house."

Chapter Forty-Five

Although Charlie did not fancy himself a tracker in the traditional sense of the word, he did pride himself on being observant. That was one of the ways he had made a success of his own small corner of London. He knew when something was out of order, a doorway propped open or a man who would not meet his eyes. He employed the same skill in the woods and was rewarded when he found a small trail that led from the edge of the woods to the graveside and then to the main road. The path was narrow, so that the undiscerning eye might not even notice it, but Charlie could see where the branches were bent and the plants were trodden. Someone came this way often enough to beat a tiny trail, and Charlie would lay odds in one of his gambling hells that it was the so-called ghost.

Unfortunately there was little else to be learned from the trail once it disappeared at the main road, so Charlie then turned his attention to the staff. Many had already shared their encounters, but this time he asked for more details. While the most common sightings were of her outside in the forest, three of the older maids had also seen the ghost at night in the corridors of the house. This hadn't happened in several years, but they all swore that at one time or another, they'd seen Catriona within the walls of the manor. This intrigued Charlie most of all, because a spectre needed no key or doorway, but a flesh and blood person would. There must be some way this person had gained access to the house.

As Charlie prowled the rooms of the great house seeking clues and mulling this conundrum over in his mind, more memories of his childhood came back to him. Their home in India had been similar, with massive rooms and ornate furnishings. It had just been the four of them most of time—too much space with not enough people to fill it. Charlie had been too young to understand it then, but now looking back he understood that his mother's parents had been unsupportive of her unplanned pregnancy with a British soldier she wasn't even married to. Charlie's father had allowed her to live with him, even having a second child with her, but there had been no official commitment, and their life together must have felt very isolating for Katy.

Despite this, Charlie remembered his mother had been happy. He remembered her laughing, at least. Charlie had been happy too.

Then one day they weren't. But the thought lacked the familiar bitterness that usually accompanied it. For some reason, being here in the country, here in this house, softened his anger.

In the quiet of the mostly vacant house, with only his own thoughts for company, Charlie remembered something else about his father's home in India—secret passages.

As a boy he had stumbled upon them. That house was near the sea, and the passages undoubtedly had been used for smuggling at some time in their history. But Charlie had used them for pranks, or to disappear when his mother ordered him to do chores, or to take Savi on an adventure. He wondered if Cedarbrook held any secrets of its own . . .

Charlie started in the study, setting on the desk the small lantern he'd brought along in case he found what he was looking for. The old man toff had taken himself out for a horseback ride earlier and, if custom held, would not arrive home until near dark, but Charlie didn't want to risk crossing paths with him. Charlie had watched as the toff son met up with Quinton and John, already deep in his cups. They would have their hands full for a while with that one. If his search of the study proved unsuccessful, then he would move on to other rooms.

Charlie walked the length of the full bookcase. It centred on the west wall of the room, taking up at least three quarters of the wall and rising to the ceiling. The books were all dusted, meaning the old man let the maids in the room. Nonetheless, if there was a passageway, there would be a way to find a lever or catch to unlock a door.

Charlie stepped back, going as far as to the opposite wall. The books were grouped by their covers and size, more for looks than use. But . . . there it was. Charlie's eyes alighted on a book with leather covers that was taller than its neighbours, and on the open end, not against the side of the bookshelf as taller books usually were. Charlie walked over and felt the book on each side carefully, finally pulling it toward him. And silently the inner bookshelf swung open.

Pleased with himself, Charlie entered the passage with a satisfied smile, bringing along the small lantern. Closing the bookshelf behind him, he was immediately encompassed in darkness. If it weren't for the lantern, he would have been blind.

The hall ahead was small but easy to traverse, and he found the passage led past the sitting rooms and down to the kitchen area, before finally coming to a stop at a tight door on an outside wall. Charlie turned the handle and pushed hard, and the door swung silently open to the side of the kitchen garden, very near where he had seen the ghost earlier.

Taking a deep breath of country air, Charlie stepped out and shut his hidden passage door, admiring how it fit perfectly into the wall of the house, making it almost invisible. Impressive craftsmanship.

Now he knew how the ghost was gaining entry, but still not

how they knew where the passageways were. It would have to be someone who at least at one point had had regular access to the house. There was one person in particular who he suspected would have both the means and the motive to breach the walls . . .

Chapter Forty-Six

The whiskey was poured and the wine opened as everyone settled in the parlour late that evening. Both Philip and Montgomery had been informed of the gathering, but only Montgomery came. Zoe watched him closely, having been briefly informed by her husband of the man's overindulgence earlier in the afternoon. But he seemed none the worse for wear, probably having slept most of it off, and helped himself to a glass of whiskey without hesitation. Though Theo had wanted to be here as well, the long day had taken a toll on her aunt. And while she was loath to admit it, Theo had agreed that an early night was in store for her, and Katy had followed, a bitter tonic no doubt part of their evening plans.

After those present had settled in, Hugh spoke first. "The magistrate was excellent company yesterday, and I definitely have a broader picture of Ellis Langford. Mr. Dandridge couldn't prove it, but he believes Mr. Langford made a habit of using bits of information about people to his own advantage, and having heard his reasoning, I am inclined to agree."

"Well, that broadens the pool as far as motive goes." Quinton leaned back in his chair, clearly absorbing this information. "Blackmail is not good for one's health."

"Indeed," agreed Hugh. "Some people can only be pushed so far. If Langford tried to push his luck with one of them, it may very well have ended badly for him."

Interesting, but Zoe was more interested the original purpose of their journey. "What about the missing footman?" she asked.

Hugh nodded enthusiastically. "Yes, the footman. It's an odd story, and Dandridge and I agreed it had some holes. According to the aunt and uncle who raised him, this young Maxwell was employed here at Cedarbrook as a footman. But then one day, about the same time as Catriona disappeared, Maxwell went off rather abruptly to London to be an actor."

"Did they hear this from Maxwell himself?" asked Zoe, hoping for more.

"Well, here's where it gets murky." Hugh took a drink from his glass before continuing. "Apparently all this was heard from the lips of his twin brother Mac."

The group quieted at that. Zoe leaned forward. "Have they ever heard from Maxwell again?"

Hugh glared at her. "If you would stop interrupting me, I would get to it. To answer your question, they have gotten a few letters over the years, along with some money on occasion. But Maxwell himself has never resurfaced in person."

Zoe tried to prove her patience by waiting, but Hugh said nothing more.

"Is that all?" she finally asked.

"What do you mean 'is that all,' I thought that was quite a lot," responded Hugh indignantly.

"Well, I didn't want to interrupt you again, but if you are quite finished—"

"Darling." Quinton placed a light hand on her shoulder, and Zoe let it go, though still annoyed.

"How strange." Mary strummed her fingers against the arm of her chair. "So then do we believe it is Maxwell in the grave?"

"It's certainly possible." Hugh shrugged. "It seems unlikely to me that the man would not return home at all in all that time."

"But thirty-eight years is a long time," said Simone softly. "If Maxwell has not been the one sending money and letters, then someone else has been keeping up the ruse. That's quite the commitment on their part."

Zoe considered this. Her mother raised a good point. Only guilt or love would motivate someone to keep up such a pretence for so long.

After a few moments of silence, Quinton gestured toward John. "Why don't you tell us your findings?"

John cleared his throat. "Well, as I've stated, I do believe Catriona made it as far as London, staying with relatives briefly. After that, the trail went cold . . . until Quinton and I discovered something in the attic."

He related the discovery of the paintings in the attic, as well as his belief that there were paintings done in the same style at Mr. Pearson's seaside home.

"He claimed he hardly knew the girl at all," finished John. "But I don't know how else he would come to have so much of her artwork. I couldn't swear to it, but some of the landscapes looked like the seaside there, meaning she must have been painting from the same view."

Zoe absorbed this information, connecting the dots rapidly in her head. "You're saying Catriona and her brother's tutor ran off together?"

"But Mr. Pearson did not leave his post for another year or two," countered Hugh.

"Love is begun by time. And time qualifies the spark and fire of it." The words were said with a smile, but Zoe could see a far-off look in Rory's eyes. She wondered who he was thinking of when he said the words from Hamlet.

"I remain unconvinced," said Montgomery suddenly. Zoe had forgotten he was in the room at all. "I find it hard to believe that Cat has been alive all these years, a few hours' ride from this very spot, and none of her family was aware."

Hard to blame the man for his doubt. It would be a blow if

his sister truly had lived a relatively short distance from their family home and chosen never to contact him.

"Regardless," started Quinton, perhaps also sensing Montgomery's discomfort. "As fascinating as this all is, none of it explains Langford's death, or what happened to Maxwell, if it is indeed him in the grave."

"I see a connection, and it's wrapped in a ghost." This bold statement came from Charlie, who sipped unapologetic on his whiskey with a look that made Zoe think he knew something the rest did not. Sometimes he and Oscar looked more alike than Charlie would like her to point out.

Montgomery groaned. "Not this again. Even if it does exist, which I'm not conceding it does, it proves nothing—except perhaps my point. Catriona has long since been dead."

"Don't be so quick to dismiss that which you can't explain." Mary spoke confidently, and Zoe had to admit there were things about Mary herself she couldn't explain but still believed in.

"She's right." This surprised Zoe, coming from the most grounded woman she knew—her mother. "We are all haunted by some old history, in our own way. Who's to say what form those hauntings might take?"

Charlie stared at Simone for a moment, as if unsure how to proceed. Zoe was equally taken aback. She would not have thought her mother, of all people, would believe in such things. She made a mental note to ask Simone about this more.

After a brief pause, and seeing that no one was coming to his rescue, Charlie continued. "Well, in this case, I believe this ghost's form is more physical than spiritual. I have found how she enters the house and the only place in the woods she stops."

Zoe noted the choice of pronouns for the ghost. The room was quiet as Charlie explained how he found the secret passage and where it led.

"It makes sense as to why I could not find her the day I saw her by the kitchen garden. She must have slipped inside the passage and waited for us to disperse."

Glancing at Montgomery, Zoe wondered if he knew about these passages, but he seemed as surprised as the rest of them.

"What did you mean by where she stops in the woods?" queried Rory.

"The path starts at the game trail at the edge of the West Wood, but it doesn't stick to that larger trail. It takes a detour deeper into the woods." Charlie paused, taking a fortifying sip of whiskey. "The path stops at the grave. There is only one person I can think of who would have reason to visit the burial site and would have prior knowledge of the passages—Catriona."

A silence descended as the group took in the bold assertion. But it made sense. Zoe found herself nodding as she added up the information in her mind.

"It tallies with the necklace being left with the babies," said Simone softly. "If the babes were hers, she would feel compelled to visit them."

"Agreed." Quinton leaned forward, his expression dark. "But this leads us to another possibility. The babes were not alone in the grave, and someone killed the man with them. If Catriona has been alive all this time, that makes her a suspect."

It was a dark thought, but before Zoe could voice her doubts, Rory beat her to it.

"Hold on there, Quinton." Rory spoke smoothly, putting his empty glass aside. "I find it hard to believe a seventeen-year-old girl—who had likely recently given birth—overpowered a strapping lad, snapping his neck, then dug a deep grave, moved the lad's dead body to the gravesite, and buried them all without any help."

"He's right. We don't know what happened." Zoe wondered why she was so quick to defend a woman she had never met. Maybe because the lady was not here to defend herself.

"Fair points, but even if she didn't kill him herself, it can't be a coincidence that all three were buried at the same time," countered Quinton. "She must know what happened, at the very least."

True, but Zoe's mind had already turned elsewhere. She looked over at Charlie. "You said this connected to Langford's death as well? How so?"

"Well, it seems likely at this point that Langford made a habit of blackmailing people." Charlie tapped his fingers against his nearly empty glass. "We know he was around during the time in question. Perhaps he decided to play his biggest card yet, hoping to cash out before he left for good, but underestimated what the killer would do to keep his secret."

Another silence draped the room, and Montgomery stood, as if suddenly filled with violent energy. "All this surmising is good, but it has a limit. If you are right, then there is one person at least who can tell us for sure what happened." He turned to Quinton. "If Catriona is alive, then she has all the answers we need. Tomorrow we go to Hartlemond."

Chapter Forty-Seven

Quinton leaned back in the most comfortable chair in the manor and let his mind replay the nights events. Everyone else had retreated to bed, even Zoe, exhaustion showing in her blue eyes. But Quinton knew with the day ahead to think about, sleep would elude him.

This particular chair was oversized, which fit his frame perfectly, and resided in a small room on the same floor as the family bedrooms. Small by manor standards, that is. The room still had space for several other chairs and a desk, as well as a wall of bookshelves and some small tables. Quinton had found the room while exploring and suspected it had been used by some past member of the household as a study. He had started to come here for a solitary moment when he could, and had begun to think of it as his own oasis of quiet.

As if to counter that thought, the closed door swung silently open and John and Charlie sauntered in without knocking. Charlie was carrying an unopened bottle of whiskey and John had three clean glasses. Without apology or explanation the two pulled up chairs on either side of Quinton, and Charlie poured them each a finger of whiskey, handing out glasses.

To Quinton's surprise, Charlie raised his in a toast. "To family that is lost, and family that is found."

John and Quinton clinked their glasses, and Quinton suddenly felt completely at ease, reminiscent of the many nights the three men had spent in his rented rooms, sharing cheap whiskey and each other's secrets.

Except this was definitely not cheap whiskey. Quinton nodded to the bottle. "Heaven help us. You found the wine cellar."

Charlie shrugged. "Don't tell the bloody Scot but I hid the last two bottles of our brew. We are in the land of plenty and we should enjoy it." He paused and took an appreciative sip.

"He's right, Q. This is nectar," John interjected.

Quinton nodded. "It should be. It's been aged twenty years."

"Perfect," replied Charlie without a pause.

All three men let a comfortable silence stretch for several minutes. Then John asked quietly, "How are you really, Q?"

Quinton took a deep breath, suddenly grateful for old friends. "Honestly, I'm not sure. Besides having found myself in a mind-boggling change of circumstance, tomorrow I might meet a woman who was my dead father's best friend, missing for decades. It's overwhelming." He paused and his friends let him search for words. "Besides which, this mystery was buried in the deepest hole my career as an agent has ever seen, and I deeply enjoyed digging it out. I fear the act of unearthing has given me more purpose and meaning than my newfound wealth or position ever will. What am I without the dig? Perhaps I am an agent, not a noble." Quinton looked at the whiskey in his hands, then finished it in a single shot.

Charlie's voice was surprisingly quiet. "I think you can, in a way, be both. You weren't raised to spend idle days in luxury."

John continued Charlie's thought. "I think it's the same with all of us. We all came here looking forward to relaxation and being waited on. But at the first opportunity, we all immersed ourselves in what amounts to work. But work that we enjoy. Work with a purpose." He drained his own glass and looked around for the bottle. "Even Savi found a way to use her skills, and even I see that purpose makes her happy."

Charlie refilled all three glasses as he spoke. "All of us came from the streets. We have fought our way to where we are, every one of us. There is a place for a step back, but truthfully Q, it's part of who we are at this point."

Quinton looked at each of his friends, brothers really, and felt a peace come over him. These men had seen him at practically every stage of his life and could see what kind of a man he had become. Their belief in him steadied him.

He leaned back again in his chair realizing he was finally finding his own way, a way he could not only live with but be proud of. He felt Charlie stir next to him.

"But seriously, this bottle was on the sideboard in the sitting room. Where's the wine cellar? "

Chapter Forty-Eight

He hadn't realized it at the time, but Quinton's mother had spent the short time she had with him preparing him to take his place one day among society. As an actress, she'd rubbed shoulders with all sorts of people, and in the business of theatre, one could find someone to teach just about anything. As a result, Quinton could dance with proficiency, speak the King's English well, understand which fork to use for what, and—most importantly at this moment—ride a horse.

His experience had been limited, but it was enough of a start that the horses of the manor held no fear for Quinton. But that was not the same as being an exceptionally skilled rider, and Quinton was beginning to understand this as his spirited beast danced around in a circle, very nearly unseating him.

Taking a tighter hold on the reins, Quinton guided his mount back beside his uncle. Montgomery raised an eyebrow. He looked completely natural and at ease on the back of his horse, Quinton noted with irritation.

"Feel the beast, Quinton," advised Montgomery. "You have a seat like a load of bricks. Lean into the saddle and feel the gait."

Squashing his annoyance, Quinton tried to apply the advice. It did help to lean forward, and Quinton relaxed slightly. Feeling the beast might take some time, but right now he was pleased to remain upright.

Glancing over at his companion, Quinton tried to gauge the mood of his uncle. The older man had a determined set to his jaw and a faraway look in his eyes. When they'd made plans to make the journey the previous night, Montgomery had been eager to speak with his long-lost older sister. But apparently a night spent thinking about it had dampened some of that enthusiasm. Now he seemed less eager and more resolved—much like how Quinton felt about riding this horse.

The ride took three hours, and by the time the seaside village came into view Quinton was quite certain he would not be able to sit down for a week. Wincing as he dismounted, a similar thought arose about standing. He stamped his feet into the ground, trying to force feeling back into the limbs.

Montgomery dismounted fluidly, without a single pang of discomfort as far as Quinton could see. Considering his uncle was a full decade older than Quinton, this was as impressive as it was irritating.

They walked their horses without haste toward the festive home by the sea. Quinton understood what John had meant in describing it as happy. The colourful porch, striped chairs, and haphazard collection of seashells gave the distinct impression of joy.

In response to the knock on the door, a still-handsome man in that land between middle-aged and elderly answered. His eyes widened as he caught sight of Quinton. "Oh," he said with a sharp exhale.

Montgomery glanced between the two men. "Good morning. I am Montgomery Coleville and this is—"

"I know," interrupted the man. "I know who he is. No one who knew Graham could doubt it." He paused briefly, then without words stood aside and extended his arm to the inside.

Once they had entered, he extended a hand toward Quinton. "I am Mr. James Pearson, but I suspect you already know that."

Intellectually, Quinton had known that Pearson knew his father, but it had not crossed Quinton's mind that an emotional connection might have been forged as well. But looking at the expression on Pearson's face, it dawned on Quinton that the man had spent years as his father's tutor. Seeing Quinton now must be quite a shock.

Taking the extended hand, Quinton smiled. "Yes, Mr. Pearson. It's a pleasure to meet you."

"Even the voice . . ." Pearson shook his head. "I apologize, but the resemblance is uncanny. I was very fond of your father. I'm sorry you weren't able to get to know him yourself."

A simple sentiment, but Quinton found himself touched at the man's genuineness. "As am I," he responded.

Standing to the side, Montgomery cleared his throat, and Quinton suddenly remembered his uncle was here too.

Pearson seemed to have the same realization. He extended his hand to Montgomery as well, with a respectful incline of his head.

"Please, sit, gentlemen." He gestured toward the chairs in the living area.

He followed Pearson into the room, but instead of sitting down, Quinton found himself drawn to the paintings John had described. He stood in front of the wall of art, these framed cleverly with driftwood. John was right—there was no mistaking it was the same artist. The emotion of the pictures was as strong as the rolled canvasses in the Coleville attic.

"She knew you would come," Mr. Pearson said, breaking Quinton's connection with the art.

Quinton turned to see the older man studying him carefully. He wondered if Pearson was seeing him or his father standing there.

"Catriona?" he asked, even though Quinton was fairly sure of the answer.

"Yes." He said the word in a matter-of-fact manner. "After the other two came around asking questions, Cat knew it was just a matter of time before you figured it out."

"Is she here?" Montgomery leaned forward, an intensity in his eyes.

"Something you will learn about Cat is that she does things in her own time, and in her own way," responded Pearson, avoiding answering the question directly.

"Then she does want to meet me—us?" Quinton asked.

Pearson appeared surprised at the question. "Of course. But I'm afraid that won't be today. I am sorry you gentlemen have wasted your journey."

The statement was said with a finality that told Quinton the topic was not open to discussion or debate. Disappointment well up inside him, but Quinton quickly dismissed it. He couldn't force his aunt to speak with him.

Montgomery apparently didn't pick up Pearson's meaning. "I understand, but there's actually a few questions I would like to ask her—"

"I'm sorry, Lord Coleville." Pearson turned his gazed toward him, his tone mild but unyielding. "But you will not be able to speak to her today."

Blinking, Montgomery seemed taken aback by Pearson's unwillingness to give in. Quinton suspected not many people had told the lord no in his life. Where disappointment was common place for Quinton, for Montgomery it must be a new sensation.

"We didn't mean to intrude," said Quinton smoothly. "We would be happy to come back at another time, or she would of course be welcome at Cedarbrook at any time."

"I think she would argue that sentiment." Quinton didn't know if he had ever seen a man speak so mildly while at the same time be so firm. It was quite a skill.

"I realize it has been some time since she was invited inside the boundaries of Cedarbrook," Quinton acknowledged. "But she is welcome now."

Mr. Pearson cocked his head, his gaze once again studious, then arose and ambled to a sideboard with an array of bottles and glasses. "Whiskey or brandy?"

TAYLOR PREISLER & SANDRA PREISLER

Glancing back as they answered in favour of whiskey, he poured a generous amount in each glass, then handed them back to Quinton and Montgomery.

As he settled in, Quinton shifted the conversation. "Would you at least tell us your part of the story?"

Pearson considered this. "I will tell you what I can. But Cat's part in it is her own. I'm sure she will tell you herself when she is ready."

Quinton leaned back, intrigued by what the former tutor would have to say.

"I told the magistrate and his companion the truth, at least in part," Pearson started after taking a sip of whiskey. "During my time in the Coleville employ, mine and Cat's paths rarely crossed, and we spoke only in passing. She was much younger than I, still a child then, absorbed in her own dramas and imaginings, and my time was taken up with my student. Graham was such a pleasure to teach and I found the work very rewarding. Then one day something happened and everything changed . . ." Pearson paused, gazing off into the middle distance as if lost in some memory. After a moment he shook himself and continued. "The reasons and details of her departure are Cat's to tell, but I will say I was the one who took her to the coaching inn, at Graham's request."

"And you didn't say anything to my father about it?" asked Montgomery.

"They both asked me not to, and the circumstances were such that I agreed with them."

Pearson paused again, taking another drink of his whiskey. Quinton followed suit, wishing very much that Catriona was there to fill in the blanks that Pearson clearly would not.

After a moment, Pearson cleared his throat. "After Cat was settled with her cousin in London, Graham asked me to stop in and deliver a letter He didn't wish to use the messengers, for fear of his father finding him out, and I had family in London which I visited a few times a year, so it wasn't a great burden for me. When

I stopped in, I found her quite despondent. The events leading up to her leaving had taken a heavy toll, and seeing as I was a person already privy to the details, she felt safe to share her private griefs with me. We spoke at length and then I took a letter from her back to Graham." Pearson shook his head. "I honestly thought that would be the end of it, but I couldn't get the girl out of my mind. As much as I enjoyed my work, the life of a tutor is isolating, and I realized I was quite lonely."

"I stopped in again the next time I was in London, and found she had moved to a boarding house, not wishing to embroil her cousin in any scandal." Pearson snorted in dark amusement. "Turns out they didn't need her help anyway, but that's beside the point. I began calling on Cat at the boarding house whenever I was in London, just to check in on her and to pass letters between the siblings. Cat and I became friends out of necessity at first—a light in the darkness of mutual loneliness, if you will— just someone to talk to about the trials of life who already knew all the history leading up to it, and then eventually, after a few years, it turned into . . . something else." Gesturing around the room, Pearson smiled. "And the rest I'm sure you can infer."

Montgomery sighed, running his fingers through his hair. "I am pleased she was able to build a life, but I am just sorry she never came back. As difficult as my father is, whatever it is that happened, I'm sure they could have worked it out eventually."

Pearson gave him a hard look but said nothing to this. Quinton watched the exchange, wondering what else Pearson was leaving out of his story. He supposed he would have to wait to find out.

"Graham remained a part of your lives?" asked Quinton instead.

"Yes, as well as her mother's parents, for as long as they were with us." Pearson took a long look at Quinton. "We actually met you once, when you were a baby, as well as your mother."

That, Quinton hadn't expected. "Oh," he said, simply.

"Yes. When Graham died, Cat stayed in touch with your

mother. But then when she died . . ." Pearson glanced away. "I'm afraid by the time she got to London, you were already gone. Cat did look, but she couldn't find you. It always tore her up, thinking Graham's son was out there somewhere. You should have seen how happy she was when she heard you were found and coming to Cedarbrook."

Quinton swallowed a lump in his throat, strangely affected by the idea that his aunt had cared so much.

"How did you end up here?" Montgomery was once again not reading the emotion of the room correctly, but Quinton was grateful for the change of topic.

Pearson turned to him. "Well, we were wed after Graham went to boarding school and I was let go from the earl's employ. After that, we knew we didn't want to stay in London. I had a few cousins in this area and I knew she wanted to be close to her . . . regardless, my cousin wrote, saying there was an opening for a teacher at a school in the village."

The man rose, moving easily, and looked out the large front window, the sea in full view. "We arrived at sunset, and Catriona was immediately enchanted. She found peace here, at least as much as she could, continuing to paint and learning how to be a healer of sorts. She found purpose in helping those around us."

Mr. Pearson remained standing in silence for several minutes, long enough that Quinton wondered if it was their invitation to leave. But then the older man ambled easily to the wide window sills, with pencil drawings and shells vying for space. He chose a drawing and handed it to Montgomery.

"Your brother," he said simply.

Montgomery stared hard at the picture, and Quinton saw the emotion well up. After a few moments, Montgomery blinked and handed the drawing to Quinton.

The picture showed his father Graham with his head thrown back just a bit in laughter, but he was young, still just a boy, and next to him was girl with fire-red hair, a smile on her face. Catriona.

"I would very much like to meet her," Montgomery said, his voice thick with emotion.

Pearson smiled sympathetically. "I assure you, you will get the chance."

"Thank you for telling us your story, as well as allowing us to peer into your lives just a bit." Quinton set the paper down on the table. "I don't suppose there's any chance you'll expound on Catriona and her hauntings?"

Pearson's eyes shone with amusement. "No, I'm afraid that is still Cat's tale to tell."

Quinton nodded and finished his whiskey. He sensed they had reached the end of the discussion. He stood up, and Montgomery followed suit. Pearson nodded and made his way to the door, opening it up for them.

As Quinton walked through the threshold, he paused and met Mr. Pearson's eyes. "This family has made many mistakes. There is no denying that. But it is a new day and a new way in the family now. When she is ready, I would welcome the chance to introduce my own family. The choice is hers."

The older man nodded, and Montgomery paused as well. "My father has a great deal to answer for, but I, too, have a family I welcome her into. Please let her know."

"I will."

As Quinton walked back to his horse, already dreading the long ride back, he reflected on the conversation they'd just had. Of everything he had learned, the thing that stuck out the most was the life Catriona had managed to build, despite her sorrows. She had found love and happiness and a purpose, and Quinton couldn't help but admire her tenacity. He hoped one day he would have the opportunity to tell her in person.

Chapter Forty-Nine

The early afternoon sun streamed in the parlour windows, making the room warmer than most preferred. Mary pulled a chair out of the stream of sunlight, but across from her Zoe did the opposite, pulling her chair into the square of sun. Just like a cat, that one.

Mary sipped from her glass of whiskey, pleased that Zoe had arranged the day so they would spend it together and do some sorely needed catching up. Savita, Katy, Theo, and Simone were all taking a turn about the garden, while Charlie, John, and Rory had taken the afternoon to do "research" into their budding distillery business. And Quinton and Montgomery were off to find Catriona. Mary had seen that Zoe wanted to go, but she had instead opted to stay behind with her friend.

"Your hair looks . . . rebellious," Mary started.

Zoe laughed. "I agree. The rebellion is in full swing. Camille had a better hand with my curls, but they confound Louisa. She is learning."

"I'm sure she will get better with experience." Mary took another sip. "Have you heard from Camille at all?"

"Yes." Zoe nodded. "She wrote not long ago. The baby is

faring well, and Camille is enjoying her new occupation at the apothecary."

"Good, I am glad to hear it."

"How are your parents faring?" Zoe asked, changing the subject, eyes closed as she basked in the rays of the sun.

"They are well. Four of my sisters are in service now, so their money worries are considerably less." Mary leaned back as well and mentioned casually, "They suggested I move home, now that you have married."

Zoe's eyes flew open and she laughed out loud. "Whatever did you say?"

"I did not say that hell itself would freeze over before I moved home to share a room with two sisters and be constantly berated by my mother." Mary sighed. "They have a point, though. You hardly need a companion any more now that you are a wife."

Zoe sat upright and glared at Mary. "No, but I need my friend, Mary. I need you." She leaned towards Mary and continued more softly. "I know everything has been at sixes and sevens since you arrived. But you are still my dearest friend, even if I haven't been much of one lately."

Mary laughed. "I know you are lost without me. Who wouldn't be?" She took a sip of the whiskey. "But you must admit, it is a poor friend who must be paid for her friendship. I cannot continue to live in your parents' home as a hanger-on, contributing nothing. I will need to find own my way."

"I would never call you a hanger-on." Zoe shook her head. "But I do understand the need to adapt to change. It has not been easy for me either."

Saying nothing, Mary waited for her friend to elaborate. She didn't have to wait long—Zoe was never a patient one.

"The coming years filled with my responsibilities as a wife and eventually a mother have begun to loom in my mind. It's not that I don't love Quinton—I do, but the reality of it all is sinking in. And speaking of mothers, mine keeps telling me that the job of running the domestic part of the estate, tallying expenditures and ordering wine and hiring servants, will fall to me. She tells me I will have plenty to occupy my ever-wandering mind."

That made Mary laugh again. "You need a puzzle, not an accounting book."

Zoe laughed as well. "Perhaps we should put our heads together on this puzzle of Langford and the bones. We have always been good at working through these things, just the two of us."

Raising her glass in a mock toast, Mary nodded. "A splendid idea."

Dashing over to retrieve one of her artist's pencils and a piece of embossed stationary, Zoe quickly returned to her seat. "It seems to me there are three different deaths here, grouping the babies as one."

She drew three wide columns on the paper and headed the first with *Mr. Langford*, the second with *Man/Maxwell?* and the third with *Babies*. Then Zoe wrote *Catriona's necklace* under the *Babies* heading.

"The necklace is significant," mused Zoe. "The poor babes must have been hers, though how she hid the pregnancy for so long I do not know."

"A woman will do extraordinary things to survive," replied Mary. "Rory said the babies were most likely stillborn, right?"

"Yes. He saw no injury to the babies themselves, but it is possible Cat suffered a blow that sent her into an early birth. There's no way to know without Catriona herself telling us what happened."

Zoe wrote *stillborn* and *foul play?* under the 'Babies' column.

"We know a bit about the *Man* column." Mary cocked her head, thinking back. "Hugh said this Maxwell fellow ran off to London, but the story sounded full of holes, right?"

"That's right." Zoe wrote down *London (dodgy)*. "His brother was the one who told his aunt and uncle that."

"We really ought to track him down. See if he came up with that story if or it was told to him by someone else."

"True," affirmed Zoe as she added *brother (liar?)*. "What was his name? Mac? There's something familiar about that, but I can't place where I heard it before."

Something occurred to Mary. "But when Quinton asked the earl about it, didn't the old man say Maxwell resigned in person, days after Catriona ran away? That doesn't track with him being dead before she left."

"No, it doesn't." Zoe tapped the pencil against her paper. "So where does that leave us?"

Just then a knock came at the door and one of the footmen entered.

"Pardon me, my lady, but Mrs. Foster wished to know if you'd like fish pie for luncheon?"

"Yes, that will be fine," responded Zoe.

As the man retreated, Mary shook her head. "I still for the life of me cannot always tell those two apart—not unless they're standing right next to each other."

"I know. Montgomery was telling me they're cousins, but they could be twins as far as I'm concerned." Zoe paused and met Mary's eyes, and Mary knew they had just had the same thought. "Maxwell's brother was a twin, was he not?"

"Yes." Mary's mind raced. "So maybe it wasn't Maxwell at all that resigned."

Zoe nodded and wrote down *twin* and then a line connecting it to *resigned?*

Both women were quiet a moment, thinking on this possibility.

"Alright, what about Langford?" asked Zoe, not one to sit in silence too long.

"Put *blackmailer*." Mary's nose wrinkled. "Loathsome man."

"Indeed." Zoe wrote it down. "I wonder what he knew that got him killed."

"It might be about the dead man and the babies, but then, it could be a coincidence," said Mary with a shrug. "Too bad we can't ask old Mac about it. I suppose we'll have to go back to the farm and ask the aunt and uncle what his current address is."

Zoe sat bolt upright, her face suddenly white as a sheet.

"What?" asked Mary with concern.

"I just remembered where I heard that name." Zoe met her gaze. "It was at the market. One of the troupe called Evans 'Mac.' His first name is Malcolm. I'd forgotten that."

Mary's blood ran cold. "So that would make Evans Maxwell's brother?"

"It's too large of a coincidence to be just a coincidence, don't you agree?"

"Yes." Mary nodded slowly. "He's the right age. Charlie said he started as a footman. It can't be a coincidence."

Putting the pencil and paper aside, Zoe leaned forward. "Agreed. I never liked him from the start. I hated him sowing doubts in Quinton's mind as to his motive for the investigation. Now I wonder if he wasn't just being subordinate but was actually trying to stymie the investigation."

"Charlie said Evans accompanied him to the ruins after the murder of Mr. Langsford. Charlie didn't find it all that odd, but why would a butler do that? Or really any servant, follow after a guest of the manor?" Mary added, her excitement building.

"Yes, you're correct, that is odd." Zoe suddenly shook her head. "But on the other hand, to kill one's twin . . . that is an act of pure evil. It would be like cutting out a piece of your own soul. I don't like the man, but I don't know if Evans is capable of that."

"I'm not so sure." Mary took a long sip of her whiskey. "I don't have a twin, I'll grant you, but I've come to actual blows more than once with my oldest sister. No one gets under your skin like a sibling." Mary absentmindedly rubbed her upper arm. "But as you said, it might have been an accident, a heated discussion that just went too far. Perhaps even it was Maxwell who was the instigator."

Zoe nodded. "That is true. But whatever happened, we need to ask 'Mac' about it. That dirty rotter has been holding out on us, and there's no good reason to do that unless he is keeping one hell of a secret."

"I agree." Mary thought of the dead blackmailer. "Though I don't know if this helps us with Langford's murder. If Langford knew all these years what Evans had done, that's a long time to bide one's time."

"It is." Zoe refilled their glasses. "But we know Langford was cleverer than we gave him credit for. This isn't your run-of-the-mill affair or guilty indulgence. If he happened upon this knowledge, one way or another, Langford would have to know this was winning card to play. He must have saved it until he felt he needed it, when he resigned."

Mary could picture their hypothetical scene playing out. "And then Evans decides the price was too high, or that he can't risk Langford continuing to know for any price."

Nodding, Zoe returned to her note-taking, writing *Evans?* in the *Man* column. She paused a moment, then wrote *Mac* beneath.

Both women leaned back and took identical long sips of whiskey.

"Of course, none of this proves anything," said Zoe with a sigh. "It's a story that fits, but it is still just a story."

She wasn't wrong. After all these years, there was no way to know for certain what happened that day unless one of the parties involved chose to reveal that information. It seemed unlikely to her that Evans would choose to do so, but Catriona on the other hand . . .

Mary stilled. "Cat knows what happened back then."

"Yes." Zoe met her eyes, once again understanding dawning in expression. "If you had committed a terrible crime and only one other person was actually there when it happened, you might want to make sure that person was still going to remain silent."

"Does Evans know where Quinton and Montgomery went this morning?"

"I don't know. They left quite early."

Mary was quiet for a full minute, thinking. "We can't let him leave," she said finally.

"We don't have proof," pointed out Zoe.

"I know, but we can't risk it," said Mary emphatically. "If he puts the pieces together, he'll try to silence Catriona and anyone else she may have told."

That did it. The idea of Quinton's life being risked was enough to bring Zoe around. "Very well. If we're wrong, we'll make it up to him. But what can we do to stop him from leaving?"

"Maybe we could get the key from Mrs. Fox and lock him in his office."

Biting her lower lip as she considered it, Zoe shook her head. "Won't he have his own key?"

"Well, yes, I suppose." Blasted Zoe and her logic. "Can't one of us go down there and surreptitiously just slip them off the hook before he notices?"

"I mean, maybe. But the two of us would draw too much attention." Zoe paused, as if an idea had just occurred to her. "But I can think of someone who wouldn't."

Chapter Fifty

"Y̶ou want me to do what?"

Zoe sighed. She'd expected Darrow to be confused, but she wasn't sure how else to explain it to him.

"We just need you to go downstairs and take Mr. Evans's keys off the hook in his office. Quietly. Without him noticing."

"Oh is that all?"

The tone was sarcastic, but Zoe let it slide given the circumstances. She knew it was an unusual ask, but she didn't know who else to enlist. Louisa was too nervous of a creature to put the burden on, and she didn't have a relationship with any of the household servants. Mary had suggested the new land steward, but he had no more business being downstairs than they did. Mrs. Fox might be talked into giving up her key, but Zoe doubted she would do it if she knew what the purpose was. So that left Darrow.

"Darrow, we're wasting time," snapped Mary. "Are you willing or not?"

"And you won't tell me why you need me to take the keys?" he pressed.

"Not yet." Zoe suppressed another sigh. "But it is important, I assure you."

There was a long pause while he considered it.

"If he catches me, do I lose my job?" he finally asked. "I've never found it beneficial to anger the butler of the house I'm working in."

"You work for my husband, not Mr. Evans," Zoe retorted. "So will you do it?"

Darrow let out a slow breath. "Fine. I suppose Lady Dovefield did warn me."

"What's that?"

"Nothing." Darrow held up a hand. "Wait here. I'll return shortly."

With that he turned on his heel and stalked out of the parlour.

Zoe turned to Mary. "Well, that went better than expected."

As the minutes ticked by Zoe began to pace, her nervous energy needing somewhere to go. Perhaps nervous wasn't quite the right word. Her body felt . . . alight, but at a certain point fear and nervousness and excitement and anticipation all blended together, and all she really knew was that she felt completely alive and wound as tight as Quinton's pocket watch.

"You're going to wear a hole in the rug if you keep that up," said Mary nonchalantly.

"How can you be so calm," asked Zoe as she collapsed back into the sofa.

Mary shrugged. "He'll either come through or he won't. Worrying about it won't change anything."

Zoe wasn't sure when Mary had become so calm and collected. Or maybe she always had been. Zoe couldn't quite remember.

Just then the door opened and Darrow stepped inside. Zoe leapt back up to her feet.

"Well?" she asked, unable to wait for him to speak.

He held up his left hand, showing off the ring of iron keys which jingled with the movement. "I got them."

"Fantastic." Zoe clasped her hands together. "What of Mr. Evans? Did you see him at all?"

"No." Darrow lowered his hand. "That's the unfortunate news. I don't know what your game is, but Mrs. Fox told me Mr. Evans hasn't been seen in about an hour. She didn't know where he might have gone."

Zoe cursed, not as under her breath as a lady should.

"Do you think he heard Quinton and company were going to see Catriona?" asked Mary.

Darrow frowned at that. "What's this?"

"I'll explain later." Zoe waved a distracted hand as she thought of what to do next. Evans's absence might be unrelated to her husband's errand. But the risk was too great to assume. After a moment, she muttered, "I just don't see any choice."

Turning to Mary, she continued, "You and I will have to give chase. If the worst is true, he is headed to Hartlemond. Perhaps if we go quickly, we can catch him before he does harm."

"Are you mad?" Mary stared at Zoe in astonishment. "What would we do if we did catch up with him? Overpower him, just the two of us? Hope he isn't armed in some way? And besides all that, I can't even ride a horse."

Watching the exchange, Darrow broke in. "Pardon my forth-rightness, my lady, but what do you suspect the man of doing to justify your inclination to pursue him?"

"It is no concern of yours," snapped Zoe, annoyed at Mary's logical arguments against her plan.

"Considering you have already involved me in whatever this is and have no plan aside from foolhardiness, I would say it very much is my concern now."

Zoe started at his forthrightness. The servants she had grown up with would never speak to any of the nobles of a house in such a manor. To offer any criticism of their employers would be grounds for dismissal, and this man had barely gotten his feet wet in his job.

"You are impertinent, sir," she said sharply.

A smile tugged at Darrow's lips. "I can offer little defence to your assertion, my lady, but for now, I also seem to be the only able-bodied man in sight who could help you in this quest."

"He's right." Zoe glared at Mary, annoyed at her betrayal, but Mary didn't meet her eyes, still speaking, "We need him, and we have no time to waste on arguments over manners."

Zoe let out a long, deep breath, but once again she could not fault Mary's logic. "Fine." Zoe snatched the paper off the table and handed it to Darrow. She gave him the abridged version of events, not wanting to waste any more time on this.

When she finished, he nodded slowly, still staring down at their careful scribbling. "Downstairs has been abuzz with gossip about this. The staff have been speaking of little else besides the discovery of graves—which held between two and eight bodies, depending who you ask—and the death of a land steward, who most believe died by his own hand. I honestly thought most of it was fabricated or exaggerated."

"I know it's a wild tale, but it's true." Mary glanced at the door, as if afraid someone might be listening. "We believe 'Mac' to be Malcolm Evans, and if he thinks Catriona will expose whatever happened all those years ago, he could very well mean her harm. That's why we need to go—now."

Darrow nodded again, setting the paper down and running his fingers through his hair. A notion—a semblance of a thought floating right on the edge of her field of understanding—occurred to Zoe, but she didn't know what it meant. She pushed it aside, needing to deal with the here and now.

"Very well." Darrow met her gaze, his brown eyes dark with an emotion Zoe couldn't identify. "We should get to the stables."

Realization crystallized in Zoe's mind, and she gave a soft gasp as the muddy connection her mind had been grasping at suddenly became clear.

If she was right, it would explain a great deal about this impertinent so-called valet.

Chapter Fifty-One

As Zoe, Mary, and Darrow hurried down the flagstone path to the stables, Zoe forced herself to concentrate on the present. There would be time to sort the rest out later . . . at least, she hoped there would.

"I meant what I said, Zoe." Mary glanced over at her. "I'm not a skilled enough rider to manage the pace you will need to keep."

"I understand." Zoe's mind raced. "Take the carriage to the village and find John, if you can, or my father. We need the magistrate, and they'll know how to find him. Tell them where we're headed and to meet us there."

Mary nodded, her expression serious. "Very well."

"And you are certain your skills are up to the task, my lady?" asked Darrow, not slowing his pace. "If what you've said is true, speed will be crucial, and we can't afford delays."

Zoe's blood boiled—yes, there was only one explanation for this man's ability to get under her skin. "There is no need to concern yourself with my skills, Mr. Darrow. You need only make sure to keep up with me."

Darrow raised an eyebrow but refrained from further comment on the matter.

Glancing at the sun, already moving lower into the sky, Zoe

growled. "How far is Hartlemond? Three hours? Blast it, we're going to have to have to push the horses flat out."

"I know a path through the woods that is a considerable shortcut," offered Darrow. "I think we can beat him there, if he's taken the main road."

"You know a shortcut to Hartlemond, specifically?" Mary's eyes narrow. "That's awfully coincidental."

Darrow opened his mouth, but then shut it again. He met Zoe's eyes, and she knew she was right.

"He is trustworthy," Zoe said before Mary could say more. "I will explain later."

When they reached the stables, Zoe called for the stable boy.

As they waited, a cheerful voice greeted them in French. *"Bonjour! Comment allez-vous tous?"*

Looking in the direction of the voice, Zoe saw the new land steward, in the process of hitching a bay horse to a cart. The beast shook his head and whinnied, obviously unimpressed with the direction his day was taking.

Tying the horse's reins to a post, Mr. Baptise smiled and walked over to the group. "He is not impressed to be a cart horse for a day, but I have need of a strong *cheval* for my work."

Mary glanced from Zoe to Baptise and back again. "Faster than getting the carriage hooked up. From my lips to God's ear. I'll take it from here."

Mr. Baptise looked confused as Mary took his arm and guided him back to the cart. As Mary pointed toward the village, speaking in a low voice, Baptise nodded. Zoe believed her friend was in good hands, so she turned back to her own transportation.

Darrow was assisting the stable boy in saddling two horses. Despite her London upbringing, Zoe had attended a prestigious riding school through much of her youth, and she considered herself a good judge of horseflesh. Darrow had chosen well, both beasts built for speed and endurance, not show.

He turned to Zoe as he tightened the girth. "At the continued risk of sounding impertinent, I chose an astride style saddle for you. Your attire should allow it, and we'll be able to make better time than if you ride aside."

Her present attire would indeed accommodate his suggestion. Zoe was far more experienced riding side saddle, but she understood the mechanics enough to ride astride. It was a good suggestion.

"Very well."

Zoe stepped up onto the mounting block, then threw her leg over the back of the horse, mounting it in one fluid movement. It was most definitely not a ladylike position, but social niceties had never been Zoe's strong suit anyways.

Mounting from the ground, Darrow quickly turned his horse toward the woods, carefully following a path that branched off the game trail.

As their pace quickened into a fast trot and then a gallop, Zoe turned her thoughts to the road ahead. She fervently hoped they were not too late, both for her sake and for Darrow's.

Chapter Fifty-Two

The sunlight was beginning to wane as Quinton rode down the trail, the light streaming through the tree branches and leaves casting a low dappled pattern across the ground. He was tempted to put his jacket back on, which currently laid across his lap. He'd taken it off when Montgomery had gone off on his own, the warm summer air making the constricting fabric feel unbearable, but now the warm air was cooling down enough that he was comfortable, if not slightly chilled. Still, he wanted to enjoy the lack of constraint while he could.

Quinton had planned on his uncle accompanying him on his journey back to the estate, but after leaving the seaside home without having a conversation with Catriona, Montgomery had excused himself. Whether it was to contemplate their failure in private or to get absolutely blasted in the pub, Quinton wasn't sure. He'd considered staying behind to keep an eye on him, but then decided that Montgomery was a grown man. He'd taken care of himself for years before Quinton came around, and he didn't need to a nursemaid to follow him around. Quinton would just have to trust that he could make his own way.

If it weren't for the disappointment at the result of their

mission, the casual jaunt on horseback might have been pleasant. Without any eyes on him, Quinton felt more himself than he had in months, even though he was still frustrated at not being able to speak to Catriona.

This wasn't the road they had taken to the little seaside village. When Quinton had stopped for a mincemeat pie on his way out, the baker had told him there was a faster path through the forest and how to get to it. Sure enough, he had found it without much difficulty. He wondered if it was the same one his aunt took when she visited her family's grounds. He could picture her all those years ago, young and fragile, clinging to her horse's reigns as if clinging to life itself, making the journey filled with grief and anger. He hoped that over the years the rage had waned, replaced by peace and contentment with the life she'd built, rather than festering and hardening in the centre of her chest, forever freezing her at the worst time of her life.

As Quinton mused on these thoughts, he nearly failed to hear the clopping of another horse's hooves on the path until the rider was almost upon him.

The look on Evans' face as the blood drained from his features matched the surprise Quinton felt as he saw the butler round the corner. Evans pulled on the reins of his horse, stopping dead in the middle of the path.

"Good afternoon, Evans," said Quinton as he halted his own horse. "I'll admit, I didn't expect to see you out here so late in the day."

"Nor I you, my lord. This path isn't known to many who aren't local." The words were well controlled and respectful, but they didn't match the stiff posture or the pale countenance of the man across from him. Where Evans had always seemed so proud and dignified, now there seemed to be something else there— something cold and rigid and directed at Quinton. He wasn't sure if it was fear or anger, or something in between, but it unsettled Quinton.

"Where are you headed, Evans?" he asked, years of instinct compelling him to push further.

Evans didn't say anything for a long minute, just stared at Quinton with an intensity that made Quinton squirm.

"Did you speak with Lady Catriona, my lord?" he finally said.

Quinton's eyes narrowed. "I don't see how that's any of your concern. How did you know where we were going?"

"Hard to keep secrets at Cedarbrook." Evans continued to stare. "The walls have ears."

"I see." Quinton couldn't shake the feeling that something was very wrong. "Do you come this way often, Evans? Doesn't seem to be a very well-travelled trail . . ."

"Did you speak to her?" Evans asked again, ignoring Quinton's question.

"What's your interest?" Shifting in the saddle, Quinton tightened his grip on the reigns. "Why does it matter if I spoke to her or not?"

"It matters, I assure you, my lord."

The weather which had felt so pleasant just minutes before now suddenly felt uncomfortably cool. A chill ran up Quinton's spine as he looked into the butler's hard eyes. He had seen eyes like that before. Over the years he had spent living on the streets, Quinton's body had become attuned to the darkness around him. The ability to identify a threat quickly was the difference between an urchin who survived and one who didn't. The eyes staring across at him now . . . they were the eyes of a predator, sizing up their prey and deciding the best line of attack. Every fibre of Quinton's being told him he needed to flee—now.

"I'm going to be on my way now, Evans." Quinton nodded curtly and tapped his heels against his horse's side to move the gelding along. "Good evening to you."

He was so distracted contemplating Evans' darkening eyes, Quinton had failed to notice that the butler's left hand was hidden on the other side of his horse. It wasn't until he saw the flash of gold and dark-stained wood as Evans moved his arm that Quinton realized what was happening.

He heard the shot, loud enough to make his ears ring, at the same time as he felt the pain of the lead ball ripping through his shoulder. The sulphur scent of gunpowder filled the air, making his eyes prick. The impact knocked him backward, toppling Quinton off the horse. The horse reared up, terror in the whites of its eyes at the explosive sound, and Quinton was forced to roll away to avoid being trampled. It took off running, ripping its reigns out of Quinton's hand, leaving behind leather friction burns that would have made him wince if it weren't for the blinding white pain already pulsing through his body.

Pushing himself up with his left forearm, Quinton glanced over and up at Evans. Though his horse was also distressed and prancing, Evans had managed to remained seated and in control. He held the pistol aloft, smoke billowing upwards from the barrel. Though Quinton's eyesight was beginning to blur, he could tell it was a single barrel—only capable of firing a single shot without reloading. Then he saw Evans shove the gun back into his saddle bag and pull out another identical one. Of course. What noble estate was complete without a set of duelling pistols?

Quinton forced himself to his feet and darted into the forest. His vision blurred at the edges and he stumbled as he moved, but he did what he could stay upright. He knew if he stopped or fell, he would die. He had to find cover. He had to get away.

He managed to find cover in the thick underbrush, scrambling down an embankment, past trees and rocks in an effort to put distance between himself and Evans. He could only hope that the foliage was too thick for the butler to manage on horseback and that he would be forced to follow on foot.

Pausing for breath against a large tree, Quinton looked to his right and saw blood, red and hot, seeping down his arm and chest. Quinton tried to move the dangling limb, but the sharp pain that shot through him discouraged him from trying again. He clenched his teeth together hard enough he thought they might crack as he stifled any noise. If a groan gave away his position, Zoe would never forgive him for dying so pointlessly.

"Lord Coleville!"

The shout came from far too close for Quinton's liking. He pushed himself up off the rough bark, forcing one foot in front of the other once again. Even in his weakened and disoriented state, he knew his footsteps were too loud as he trampled over sticks and leaves, the crunch underfoot seeming to echo in the thick summer air.

"Lord Coleville, stop! I only wish to talk!" came Evans's voice again, still far too close.

Did anyone ever actually fall for that? How stupid did he think Quinton was? No one who only wished to talk started the conversation with a gunshot.

He didn't stop, of course. But as he continued to run, breathing became more difficult. Quinton stumbled, his knees slamming into the ground with jarring impact, his left hand pressing into his seeping wound instinctively. Looking behind him, he could see a clear trail of blood following his path, dripping off his fingers in a steady stream.

If he'd known he was going to die today, Quinton would have done things differently. That was the thought which was circling round and round in his head. There was little left unsaid between himself and Charlie, or John, or Rory, but he would have told Katy how much he appreciated everything she'd done for him growing up. He would have told Theo and Simone how grateful he was for their meddling in his life. He would have shaken Hugh's hand and thanked him for all his support.

At the very least he would have held his dark-haired, blue-eyed wife in his arms and told her how much he loved her one last time.

That was Quinton's last thought as he sank down to the ground, his mind going black as he lost consciousness.

Chapter Fifty-Three

"I always knew you were unfeeling, Mac. I just did not realize you were also a coward."

Those words were the first thing Quinton became aware of as he regained consciousness. The woman's voice was unknown to Quinton, but at the same time somehow familiar. Quinton opened his eyes, pushing himself back up onto his knees. He didn't know how long he'd been out of it, but any time spent immobile was time Evans could catch up. He tried to get to his feet, but he only made it a few steps before collapsing weakly in a heap at the base of a tree.

Fleeing was no longer an option. Whatever fate awaited him, the die was cast. Quinton leaned his back against the obliging tree, fighting to stay awake this time.

"Don't test me, Cat." This voice Quinton recognized—Evans. "If I was truly as unfeeling as you believe, I would have put you in the ground with Max all those years ago. You know the stakes here, better than anyone. If you didn't want to put your nephew's life in danger, then you shouldn't have told him the truth."

The truth? What truth? Quinton wasn't having a hard time thinking straight. Evans called the woman Cat. Cat was here?

"I didn't tell him anything," snapped the woman—Cat. "I

honoured our agreement. You are the one who has exposed yourself."

Quinton could hear the hoof steps of horses circling nearby, but getting fainter as the seconds ticked by. He couldn't tell if Cat was keeping herself out of sight, leading Evans away, or if they were having this conversation in full view of the other, a desperate bid to save Quinton's life. He hoped it was the former. He didn't want Cat to die on his account.

"What choice did I have?" Evans' voice sounded different that Quinton had heard before, more desperate and raw. "That bastard nephew of yours won't stop picking at the wound, Cat. He found the grave, figured out the body was Max's. He even found you. Why couldn't you just leave the estate alone? I let you go, but why did you have to keep coming back, keeping this ridiculous ghost story alive?"

"You know why." Cat's tone was softer than before. "You could no sooner leave Max than I could leave my children."

There was a long silence after that, with the only sounds to be heard the faint stepping and breathing of the horses.

"You know I never wanted this." Evans' voice broke. "I fought so hard for this position. We were so lucky, orphans from the village, to be hired as footmen for the manor. It was a golden opportunity; one we would never get again. Max knew that. If he had just kept to his station . . . if you had stayed away from him . . ."

"I never wanted this either." Cat's voice was also mournful. "But I was young and angry and ignorant and in love. We didn't mean any harm."

"But you caused harm nonetheless!" shouted Evans. "You put everything my brother and I had at risk with your foolishness. Carrying on together was bad enough, but then . . . can you imagine, if your father had found out whose children you were pregnant with? Max would have been ruined, a black mark across his name for any position he applied for again, and me also by association."

There was another silence before Catriona responded. "I may have been ignorant and foolish, but I'm not the one who hurt Max."

Quinton heard the pain still in Cat's voice after all these years.

"I wouldn't have had to if you hadn't put him in that position." The pain was present in Evans' voice too, but with a bitter edge of resentment.

Cat scoffed. "I was *dying*, Mac. Our children were *dying*. Max was willing to give up everything to try and save us, to get help, even if our secret came out. All these years later, and you still don't understand that kind of love?"

"Don't talk to me about who loved Max more." Evans laughed darkly. "He's the one who turned his back on me."

"Max loved you, Mac, always. Even at the end. He wouldn't want this for you." Quinton could hear the desperation in Cat's voice. She was trying to calm Mac down—one last bid to talk him down.

"If Max really cared for me, he wouldn't have tried to tell your father the truth." Evans's tone was no longer sad or raw—now all Quinton heard was the bitterness. "His life wasn't the only one on the line. In the end, he had to make a choice, and he chose you."

There was another brief pause.

"Yes, of course. I've heard all this before. Poor, poor, Mac. Backed into a corner with no choice other than to kill his own twin." Cat's tactic had clearly shifted from placating to provoking. "The truth is, Mac, you're selfish. You always have been. You'll do whatever it takes to protect your precious position, even kill for it."

"What happened with Max was an accident and you know it." Evans's tone was darker, sharpened by Cat's accusation.

"What about Langford?" The sounds of the horses were getting closer again. "Yes, I heard about his untimely demise. That wasn't an accident, was it?"

"Langford was greedy and deserved what he got," snapped Evans.

"Always an excuse with you." Cat's voice was disgusted. "Have you ever taken accountability for anything in your life?"

Quinton couldn't hear Evans's reply. His vision blurred, and he realized he was drifting back off into unconsciousness. Panic started to set over him.

Hadn't Rory once told himself something, about breathing? Quinton struggled to remember.

"Deep breaths, my boy, anytime you feel unsteady. Breath in, count to four, and breath back out. They say it worked for the bard himself..."

May God bless that crazy Scot. Taking a deep, shaky inhale, Quinton tried to force himself to stay awake, concentrating on his breathing and counting. After a few moments went by, his heart-beat slowed and the dizziness passed.

". . . my brother is dead because of you, and soon you and your blasted nephew will join him!" Evans's voice had passed shouting, having entered the realm of unhinged ranting.

Cat must be trying to rattle the man, to throw him off and get him to make a mistake. If Evans fired his shot and missed, it would level the playing field considerably. A risky gamble, but one with a huge payoff. Quinton hoped his aunt knew what she was doing.

Without warning, a horse suddenly burst from the treeline, shocking Quinton. The rider galloped past him, barely a blur, especially to Quinton's hazy vision, but the impression was distinct.

What the bloody hell was his valet doing here? Did blood loss cause hallucinations? Quinton made a mental note to ask Rory, should he get the opportunity again.

Mere seconds later a familiar figure dropped from a second horse, and he felt warm arms around him. Tears streamed down Zoe's face as she shouted at him. "Don't you dare die, do you hear me? I won't stand for it, so just put any thought of it out of that stubborn skull of yours."

Quinton laughed, despite himself, wincing at the pain which shot down his arm and chest as a result. "Well, now that you've said it, I'll be sure to do so."

In the distance he could hear shouting, though Quinton wasn't sure if it really was far away or if it just seemed distant to his fading body.

A single loud gunshot rang out, followed by a long, terrible silence.

Zoe looked up at the sound of the shot, but if she'd seen what had happened, Quinton couldn't read it from her expression.

"Darrow, I need your help!" she half shouted, half screamed.

The pain had faded now. Quinton couldn't really feel anything anymore, except for Zoe's hand grasping his own. He tried to hold on tighter, but he couldn't seem to make his fingers move.

"You stupid, stupid man," Zoe muttered. "You stubborn, inconsiderate, selfish—"

"I love you too, Zoe."

The words were no more than a whisper, but his last thought as he drifted back into the darkness was that he'd gotten his final wish. That in itself was enough.

Chapter Fifty-Four

Watching Quinton's eyes slide shut, Zoe felt an overwhelming compulsion to scream and pull her hair out. She had never felt so helpless in her life.

Her conversation with Katy suddenly popped into her mind. They had talked about stemming blood loss, hadn't they? Zoe pulled the skirt of her day dress up, exposing her petticoat. Taking the thick white fabric firmly in her hands, she tore away a sizable strip.

Pressing the fabric firmly against the ragged wound in Quinton's shoulder, Zoe tried to remember what Katy had told her. She needed to keep pressure on it, that much she knew, but Zoe couldn't think of what else. There must be something else she could do, right?

"Darrow!" she screamed again, tears clouding her vision.

Despite her best efforts to press her body weight into it, the bright red blood still soaked through the strip of petticoat, seeping over Zoe's fingers. It was warm and sticky, and Zoe's stomach turned as the metallic scent filled her nose and lungs. She didn't talk to God often, but in that moment, she prayed like she'd never prayed before, begging for her husband to be spared and promising anything in return.

"Release the pressure while I pack the wound with comfrey," said a woman's voice from behind. "While I do that, you tear off another strip of your petticoat, then I'll apply it to the wound."

Looking up, Zoe saw the brilliant blue eyes of a woman around sixty, her red hair streaked with grey and held back in a loose bun. Behind her stood Darrow, his face drained of colour.

So grateful to have someone else who seemed to know what they were doing take charge, Zoe did as she was told. She stood aside, allowing the woman to kneel by Quinton.

"You're Catriona," said Zoe dumbly, her voice sounding distant to her own ears.

"Yes," responded the woman, her eyes still on Quinton as she took a pouch out of the cloth bag tied around her waist.

Zoe knew she was supposed to be doing something, but she couldn't think what it was. Her body felt numb to her, foreign, like it belonged to someone else. Suddenly Darrow was crouching by her side. He took the outer layer of her dress and pulled it up, holding it up towards Zoe's hand. Wildly inappropriate, but Zoe couldn't bring herself to care.

"Hold this," he said after she did nothing.

Grasping the outstretched fabric, Zoe watched as Darrow took her petticoat and tore another two long strips from it. He quickly passed the strips over to Catriona, whose deft fingers were pushing something plantlike into Quinton's wound. Once finished, she took the strips, folding one and pressing it against the bullet hole, then taking the other and wrapping it around Quinton's shoulder to hold the first in place. He was still breathing, if only just.

Standing up, Catriona sighed and wiped away sweat from her forehead, leaving behind a streak of blood. "I added wild calendula as well to prevent infection, but we need to get the wound closed as soon as possible." She glanced at Darrow, and a silent exchange passed between them. "Cedarbrook is closest. We'll go there."

Turning to Zoe, Catriona's eyes flicked up and down,

seeming to properly appraise her for the first time. Realizing she was still holding her day dress, Zoe quickly let it go, the fabric fluttering back into place, now smeared with red. She flexed her hand, the blood drying tacky on her fingers.

"Can you ride?" asked Catriona.

"Yes." The answer was automatic, although Zoe was actually feeling quite lightheaded and cold. Another thought occurred to her. "What of Evans?"

Another silent exchanged passed between Darrow and Catriona.

"He is no longer a factor." Darrow moved past it before Zoe could ask further questions. "We need to go, now, for Quinton's sake. I'll take him with me on my horse."

"Right." Zoe nodded, feeling as though there was a heavy wet blanket weighing her down. "Yes, we should go."

As she turned to take her horse's reigns, Zoe heard Catriona say, "Don't think I've not noticed, Finlay. We will have words about your actions, and how you came to be at this place and in this time."

Whatever reply "Finley" might have had was cut off by the sound of nearby voices.

"Zoe!"

The shout sounded like Mary. The realization pierced through the fog in Zoe's mind.

"Over here!" she called in response.

The sound of rustling leaves and footfalls got closer, and then Mary and Mr. Baptise appeared from the thick underbrush. Mary raced over, her face pale.

"My god, Zoe, what happened?" asked Mary, her voice thick with emotion.

"How did you find us?" responded Zoe, still feeling like she couldn't think properly.

Mr. Baptise answered. "We were en route to the village, but then it was as if lightning struck *Mademoiselle* Mary. She felt very strongly we must redirect in this direction, so redirect we did."

Mary nodded, her eyes on Quinton. "We heard the shot from the main road and followed the sound from there as close as we could." She finally tore her eyes away from Quinton. "Will he live?"

"There is still hope, but we must get him to Cedarbrook as fast as possible," said Catriona in response.

"My *cheval et ma charrette* is nearby." Mr. Baptiste pointed in the direction they'd come from. "The forest was too thick to bring it *tout au long du chemin.*"

"Good, it is better than being jostled on the back of horse." Catriona nodded toward Darrow/Finlay. "Take his shoulders, and you Mr. . . . ."

"Baptiste."

"Mr. Baptiste, you take his legs."

The two men followed Catriona's instructions, carefully carrying Quinton's considerable weight to the waiting cart. Mary walked alongside Zoe, taking her arm and guiding her in the right direction. After Quinton was loaded in the cart, Catriona clambered up next to him, her attention focused on the bandages which were already stained red. Mr. Baptiste followed suit, climbing into the driver's bench.

Catriona's piercing blue eyes met Zoe's. "Speed is essential. We'll go ahead as quickly as is possible, and the rest of you will follow on horseback once the horses have been retrieved. Do you understand?"

Even in her current state, Zoe's body screamed in panic at the idea of being separated from her husband. But she understood that there was no time to argue, and another body in the cart would just slow them down. "Yes," she said, her mouth dry as cotton.

Catriona nodded at her response, and the cart lurched forward. Zoe watched it disappear down the path, wondering if this was the last time she would ever see her husband alive. The cold which had settled in the centre of Zoe's chest seemed to deepen, as if ice was flowing through her body, freezing her in place.

Darrow ran back into the woods, returning after a few minutes with the horses in tow—his and Zoe's, as well as Evans's. Zoe noticed a spray of blood splattered across the third horse's neck and mane, but she didn't ask about it. There would be time for that. Or maybe there wouldn't. Maybe it didn't matter. Maybe nothing mattered at all.

"Zoe?"

Mary's voice brought Zoe back to herself, and she realized she needed to mount. Darrow knelt down, interlocking his fingers to make a makeshift step. As she stepped into it, he heaved up, helping Zoe up onto the beast. He then quickly did the same for Mary onto his own horse. Her friend's expression was set somewhere between terrified and horrified, but she refrained from complaining. Brave, brave Mary.

Not for the first time, Zoe was deeply grateful for the unusual intuition which had brought Mary there. Where would she be without her dear friend?

They rode along at as fast a pace as they could manage. Mary sat in front of Darrow, with Evans's horse in tow and Zoe on her own. It was all Zoe could do just to hang on, but fortunately for her, the beast knew the way home and made its way without much guidance from her.

She thought back to the whispered words from Quinton. Instead of bringing her any joy, they filled her with dread. They were the words of a man who thought he had no more words left to say.

That blasted man better not die on her. She would never forgive him if he did.

Chapter Fifty-Five

T his whiskey had a smooth finish; Rory would give the old earl that. Rory was the first to admit he and Charlie's offerings along that line were not yet up to snuff. If the stubborn mule would consider making true Scotch, that would certainly be an improvement. Yes, there were challenges in importing the necessary ingredients, but nothing good came without a cost.

Sinking deeper in the comfortable chair, Rory closed his eyes. He was flanked by John and Charlie on either side. They had started the afternoon at the local taverns, debating the merits of several whiskeys. But it wasn't too very long before they decided Cedarbrook had better whiskey and better food, so they made their way home early. The sun was low in the sky but not yet set while the three of them happily sipped the earl's best, their largest concern debating whether they should call for a repast or ought to wait for Quinton.

"What on earth . . .?" The tone of Charlie's words immediately set Rory on edge.

He opened his eyes to see Charlie perched on the edge of his chair, staring out the large window into the deepening dusk. Rory followed his gaze, a sinking feeling coming over him.

A horse and cart were racing across the grounds, not stopping at the stables but continuing on at a breakneck speed toward the house. Rory could just make out the new land steward on the driver's bench, but there were also two figures in the back of the cart, one sitting and one laying prone. He didn't know what had happened, but Rory knew something was wrong—terribly, terribly wrong.

Setting his drink down hastily, Rory bolted for the door, John and Charlie close on his heels. By the time they reached the garden, the cart was just pulling up. The Frenchman skilfully stopped his horse right next to the house, lather coating the bay beast.

Once Rory finally caught sight of the back of the cart, his heart dropped. "Quinton," he said softly.

His friend was laid out on his side, his upper shoulder dark with blood. Quinton's eyes were closed, and for a long, panic-filled moment, Rory couldn't tell if he was breathing or not. But then he saw his chest rise and fall, and a wave of relief washed over Rory. If Quinton was still alive, there was still hope.

The other figure in the back with Quinton was an older woman who stood when the cart stopped. Forty years might have passed, but Rory recognized her immediately from the portraits.

"The musket ball entered through the right shoulder, but I couldn't find an exit hole," said Catriona, her manner that of a surgeon performing triage. "I packed the wound with comfrey and calendula but the bleeding has continued. He is in need of a surgeon if his life is to be saved."

"I can do the surgery." The seriousness of the situation had instantly sobered Rory, and the only thoughts going through his head were how to save his friend's life. In a perfect world, he'd have some kind of assistance, perhaps from Katy or Savita as women familiar with medicine, but he didn't have time for them to be tracked down. He met Catriona's intense gaze. "You're familiar with wound care and herbal remedies?"

Catriona nodded. "Yes."

"Then I could use your assistance." Rory glanced at Charlie and John. "Help me get him inside and onto the staff's kitchen table."

They quickly complied, gently lifting Quinton and taking him inside to a large table the kitchen staff used to eat their meals. As Rory carefully began to examine the skilfully secured bandages with steady hands, he prayed fervently to whatever god was listening that his knowledge and skills would be enough.

Chapter Fifty-Six

Hugh rose as Simone entered, his arms opening to receive her. "How is Zoe?" he asked as he drew her close.

Letting him lead her to the settee, Simone wearily sat down. "She has bathed and changed. She will not rest until we know how Quinton fares."

Simone shuddered as she thought back to the sight of her daughter riding up, her hands and dress covered in blood and her face white as a sheet. It was an image Simone suspected would haunt her nightmares for many years to come.

At first Zoe had been quiet, then almost hysterical, then quiet again. Simone had finally managed to convince her to wash the blood off, and had only just left her side a few minutes ago while Louisa changed her clothes.

After a few minutes had passed, Zoe entered the parlour as well. She still looked pale, her eyes vacant and her expression blank. Simone recognized the signs of shock and trauma because she too had experienced it. Zoe had gone into survival mode, just trying to get from one moment to the next. The warm bath should have helped, but her daughter still needed someone to make sure she ate and drank something to keep her strength up.

Mary followed close behind. Her gaze met Simone's, equally concerned. Simone knew as long as Mary was by her daughter's side, Zoe would be alright. If not alright, then at least cared for.

The two sat in the chairs near the window, Mary having to take Zoe's elbow to guide her there.

Looking around, Simone noted the rest of the people in the room. Charlie leaned against the mantle, his expression stoic but his shoulders sagging, while John and Savi sat near Katy and Theo. The two midwives had been paying a visit to the house-keeper's expectant niece when Rory had begun the surgery. Simone had to hope Catriona was as skilled as those two.

The room was oppressively silent, with no chatter or small talk. What was there to say, until the extent of the tragedy was known?

In the corner of the room stood the outlier, Darrow, the valet Simone herself had hired, who apparently was neither Darrow nor a valet. Apparently, she wasn't as good a judge of character as she had thought. So much for an open and honest soul. That would have to be addressed eventually but now was not the time.

Her precious, darling husband handed her a glass of claret, and Simone didn't know if she had ever loved him more than in that moment. She leaned against his shoulder, finding comfort in his steady warmth.

Simone knew she didn't always appreciate Hugh as much as she should. He was a man who loved his profession, passionate about the law and defending those who had no other advocate, and while Simone appreciated his passion for his work, there were times when she wished he looked at her the same way he looked at a court summons. But Hugh was a good and reliable man who had cared for her and helped raise her daughter for fifteen years, and who Simone knew she could always rely upon. He was a place of safety, and even now, in the midst of tragedy and grief, Simone was comforted by his arm around her shoulders. She could ask for little else.

Her musings were interrupted by the door suddenly opening.

Rory stepped through, his expression unreadable. Simone grasped Hugh's hand, drawing on his strength to hear whatever came next.

"He survived the surgery."

With those four words, an enormous weight lifted off Simone's chest, and she took in a deep breath of relief. Across the room, Zoe let out a sob, but Simone recognized it as the much-needed release of all her pent-up terror and dread.

"He's not completely safe yet. We were able to remove the musket ball, but the blood loss was significant," continued Rory. "At this point, we've done all we can and will just have to wait and see."

Simone appreciated his honestly. She knew there were no guarantees in a situation like this, but she was grateful that Quinton had a fighting chance. He was a strong, determined young man—hopefully that would be enough.

"Well he can't stay on the kitchen table. I'll prepare a bed for him." Everyone in the room turned to look at Darrow, but he appeared unfazed. "I am still his valet."

Exchanging a quick look, John and Charlie followed him out of the room. Zoe stood as well, but John raised a hand at the threshold. "Stay. You should rest for now. We'll get him settled and then send for you."

Hesitating briefly, Zoe nodded and sat back. It was the course of wisdom. There would be plenty of time for her vigil by Quinton's bedside.

Rory had also left with the three men, no doubt to supervise the transfer of his patient. A few moments later, the door opened again, this time to admit their most unusual guest—the long-lost Catriona, back from the supposed grave. She looked worn, her greying red hair falling forward from her bun in loose wisps, and the front of her dress covered in blood dried reddish brown. But there was still a compelling, striking quality to the woman. It had been nearly forty years since she walked these hallways, but

Catriona still carried herself like the aristocrat she was born to be—proud and dignified.

Hugh stood first, extending his hand. "Hugh Dovefield."

She grasped it. "Catriona Pearson."

Simone followed suit, though instead of extending a hand she just stood and inclined her head. "And I am Simone Dovefield. It is a pleasure to meet you . . ." She trailed off, uncertain how to address the woman standing before her.

"I usually go by Mrs. Pearson these days," said Catriona with a perceptive smile. "But you may call me Cat."

"Cat." Simone returned her smile. "Then please, call me Simone."

Sitting down in an armchair by the fireplace, Cat let out a deep breath. The last few hours must have been exhausting. Simone was a decade her junior and had done hardly anything other than worry, and she still felt like she'd been hit over the head.

Hugh poured Cat a glass of whiskey without asking, handing it over before rejoining his wife on the settee.

"This will do, but I do wish my father was willing to keep a decent scotch in the cellar," Cat said after taking a drink.

"We could have Oliver run down and check?" offered Mary, ever helpful.

Cat waved her hand. "No, no. This is fine."

Theo, Katy, Savi, and Mary all then introduced themselves in turn. When it came to Zoe, Catriona spoke first.

"I know who you are," she said. "Quinton's wife."

"Yes," replied Zoe quietly. "Thank you, for what you did today."

"No thanks are necessary." Cat leaned back in her chair. "He is Graham's boy. I would trade my life for his in an instant."

Zoe looked at her with an appraising expression. "How is it you happened to be there when whatever it is that happened . . . happened?"

"I followed Quinton, after he left my home." Catriona said

the statement as if that were a perfectly normal thing to do. Simone supposed for her it was.

"I wasn't prepared to meet him today—to meet any of you," continued Cat. "I had been observing from a distance since you all arrived, learning what I could. But listening in on his and Montgomery's conversation with my husband . . . it was different. There he was, Graham's own flesh and blood, sitting in my house, only a few feet from me, and I found it more difficult than expected to be so close and yet still so far. Once he left, and Montgomery went his own way, I followed, still at a distance, but working up my courage to approach him eventually. Before I got the chance, he crossed paths with Malcolm, and things took a dark turn, as it often does—did—with Mac."

Despite the sharp criticism, Simone detected a hint of regret at the use of the past tense. The ending of a life was rarely without complicated feelings, no matter the circumstances, and Simone wondered at the history between the two.

"I take it from the turn of events that Evans is the one who killed Langford." The look on Zoe's face confirmed Simone's supposition. "May I ask what his connection was to you, Cat?"

Cat sighed, as if she'd been expecting this question but dreading it nonetheless. She succinctly explained her relationship with Maxwell, who was Malcolm Evans's twin brother, as well as the tension between the two as a result of said relationship.

"Max and I used the old ruins as a meeting place. Some of the rooms still were complete, and they served our purpose." Catriona spoke without embarrassment. "But when Mac found out, he was terrified we would be caught." Cat paused to take a slow sip of whiskey, and a hint of a smile played about her lips. "Graham and I grew up with the legend of the ruins ringing in our ears. It was he who made the ghost costume when we were younger so we could scare the servants from the ruins, making the old house our personal playground. With a candle held just right, it had an unearthly glow. It was easy enough to bring the ghost back to ensure our secret stayed secret."

She paused again, a faraway look in her eye. "Then I became pregnant . . . Malcolm had agreed to keep our secret as long as I left first, then Maxwell a few months later, to avoid suspicion falling on them. I stayed as long as I could, hiding the pregnancy with ever tighter corsets and ever looser dresses. Only my maid knew the truth about my condition, and she never asked for any details," said Catriona, her eyes distant. "But then the babies came early . . . far too early. There was so much blood. Maxwell wanted to go to my father, to send for help, but doing so would have meant revealing the truth. Malcolm wouldn't have it. When he couldn't change Maxwell's mind, he became distraught and climbed up onto the roof. Maxwell followed, fearing his brother would do something foolish. I don't know exactly what happened up on the roof, but only Malcom returned, his face white as a sheet. He always claimed it was an accident—that Max had slipped and fallen. All I know is that Maxwell died from a broken neck."

She cleared her throat before continuing. "My babies—my girls—they were born already dead. Despite all the odds, I did manage to pull through, though at the time I wished to die with them. Malcolm and I buried the three of them together, under the explicit understanding that I would never return. At the time, I thought I never would. It seemed those ruins truly were cursed." Shaking her head, Catriona sighed. "I did not know then the need I would have to be near my babies."

"I am so sorry for your loss. I am familiar with the pain that brings," said Theo.

"A mother never forgets." Catriona met her eyes. "That's part of the reason why we settled close enough for me to visit the grave."

Theo spoke again. "What are their names?"

Looking up with a surprised expression, Catriona responded, "Agnes and Annag."

An impulsive urge came over Simone to comfort the woman, but when Catriona looked her way, Simone saw no sign of the frightened and grief-stricken young girl she had once been. She didn't need their pity or their sympathy.

Charlie and John entered the room, followed by Darrow a moment later. His eyes met hers, the recognition and familiarity clear, as well as disapproval on Cat's part.

"Allow me introduce my son, Finlay," said Cat dryly.

Darrow/Finlay nodded to the group, returning to his seat without comment. If she had to think of a word for the man, Simone would choose unapologetic.

"Your son?" asked Mary.

"My son," confirmed Cat. "Who has a great deal to explain about his presence here."

"As do you, Mother," responded Finlay, again unapologetically. "I grew up hearing about stories of this place. You left out several key details."

"You certainly inherited your father's way with words, saying a great deal without answering the question asked," said Cat with a sharp edge to her tone. "It's a pity you haven't used that gift for better purposes."

Interrupting the standoff between mother and son, Charlie spoke to Zoe. "Quinton is resting comfortably. He's still unconscious, but his breathing is steady and he doesn't seem to be in pain."

"Good. That's good." There was still a vacancy to Zoe's eyes, as if she was just saying what was expected.

Charlie hesitated. "I have seen men injured worse who survived. I believe he will be alright."

Zoe looked up, as if seeing him for the first time. "Thank you, Charlie," she said with a soft smile, touching his arm gently.

John had found his way to his wife, pulling her into a tight embrace. The sentiment and emotion reflected the mood of the room.

Katy spoke to Catriona. "I was told you used comfrey and calendula on the wound. Are there any other local herbs you recommend for similar circumstances?"

Nodding in approval, Catriona moved closer to Katy. Soon the women were in an educated conversation about what grew in the kitchen gardens and the forest floor that would help Quinton recover, as well as what each had used in the past.

Several minutes passed like this, with people conversing politely as if one of their dearest companions weren't lying in a nearby room, caught somewhere between life and death. Simone supposed it was just nature of people, to find normalcy in tragedy.

Eventually Zoe stood, and the chatter quieted. "I need to be with Quinton," she said with determination, as if having finally gathered her courage.

Mary rose as well, a glass in each hand. "Lead the way."

After Zoe left, it wasn't long before the rest of the room dispersed, each weary from the difficult day's events. Arrangements were made for Finlay and Catriona to have rooms for the night, as it was far too late to travel back to Hartlemond. Even Hugh gave out, touching Simone's shoulder as he left.

Eventually it was just Simone, the final holdout, nursing yet another glass of wine—until she wasn't the alone anymore. Theo had come back, her dressing gown wrapped tightly around her nightgown. She hobbled over to a chair, dropping down into it with little grace.

"It's seldom a good idea to drink alone, my dear, though I do so more often than I care to admit." Theo set her cane aside. "Be a dear and pour me a glass."

Smiling, Simone did as Theo requested.

"Am I correct in assuming you plan to have your own vigil here, so you will be awake if the worst occurs and Zoe needs you?" asked Theo as she accepted the glass.

Simone nodded, unfazed by Theo's perception. "I know it is foolish, as I am sure I would be awakened if . . . if I were needed. But the first night is the most difficult to survive, and I will need to be present for Zoe if he does not."

"Women have held vigil for generations, my darling Simone, but it is always easier with company. I will wait for morning with you." Theo took a fortifying sip and glanced at the grandfather clock. "At this point, we are practically there already."

Chuckling softly, Simone raised her glass appreciatively, grateful for the support her sister-in-law was able to give her. Standing vigil was always easier with a companion, as Theo had said.

Chapter Fifty-Seven

W armth. Light. Softness. Pain.

These were the things Quinton became aware of as his consciousness clawed its way back to the surface. A warmth and brightness crossed his face, and his body felt enveloped in some kind of smooth softness. He wondered if perhaps he had died and this was heaven, but then, was there pain in heaven? Because as he shifted, an aching sharpness shot across his body, originating from his shoulder.

Something had happened. Quinton tried to think, but it felt as though a thick fog was enveloping his thoughts, keeping them just out of reach. He had been on his horse, riding . . . riding back to Cedarbrook. Then he met someone on the trail . . . and something had happened, but the memory was fuzzy and formless and he couldn't quite make it out.

He opened his eyes slowly, blinking at the harsh brightness. This was his room at Cedarbrook. The curtains were open, allowing the room to be bathed in warm sunlight. Not dead, then.

Turning his head to the right, Quinton saw his shoulder was wrapped in white bandages, his forearm secured across his chest by a makeshift sling to keep the limb immobile. Then he remembered.

He'd been shot. That blasted butler had shot him. Quinton recalled the sound of the gunshot and the feel of the lead ball tearing into his flesh. He recalled the impact of his body hitting the ground, the taste of blood in his mouth and the scent of gunpowder in the air. He recalled running into the forest, stumbling away in a desperate attempt to evade his attacker. And then . . . what had happened next?

Turning his head to the left, he saw what mattered most—his wife, Zoe. She was sitting in a chair by his bedside, her torso laid across the bed and her fingers clasped tightly around Quinton's left hand. Her head was propped up against her upper arm, dark curls falling all around, her eyes closed and her mouth slightly open as she slept.

As beautiful as the sight was to Quinton, he could see the toll this had taken on her. Dark circles hung under her eyes, and her olive skin had a sallow undertone. It couldn't have been long enough for her to lose any real weight—could it have been?—but there seemed to be a hollowness to her cheeks that hadn't been there before. He wondered when was the last time she ate something.

Flexing his fingers, Quinton summoned what strength he could to squeeze her hand. She stirred at the movement, her dark eye lashes fluttering as she awoke.

"Quinton?" The words were mumbled, and her eyes squinted, as if Zoe wasn't sure if she was still dreaming or not.

"Hello, my darling." Quinton's voice sounded foreign to himself, weak and hoarse, his mouth dry as cotton.

Zoe sat bolt upright, her grip on his hand tightening. "Oh, Quinton! You're awake."

"It certainly appears that way." He cleared his throat, trying to swallow. "I don't suppose I could trouble you for some water?"

She scrambled to accommodate him, pouring some water out of a pitcher sitting on his bedside table into a glass. Slipping a hand behind his neck, Zoe helped Quinton lift his head so he could take a sip. The movement, even as slow and careful as it was, still sent sparks of pain through his chest. The cool liquid on his tongue was worth it. He instantly felt revived, laying back down on the soft pillows with a satisfied sigh.

"How long have I been asleep?" he asked.

"Three days."

Three days? It couldn't have been three days.

"We didn't know if you would ever wake." Zoe pushed some of the hair from her face, and Quinton could see the puffiness around her eyes which meant she'd been crying.

"I'm sorry I worried you," said Quinton.

"You should be." Zoe sniffed, her lips turning up with a ghost of a smile. "Just don't do it again."

"I'll strive my best." The corner of Quinton's lip also quirked up in a slight smile. "I wouldn't want to be on the receiving end of your temper again, though I suppose it's inevitable considering —how did you put it again? How stupid, inconsiderate, and selfish I am."

Zoe shook her head. "You know I didn't mean it."

Quinton gasped her hand. "I know, my darling. You are my tempest, and it is because of your will and ire that I'm still alive."

Another memory came to Quinton. He'd been bleeding, leaning against tree, and there was a woman's voice. She had been talking to Evans.

"Is Catriona here?" he asked.

"Yes." Zoe nodded. "She and Katy have been taking care of you day and night."

"She saved my life."

"Yes," she repeated. "Your cousin was helpful as well."

Quinton's brow furrowed. "My cousin?"

"Darrow. His real name is Finlay Pearson." Zoe sniffed again. "You've missed quite a bit."

"I guess so." Quinton blinked, attempting to process this revelation. "My cousin?"

"I'll let him explain that to you."

Another thought suddenly occurred to Quinton. "What about Evans?"

A shadow passed over Zoe's face. "Dead. By his own hand."

Quinton wasn't sure how to feel about that. Should he feel sorry for a man who had tried to kill him? Did it make him cruel if he felt nothing at all about it?

A knock at the door interrupted his musings. Not waiting for a response, it opened to reveal Catriona on the other side.

"I heard voices." She smiled. "I am glad to see you're awake, Quinton. It's also nice to properly meet you."

This was the first time Quinton had seen his aunt. She was a striking woman, her posture straight and her gaze intense. Her eyes were blue, but not blue like Zoe's. Where Zoe's were like the ocean, deep and fathomless and ever changing, Catriona's were like ice over a lake, light and cool and unyielding. Meeting her gaze, Quinton was no longer surprised she might be mistaken for a ghost with eyes like that.

"It's nice to meet you too," he responded. "Thank you, for what you did."

"As I told your wife, no thanks necessary." Catriona walked closer to the bed, gliding across the floor with precise, smooth movements. "How are you feeling?"

"Like I got shot."

She chuckled. "I suppose that's to be expected."

Voices came from the hallway, and Catriona's head snapped toward the direction of the voices, but they kept going, passing the door and fading away whoever it was kept walking. When Catriona turned back, her expression was notably less cheerful. She glanced at Zoe, and Quinton could see something pass between the two women. Three days was a long time. Who knew what had happened in that time.

"Have you spoken with your father?" he asked.

Catriona's expression darkened even further. "We had a conversation. It went poorly. He's returned to London."

"Though he did wait until you were through the worst of it," added Zoe.

"How thoughtful of him," replied Quinton dryly. His eyelids were suddenly feeling very heavy. "And Montgomery?"

"He showed up later that night, drunk." Catriona's tone indicated her disapproval. "But after he sobered up, we also had a conversation. It went . . . better." She paused and her demeanor changed, softening. "I have spent most of my time with your family, Quinton, and I don't just mean your wife. I have heard the stories of your time on the streets, and I have seen the bond with your band of brothers. I have thanked Katy for keeping you fed during those years, and each of the men who stand by you now. You built your own family, and I am honored to be included among their ranks."

Her eyes fill with tears as she finished. Quinton reached up to touch her cheek, but his hand fell back to his side before he could reach. His eyes felt heavy.

"You should go back to sleep." Zoe brushed some of his hair back from his forehead. "I'll be here when you wake up."

"I certainly hope not." His words were softer and less enunciated. "You have better things to do than hover by my bedside all day."

"Not anymore." Zoe's voice sounded serious, and Quinton forced his eyes back open. "I spent a lot of time here over the past three days, bargaining with God. I swore if you lived, I would be better. This is my role now, and I won't complain. I'll run the household, and I'll be a good wife, and one day a good mother. This is all I need."

Quinton used the last of his waning strength to squeeze his wife's hand once again. "Darling, I love you so much. But that is utterly absurd."

Zoe frowned, seemingly taken aback by his response.

"You are already the perfect wife in my mind, and I hope one day you will be a mother, but you are so much more than just that." Quinton fought to stay in the light of consciousness. This was important, and he needed to say it before he slipped back into the darkness. "I don't ever want you to limit yourself. You need more. I want you to have more."

She squeezed back, a smile on her face. "We'll discuss it more later. For now, rest."

His eyes finally closed, and the darkness claimed him again before Quinton could say more, but he knew they would figure it out. He and Zoe would always figure it out.

Epilogue

TWO MONTHS LATER

Watching the fire burn cheerfully in the grate, Zoe reflected that it made the whole room feel welcoming. It wasn't truly cold yet, but today was rainy, and rain in London was always chilling. Now, as the day retreated, she looked forward to her friends advancing in its wake.

She had a few moments to herself before it was time for guests, so Zoe poured an early whiskey and found a seat by the warm hearth. Tucking her legs up underneath herself, her thoughts drifted back to the beginning of this path she was on, when her lady's maid, Lucy, had been brutally murdered. Zoe still felt a tinge of regret when she thought of Lucy. But in doing her best to remedy that tragedy, her choices had led her here—married to a man she loved, surrounded by people who loved her.

She remembered that first eclectic gathering, hosted by Aunt Theo—the way everyone had come, dressed in their best, still awkward and unsure of each other, to eat and drink and mingle with people they might never have crossed paths with otherwise. Now it had become something of tradition, to come together after an investigation was concluded, reinforcing those unique bonds. This was the first time Zoe had been able to host, in her own home she and Quinton shared. It was not large by noble standards, but more than enough for the two of them, and she was growing quite fond of the cozy feel of their small manor.

The sound of a door opening caught Zoe's attention, and she looked up to see Quinton come in, looking as handsome as ever in his carefully chosen suit. His tailcoat covered his brocade waist-coat, a design of blue and a soft green. Zoe's own dress was a similar blue, tailored to include slender pockets, and she knew it fit her well, with a neckline that drew Quinton's eye. The blue made her eyes stand out as well, and the use of the colours made the two of them a matched pair.

Setting aside her glass and standing to meet him, Zoe smiled, taking the lapels of his jacket and drawing him close. Quinton responded in kind, kissing her passionately. When they drew apart, Zoe knew she looked forward to continuing that kiss later, alone in their room.

Flexing his right arm, he made his way to the sideboard and helped himself to a healthy pour of whiskey. "Blast, this shoulder still aches."

"It's colder than a witch's . . . um . . . nose out there. Not even winter yet," said Mary as she burst into the room just then.

Zoe laughed. "You, who complained endlessly about the heat of London's summer not two months ago?"

Mary shrugged as she also helped herself to the bottle. "It is not my fault that London so seldom gets it right. I still live here, don't I?"

Charlie arrived alone, with Rory following soon after, and then John and Savi. She had not sequestered herself, as Zoe suspected, and she was now swollen with child. Still somehow the most beautiful woman in the room.

Now they were only waiting on one more.

In lieu of a formal dinner, Zoe had requested an early repast with a few dishes prepared and set up at a long table on the side of the room. She liked the idea of friends eating and drinking leisurely, filling their plates themselves as needed. The newly hired butler was a bit horrified at the idea, but Zoe had eventually managed to convince him.

Everyone was cheerful, helping themselves to cold cuts and the excellent whiskey from Quinton's cellars. Rory suggested they open a bottle from his and Charlie's distillery next, though only Mary seemed enthusiastic about the idea.

"How is the wing?" Charlie asked while he settled himself, gesturing vaguely at Quinton's arm. "Still gimpy?"

Quinton glared at him. "It's fine." He winced as he sat down, undercutting his statement.

"Don't fret too much, my lad." Rory spoke cheerfully, carefully tasting his whiskey. "It's honestly a miracle you have use of it this soon. Complete healing will likely take a full year."

"A year?" Quinton sounded shocked. "Please tell me you are joking."

"Instead of whining like a petulant child, perhaps you ought to be grateful that wing still flaps at all, Q." It was a surprisingly sharp scolding from Mary, and several eyes turned to look at her, but she just shrugged and continued eating.

"You are right, Mary," replied Quinton after a moment's hesitation. "And I am grateful."

"When will you see your new Aunt Catriona again?" Charlie asked, changing the subject.

Quinton glanced at the grandfather clock against the wall. "Catriona and her husband will be joining us for Christmas. But in the meantime, we are expecting one more guest."

As if on cue the door opened, and the butler came through. "Mr. Finlay Pearson," he announced.

The man in question entered, as confident and unapologetic as ever. Now that Zoe knew of their relation, she could see the resemblance between Quinton and his cousin. The colouring was different, but there was something in the bone structure and the set of their shoulders which could only be the result of shared blood. She would love to draw him. It had been too long since she'd picked up her charcoal, and her mind was eager for the creative outlet.

She glanced over at the wall, where one of Catriona's paintings was now prominently displayed. It truly was extraordinary work. Zoe looked forward to one day having a more in-depth discussion with the woman about her technique, artist to artist.

Finlay took a seat next to Quinton, shaking his left hand in greeting.

"Well, well, well, if it isn't the prodigal valet," said Charlie.

"Yes, yes, have your fun," replied Finlay, his demeanour unoffended. "I realize now that my actions, perhaps, were a bit dramatic."

John leaned forward. "Why did you do it?"

Zoe leaned back, sipping her whiskey. She and Quinton had already heard this explanation, as well as Finlay's apology, but she was content to let Finlay tell his tale again.

"My mother, as you might imagine, was a woman of secrets. I knew where she had grown up, and over the years I pieced together where she was going on her pilgrimages." Finlay accepted a glass of whiskey from Quinton. "I didn't know the full story, but I knew about my mother's brother, Graham, and the impact his death made on her. When news came that Quinton and his family were coming to Cedarbrook, I wanted to know more. My mother would not share more, so I took matters into my own hands."

Quinton snapped his fingers, as if a thought had just occurred to him. "So, was that you then I saw skulking about the treeline when we first arrived?"

Finlay nodded. "Yes, and you almost caught me. I hadn't counted on you being so quick on your feet, but fortunately you were waylaid by the land steward, may he rest in peace. I wasn't ready then to introduce myself. I wanted to get to know you from an outside perspective first."

"You forged references, faked your name, and pretended to be a valet to learn more about your cousin?" Rory laughed. "Naturally, who wouldn't?"

For the first time Zoe saw a hint of a colour come across Finlay's cheeks. "I must admit curiosity outweighed good judgment when it came to the choices I made. My mother says I am the most like Graham of her children—restless and unwilling to take life at face value. It does get me into trouble from time to time."

"No lasting damage was done," said Quinton, saving his cousin from any further embarrassment. "And it turns out Finlay followed in his father's footsteps when it came to work. He has come on as a tutor for the Dovefields."

"A good fit." Charlie clasped Finlay on the back. "But you'll have to tell me the name of your forger—"

"And what of the Grimsleys?" interrupted Savita before her brother could get too carried away. "I know what Evans did was horrible, but I can't help but feel sorry for them. Now that both nephews are gone, who will care for them?"

Quinton nodded. "The same thought occurred to us. We have arranged for a monthly stipend to be given to them, and I asked Magistrate Dandridge to officially classify Evans's death as accidental. The brothers will be buried side by side in the family graveyard, where they should be."

"Good," said Rory. "As they should be."

Conversation naturally drifted into various other subjects. Zoe lamented they'd missed Alexander and Mabel's engagement, but Quinton pointed out they would still be able to attend the wedding next week. Charlie and Rory became immersed in an animated discussion about the afterlife, with Rory bringing up several ghost sightings by reputable people and Charlie adamantly denying the possibility of any such thing. John and Savi listened in, laughing softly and offering occasional commentary. As Finlay and Quinton separated themselves out, talking about the quality of the soil near Cedarbrook, Mary came to sit near Zoe. She appeared distant and unsettled, and Zoe quickly guessed the source.

"Mr. Baptiste?"

Mary nodded. "He wrote another letter."

It wasn't the first time his name had come up between the two friends, and it likely wouldn't be the last. Zoe hid her smile behind a sip of whiskey, not wanting to embarrass Mary.

"Will you write back?" asked Zoe.

"Eventually." Mary swirled the amber liquid in her glass. "I do find him to be a likable man. But he needs time to settle there in his new position, and I don't know if I am ready for more than friendship with him."

"But you do like him?"

"Yes. I like him." Mary sighed. "I'll admit, I was feeling a bit left out there for a while. John and Savi, you and Quinton. Even Charlie has Finn and Rory, and Rory has Charlie and a new project. But with all that has happened, I realized something profound." She met Zoe's eyes. "I like my life. At times I am lonely, I will admit that. But my life is interesting. In the big picture, I am not so sure I am ready to give up what I have right now."

Zoe laughed softly. "So Mr. Baptiste must compete, not with another man, but with the life you have on your own?"

Returning the laugh, Mary leaned back in her chair. "I am complicated at best, and impossible at worst. But a man must fit into the life I have, not the other way around."

"Well, time will tell," said Zoe. "Perhaps he can."

"Perhaps he can." Mary gave her a thoughtful look. "And you? Have you found your way as well, in this new life?"

"I have been giving this some thought." Zoe paused, tapping her fingers against the arm of her chair. "Quinton wishes to focus on his present role, both here and at Cedarbrook. He realized how much he has to learn about being a good steward for the estate and the village. It will take up a great deal of his time. I have offered to help, but he feels strongly that my life should not be limited by his. He wants me to find my own passion."

Mary was silent while Zoe took a long slow sip of good whiskey.

"You realize you and I were the only two who figured out this puzzle?" said Zoe after a moments delay. "Everyone else was off doing their own thing while we unmasked the villain."

Raising her glass in acknowledgment, Mary laughed. "It was impressive deductive work, wasn't it?"

"I thought so." Zoe drew two pieces of paper from her pocket. "My father gave Quinton several notes from nobles requesting his help in some discreet investigating. Quinton hasn't opened them yet. So I did."

Taking the papers from her, Mary ran her eyes across the scribbled lines. "This one is in French," she said after a moment.

"Yes. This woman fled France at around the same time as my mother and I, and has found herself in need of aid."

Mary looked up, her gaze thoughtful. "And you want to help her?"

"Yes. Not alone, of course. That would be ridiculous." Zoe took another sip and smiled. "I want us to help her."

Also by Taylor & Sandra Preisler

The Ties That Divide

The Wounds That Linger

The Truths That Tether

About the Authors

Sandra and Taylor Preisler share a love of reading and writing, an obsession with foster kittens, and of course DNA. The Histories That Haunt is the mother daughter duo's fourth novel in their award winning Q&Z Regency Mystery Series. While both are from Casper, Wyoming, Taylor now lives in Arizona with her sister, roommate, a Pit Bull and probably some of those pesky fosters. Sandra and her husband Ken split their time between beautiful Wyoming and equally beautiful Arizona. Their two cats love the change every time and have never complained.

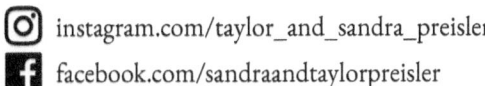

instagram.com/taylor_and_sandra_preisler
facebook.com/sandraandtaylorpreisler

www.ingramcontent.com/pod-product-compliance
Lightning Source LLC
Chambersburg PA
CBHW050013120726
47903CB00006B/1757